CLEAN START AT FORTY-SEVEN

NORA PHOENIX

Clean Start at Forty-Seven (Forty-Seven Duology 1) by Nora Phoenix

Copyright ©2022 Nora Phoenix

Cover design: Vicki Brostenianc www.vickibrostenianc.com
Models: Kevin R. Davis and David Cook
Photographer: Golden Czermak, FuriousFotog
Editing and proofreading: Tanja Ongkiehong
With thanks to my beta and sensitivity readers: Abbie, Amanda, B. Rourke, Fátima, Monica, Richelle, Stacey, Tania, and Vicki

All rights reserved. No part of this story may be used, reproduced, or transmitted in any form by any means without the written permission of the copyright holder, except in case of brief quotations and embodied within critical reviews and articles.

This is a work of fiction. Names, characters, places, and incidents either are the products of the author's imagination or are used fictitiously. Any resemblance to actual persons, living or dead, businesses, companies, events, or locales is entirely coincidental. The use of any real company and/or product names is for literary effect only. All other trademarks and copyrights are the property of their respective owners.

This book contains sexually explicit material which is suitable only for mature readers.

www.noraphoenix.com

For JP

You'll probably never read this, but I need to say this. I miss you, and I'm sorry. If I had known then what I know now...so much would've been different. I hope you're happy, wherever you are, and that you've found the unconditional love you deserve.

CLEAN START AT FORTY-SEVEN

I'm done hiding who I am.

Pretending to be straight, to be the loving, devoted husband and successful ER doctor everyone wanted me to be has been exhausting.

I numbed the pain any way I could, and in the end, it cost me everything. My job, my marriage, the relationship with my grown kids.

But now I'm in recovery, and for the first time, I'm living my true life as an out gay man.

I need to get my act together, to get healthy again. Benoni is my new personal trainer...twenty years my junior. He makes my mouth water and certain other body parts react. Oh, and he's also my son's best friend.

I'm forty-seven years old. It's time for a clean start. But where does Benoni fit in?

Clean Start at Forty-Seven is part one of a duology, an emotional and yummy romance with an age gap, first time gay, loads of hurt/comfort, and the beginnings of a beautiful Daddy/boy relationship. It contains themes of opioid addiction and religious homophobia. Please mind the trigger warnings in the Publisher's Note.

PUBLISHER'S NOTE

This is my most personal book to date, as it contains a lot of what I experienced growing up in a conservative church and coming to terms with what I had been taught there. Kinsey's story holds elements I lived through with my ex-husband, who came out as gay several years ago, though crucial details are different (eg Kinsey's addiction and contentious divorce). Please know that everyone's experiences and memories are different, so mine may not reflect yours.

The same holds true for my descriptions of addiction in this book. There's no one story and no universal experience for either. While I have tried to be accurate and authentic, this is a romance and not a non-fiction book or memoir, so obviously, I have left certain aspects out or glossed over them.

Please note the following trigger warnings for this book: parental and familial homophobia, parental and familial rejection, religious trauma (emotional, not physical or sexual), internalized religious homophobia, opioid addiction (not active but mentioned and shown in flashbacks), recovery from addiction, contentious divorce, and estranged relationship with adult children.

1

KINSEY

The wet heat slaps me in my face as I get out of my BMW, the last remnant of my old life. I lost my job, my family, my health, and my house, but I still have my old car. Well, there's me, or what's left of me at least, and I can certainly be called a remnant at this point. A relic, more accurately, one that bears a vague resemblance to the man who once was in his prime. It's hard not to laugh at that thought. My prime days are long gone, and if I would want any reminders—which I don't—all I need to do is recall the reason I'm here.

My bag is in the back seat, and I hoist it out of the car, then lock the vehicle with one click of the remote. I parked as far away from the building as I could, a healthy habit that Jerry suggested to get some extra exercise in. I doubt one could call the fifty yards from my car to the entrance exercise, but whatever. Every step adds up and all that BS. Bonus points for me for being optimistic. Or doesn't it count when you're being sarcastic at the same time?

Fun & Fit, the bright purple sign says, and I struggle to

hold back a snort at the classic example of an oxymoron, since becoming fit isn't what I would call fun. But who knows? Maybe this gym will convince me of the opposite. Ka-ching, more points for me. I'm getting the hang of that whole positive thinking. Wayne Dwyer would be proud of me. Oh wait, I guess he's as much a has-been as I am at this point. Who's the current king or queen of positive thinking? Is Oprah still cool? God, I have no fucking clue. The image of Joel Osteen pops into my head, and I shudder. Talk about the fakest smile ever. Yikes.

Anyway, I've been leaning against my car, staring at the Fun & Fit sign for a good five minutes now, so I suppose it's time to get my ass in gear and head inside. No matter what torture awaits me there, it can't be worse than this heat. Florida in August. Kill. Me. Now. Why the hell did I return here when I had the chance to move anywhere?

Right, I stayed in this cross between sauna and hell on the minuscule chance that my kids would want anything to do with me again after not talking to me for... Good god, has it been seven months already since I entered rehab?

I do a quick calculation in my head. Yes, it has been. Seven months since my son and daughter decided to side with their mother and ban me from their lives. Right around the same time their mother served me with divorce papers... while I was still in rehab. Good times, let me tell you. Nothing but great memories.

The truth is that I don't remember much from those weeks. No wonder. I was high as a kite when I entered rehab and utterly miserable the weeks after—too busy puking my brains out to be worried about my soon-to-be ex-wife. And if you wonder why on earth I'd start rehab being high, well, I figured it would be a shame to waste my last stash of Percocet by flushing it down the toilet. If I look back on that moment, the shame is so all-consuming it fills me with a deep hatred for myself. How could I have been this stupid? Alas, that's a question I doubt I'll ever find the answer to.

I need to get my shit together before I fucking melt in this godforsaken heat, and so I give myself a mental kick in the ass and walk toward the entrance. It took me six months to gather the courage to take this step. No more dallying. I use my doctor voice on myself, which, strangely enough, still works.

So does dropping the f-bomb. I was never allowed to curse or use language like that, and now that I can, it's proven to be highly effective. Fuck is such a versatile word, you know? Especially when you haven't overused it yet. It can be a noun, an adjective, a verb... The options are limitless, and childish as it may sound, I intend to fully explore them.

As soon as I open the door, cool air teases my skin, then embraces me, and I sigh with happiness. Thank fuck for air conditioning. The twentysomething brunette behind the reception desk greets me with a friendly smile. "Hello, how are you?"

"I'm good, thank you. How about you?"

"Not bad. Are you new to our gym?"

I wince. "That obvious?"

She laughs. "We're a small gym, and I work the reception almost daily, so by now, I know all our regulars. So what brings you here?"

What has brought me here? Sheesh, does she have a few hours? But no, I know damn well she's aiming for the sanitized thirty-second pitch, not the whole sorry sob story of my horrible life choices. "Looking to get back in shape again."

"You came to the right place," she says enthusiastically.

Boy, they picked the right person for this job. Her smile could light up a room.

"You came highly recommended."

"Oh? Who recommended us?"

"A friend. Jerry Fenner?"

Yeah, I'd better not mention he's my sponsor. Not how I want to introduce myself to new people. *Hi, I'm Kinsey, and up until six months ago, opioids were my best friend.* That always goes over well outside of NA, Narcotics Anonymous. Drug addicts have a bad rep in general, but opioid addicts have been in the news so much recently that people react strongly to it.

She nods. "I love Jerry. One of the most positive people I've ever met. I'm glad he recommended you to us. What's your name?"

"Kinsey. Kinsey Lindstrom."

She holds out her hand. "I'm Lynn. Welcome to Fun & Fit!"

We shake hands, and then she gives me a clipboard with a form. "If you fill this out, Kinsey, I can set you up with a free fourteen-day trial membership. After that, you can decide if you want to continue with a monthly or yearly membership."

"Sounds good."

"Did you want to start with a first training today?"

I chuckle. "I'd better before I lose my courage."

"No worries, we've got you. I'll check which one of our trainers is free to give you a tour and help you get started. I'll be right back, okay?"

The form is easy enough, and I race through the questions, then sign at the bottom before I can change my mind. Lynn is back a few minutes later and takes the form back from me. She squints at it. "Wow, you have challenging handwriting."

I almost blurt out it's a classic doctor's scrawl, but that's not something I want to announce. Doctor Lindstrom is the old me, Kinsey version 1.0, from before everything went to hell. No, before I fucked up and *made* everything go to hell. Jerry has been stressing the importance of using correct language, and as much as I hate it, he's right. Everything didn't go to hell just like that. My life imploded because of my bad choices, and I need to take responsibility for that. Still, not something Lynn needs to know.

"Sorry. Let me know if you can't read it."

She sends me another blinding smile. "I'm sure I'll figure it out. You can get changed in the men's locker room, which is down the hall and to your right. When you're done, walk into the main room, and Ben will be waiting for you. Good luck."

"Thank you." I grin. "Especially for the good luck part. I'll need it."

"Ben's a good guy and experienced in working with newbies, so I'm sure you'll settle in quickly."

I step into the locker room, where faint traces of body wash and deodorant compete with the unmistakable odor of sweat. In all fairness, it's not an unpleasant combination. A quick check shows no one is there, and I breathe out with relief. I never thought of myself as vain, but the idea of others seeing my weak, thin body gives me anxiety. And if I'm honest, so does the idea of me seeing others.

Locker rooms are nothing new to me, of course. Besides, I'm a doctor. Or I used to be. Seeing people naked has always been a part of my job, and I don't blink twice at anything anymore. After fifteen years in the ER, nothing fazes me. Any weird headline you've ever seen about something that happened in Florida? I've had it in my ER. People bitten by spiders, snakes, crocs, hell, even by a hippo—don't ask, long story. Drunk accidents, marital fights, wounds from knifes, guns, ice picks, you name it. I could go on and on. You'd be surprised at how many of those incidents involved people not wearing clothes. Or maybe not, if you've ever lived in Florida.

My point is that in itself, naked bodies don't bother me. But this is the first time I'm in a locker room since...since it all changed, and I don't know if I'm ready for it yet. What if I stare? What if my body *responds*? And trust me, that's not outside the realm of possibilities because now that I've removed the tight lock I had on myself for over thirty years, now that I've allowed myself to feel...I feel a *lot*. Everything turns me on. It's like being fifteen all over again, though even then, I had better self-control.

Jerry says it's normal and that it will stabilize, but I'm half convinced he's only saying that to make me feel less of a horny, oversexed freak. At least he's gay too, so he does speak from experience. All I can do is hope and pray it'll pass soon.

Not literally pray. Those days are long in the past, and they'll never return. God sure as fuck never answered any prayers back then, so I see no reason to keep trying. Besides, I reckon the Almighty has better things to do than listen to people trying to change things that either they fucked up themselves or that he did on purpose. No, I'm talking about the metaphorical kind. Like good thoughts, happy vibes, rays of light. Those prayers.

I pull the strings of my shorts tight so I won't have to fear them sagging down my bony hips. Good grief, I really am all skin and bones. I need to beef up and get healthy. It's the only reason why I'm here despite all my fears and misgivings. My body needs to get in better shape if I want to win this fight in the long haul. Those are Jerry's words, and after six months, I'm finally listening to him.

When I'm all dressed, I grab my water bottle and towel, take a deep breath, and head in. The main room, as Lynn called it, is rectangle, the walls gray and purple with all kinds of motivational quotes. "You miss 100 percent of the shots you don't take" and "Success is the sum of small efforts repeated day in day out" and shit like that. Machines line the walls of the room, and in the middle are the weight-lifting stations. The gym is smaller than I expected, but Jerry did mention it was intimate and personal, which does appeal to me.

"Thanks, Ben," a fiftysomething woman says to a man whose back is turned toward me. My eyes sneak to his firm ass, which is nicely outlined in the tight shorts he's wearing. His arms are a work of art too, both literally and figuratively. Tattoos of roses, leaves, and other shapes I can't quite make out cover them. They look intriguing and sexy. And man, he's in such excellent shape he must have that elusive six-pack on his stomach.

But when the woman walks off and he turns around, his abs are the last thing on my mind. My breath whooshes out of my lungs, and I'm lightheaded for a moment as I recognize him. I've known him since he was in middle school with Jonathan, but he's a man now. A sexy, confident man who makes my heart skip a beat and my mouth go dry.

His eyes light up. Of course he instantly knows who I am. It's only been, what, two years since I've seen him last? I may look like utter shit, but I haven't changed that much.

But then his expression changes, and my stomach drops. He *knows*. I wasn't sure if he's still close with Jonathan, but regardless, he knows. All I want to do is hightail it out of there, but I can't, so I raise my chin.

"Hello, Benoni."

2
2014: BENONI

"Ben, come on!" Jonathan calls out as he walks through the hallway, no doubt on his way outside, his impatience thick.

"Hold your horses, asshole," I shout back. "I'll be right there."

He's never been the patient type in the almost eight years we've been friends, and I doubt that will ever change. He, Dash, Bricks, and I met in middle school and became fast friends, and we're still close. The party is getting started for real, someone cranking up the volume of the speakers outside that blast some godawful sugary sweet pop shit. Good thing the Lindstroms have no close neighbors. One of the many perks of being rich.

Their pool is pretty sweet, especially for a party like Jonathan is throwing to celebrate his eighteenth birthday. It sure beats the hell out of my celebration, which consisted of the four of us getting shitfaced on the beach. Then again, I managed to get my dick sucked even then, so there's that.

Hopefully, my outfit should do the trick tonight as well. I might be flat broke, but my body is prime grade A, especially my ass and my dick, and the tattoos I've had done recently only add to my appeal. If I don't score a blow job tonight, I need to turn in my gay card. Jonathan invited half of the seniors in our school, and I know for a fact there's quite a number of happy cocksuckers among them, out or firmly shoved into the closet. I don't care, as long as I have a wet, willing mouth to put my cock in...or a hot ass. The chances of the latter are significantly less, but one can hope, right?

I check myself in the bathroom mirror, turning sideways to look at my ass. These Speedos are a gamble, since they practically scream "look at me being super gay," but damn if they don't make my ass pop and showcase my fat cock. A man's gotta work with what he has, which, in my case, is my body.

Satisfied I look my best, I head outside where the music is pumping, the bodies are half-naked, and the booze is flowing freely. Quite a few people are making out already, one girl sandwiched between her boyfriend and his best friend. Must be his lucky night. Or hers, depending on how you look at it.

For a fleeting moment, I wonder what Jonathan's dad thinks of us drinking, seeing as a few of us are still underage, and none of us are old enough to drink. He always warned us about the risks of drinking and especially if we'd decide to get behind the wheel. He shared this story of a teenage couple who'd gotten killed because they were drunk and crashed in a sharp turn. They were brought into the ER where Mr. Lindstrom worked, and he did everything he could to save their lives...but they still died.

Jonathan will never know, but his father's talks have made an impression on me. He's the reason why I never drink and drive. His sorrow and regret about their deaths were genuine, as was his concern about the possible damage alcohol could do to our teenage brains. Granted, I still get drunk off my ass, but I don't drive after, so one out of two ain't bad.

"Hey, Ben," someone says, their voice cracking. Look at that. Marc Hobson, a kind, nerdy guy who got into MIT... and who has the sweetest mouth on the planet. I personally tested it after a homecoming game, and I'd rate it ten out of ten for enthusiasm.

"Hey, cutie," I say with a wink, taking in his slender form with miles of pale skin in baggy surf shorts. "That pink looks perfect on you."

An hour later, I'm pleasantly buzzed as I'm leading Marc into the basement, where he drops on his knees without even asking. Good boy. "Take my dick out," I tell him, and he obliges without hesitation. The little gasp that flies from his lips as he wraps his hand around my cock is a boost for my ego.

"Y-your dick is so p-perfect," he whispers.

"Thank you. Are you gonna take good care of it?"

He nods.

"Then you may start."

His technique consists mostly of enthusiasm, but he's so goddamn eager, it's still a massive turn-on. Plus, the dude is blessed with no gag reflex. None. I sink deep into his throat, the wet heat clenching around my cock.

"Fuuuuck," I moan, only pulling back when his eyes bulge from the lack of oxygen. "You're so fucking good at that."

By the way his face lights up, you'd think I asked him to marry me.

I take my time abusing his mouth, and he takes it all, not even touching his cock, which is rock hard and ready for action. Just when I push back into his mouth, the telltale creak of the top stair tread alerts me someone is coming. Not that I'm worried or even inclined in the least to halt my activities. Everyone knows I'm gay, so if they saw me go down into the basement, they must have a damn good idea of what I'm doing here. If they want to watch, all fine by me.

But the legs that appear aren't bare ones covered in swimming trunks or a bikini bottom. They're clad in sneakers and dark blue scrubs, and I know who it is before I see his face. Jonathan's dad, Mr. Lindstrom. I doubt he knows I'm here because he's not even looking in my direction but heading straight for the washing machine in the back, where he stops and whips his scrubs top over his head, then kicks off his shoes and drops his pants, leaving him in his underwear.

God, he's so fucking sexy. Not a perfect six-pack, but a manly body, hairy and strong. He turned forty this year, and his dark hair is showing the first strands of silver, and it only makes him hotter. He's the ultimate DILF—if he were gay, which, obviously, he's not. Besides, I don't do married guys. A man's gotta draw the line somewhere.

A gurgle makes me refocus, and I cringe. Poor Marc has been deprived of oxygen a little longer than I had planned, distracted as I was by Mr. Lindstrom. I hastily draw back, and Marc gasps for air. There's no way Mr. Lindstrom didn't hear that, but I have to make sure Marc is okay first. I pet his cheek. "You good, cutie pie?"

"I..." He clears his throat. "I came."

His voice is raspy, the result of being so thoroughly abused by my cock.

"Excuse me?"

"I c-came. In my s-swimming shorts."

He came hands-free just from sucking me off? Dayum.

"You need to look into choking sex, dude. Like, seriously. You'd totally get off on that, pun intended."

He nods. "I watch it a lot in porn."

Not sure I needed to know that, but here we are. "Okay."

Marc points at my cock, which has only grown harder at the thought of having a spectator. "Can I get back to it?"

Apparently, Marc isn't aware of our visitor. Good. It would be a shame if he took off and leave me blue balled. I grin. "Abso-fucking-lutely."

It's not until I'm so deep inside his throat my balls hit his chin that I look up again. Mr. Lindstrom is still in front of the washing machine, his body rigid, his eyes glued to the show we're giving. Jonathan's dad has never been a prude, so it's not like I expected him to react with outrage, but neither did I think he'd be like this.

Fascinated.

Mesmerized.

And, judging by the way the tip of his hard cock peeps from under the waistband of his briefs, aroused. *Very* aroused.

Mr. Lindstrom might be married to a woman, but that man is not straight. Not even a little bit. And when he finally manages to tear his eyes away from my cock and raises his gaze to meet my eyes, his cheeks flush bright red. Yeah, he knows it too.

How about that?

3

KINSEY

"Hi, Mr. Lindstrom."

Benoni Healey. He'd been coming to our house since they were sixth-graders, but after that one night, I could never get that image of him out of my head: balls deep into someone's throat, looking at me in a wordless challenge to speak up and dare to stop him. I didn't. Of course I didn't. I took my scrubs right back out of the washer, got dressed at record speed, and hurried back upstairs.

I wasn't even supposed to be at home, having promised Jonathan that his mother and I would spend the night at a hotel. But I'd gotten called into work after a massive pile-up on the 75, and I'd just stopped by to pick up some clean scrubs for my shift the next day. Big mistake. I've never forgotten that scene, the confident, cocksure way he got himself off. I'd known he was gay—he'd never made a secret of that—but to see him...pleasure himself like that was still a shock.

And every encounter with him since has been awkward,

with me stuttering and stumbling and him smiling knowingly and winking at me, though as far as I know, he never spoke a word about it to anyone. No one ever mentioned it or even hinted at it, so he must've kept it to himself. He's got balls, that one.

I clear my throat. "I didn't know you worked here."

He quirks an eyebrow. "If you had, you wouldn't have come here?"

"Probably not," I admit.

He studies me for a moment. "Why not?"

Not because of that one encounter, though that may play a part as well. It made it hard to see him as my son's friend, as a young man rather than a hot, super sexy guy. But my issues with him now have a different cause.

"Don't pretend you don't know what went down." I lower my voice. Nobody needs to overhear this conversation.

"I'm not pretending at all, but I fail to see what one has to do with the other."

"Are you still close with Jonathan?"

His expression softens. "Yes. I mean, not as close as we were in school, but we hang out once a month or so."

"Then there's your answer. I don't want to put you in the middle."

He takes a step toward me, the faint smell of his sweat hitting me like a punch to my gut. "I appreciate that, and I understand where you're coming from, but don't you think that's a decision I have to make for myself? I'm an adult, Mr. Lindstrom. I may not have your life experience, but I'm not a child anymore either."

I chuckle despite the situation. "You haven't been a child for a long time, Benoni."

His mouth pulls up into a cheeky grin. "You're the only

one who still calls me by my full name. My mom always did, but to everyone else, I'm Ben."

"I never liked that abbreviation. You have such a unique name. It seems silly to shorten it to something so generic."

"My mom picked it. She'd gotten it from some book with baby names she bought for fifty cents at a flea market. My father didn't hang around long enough after he got her pregnant to get a voice, so that was that."

Benoni's situation was about as different from Jonathan's as it could get. Money was always an issue, and some of Jonathan's allowance was used to pay for things Benoni couldn't afford, like snacks, eating out, and going to the movies. "How's your mom?" I ask.

He sighs, his face tightening. "She passed away last year, right before Thanksgiving."

"Shit. I'm sorry. I didn't know. Was it the...?"

He nods. "The MS got her. She held on as long as she could, but we both knew she wouldn't grow old."

Why didn't Jonathan tell me Dory Healey passed away? Then it hits me. November of last year. That's when I told Caroline the truth, things got rough between us, and Jonathan and Judith picked her side. "Her case was very aggressive. I'm so sorry. I know you were close with her."

"She was the best mom I could've ever had. I was lucky to have her in my life as long as I did."

We stare at each other until I look away. "Is there someone else who could do this first introduction with me?"

"You really don't want me to help you, do you?"

He sounds hurt, and I sigh as I meet his eyes again. "You don't understand. It's...it's embarrassing, okay? Seeing you is a stark reminder of what I lost, of how badly I fucked up. And you have to pick Jonathan's side because he needs you."

He shakes his head. "No, I don't. Just because we're

friends doesn't mean I have to blindly support his choices. He refuses to talk about it, so I don't know anything more than the barest of essentials, and that's not sufficient for me to form an opinion one way or the other."

I scoff. "I'm a drug addict who came out as gay after twenty-six years of marriage, breaking his wife's heart. Not sure how many ways you can spin that."

"See, that one sentence raises so many questions based on what I know about you that I don't even know where to start. Not that you owe me any explanation. I'm not here as your son's friend or as your therapist. I'm here as your trainer, and my job is to help you get back into shape. And, Mr. Lindstrom, not to be rude, but it appears you could use my help."

I rub my eyes, letting out a long sigh. "Call me Kinsey. If you're gonna tell me I look like crap, at least do it as my equal."

He nods slowly. "Okay. I can do that. You need help, Kinsey. Because forgive me, but you do look like crap. It's a far cry from the man I knew years ago."

"You'll find that there's little left of that man, mostly because he never existed. He was a role, a mask, being forced to play a part he'd signed up for all those years ago."

"I can see that. The good news is that you've gotten through the part where you've accepted who you are, right? It may have taken you a while, but you're here now. That's a great first step on the path of reinventing yourself."

I frown. "Are you sure you're not a therapist?"

"My degree is in sports science, but I minored in psychology, so you get to reap the benefits from that. Though I'm sure I'm not telling you anything new, considering you're a doctor."

"*Was* a doctor," I correct him softly.

"Was?" He furrows his brows.

"Didn't Jonathan tell you? I'm banned from practicing medicine in the state of Florida. The hospital fired me and then took my case to the Medical Board. They suspended my medical license."

His eyes grow big. "You lost your job? But you worked there, like, forever."

"Fifteen years as an attending and before that, I did my residency there. But they were right. Being a doctor and a drug addict isn't a good combination."

"You were high while working?"

"Yes."

As much as I want to deny it, it's useless. One Google search will lead him to the truth. The newspapers have written my whole sad story in horrifying detail. Coming clean now saves me the shame of getting caught in yet another lie.

"So what do you do for work now?"

"I'm teaching at an online university and writing a textbook on emergency medicine. It's not the same, but at least it's still in my field."

He cringes. "I'm sorry."

"Don't be. I deserve all this...and more, probably. I hurt a lot of people, Benoni. Can't just sweep that under the rug."

He straightens his shoulders. "Maybe, but that's not why you're here. That's not what you need from me."

I cock my head. "I wasn't aware I needed anything from you."

His eyes begin to sparkle. "You may not realize it yet, but you do. I know you may still remember me as a teenager..."

A flash of that night pops up in my head. His lean lines and tight muscles packed into that sinful pair of Speedos, his body in excellent condition from years of playing soccer. The water droplets still running down his chest, dripping down that six-pack, finding his happy trail, which ran south. The way he held that boy's head, the confident thrusts into his mouth, the sheer ecstasy on his face. I swallow. Not exactly the memories I should have of a teenager, though in my defense, he was eighteen at the time. Barely, but still eighteen.

"...but I'm really good at my job. And I can help you. I can show you how to become fit again, strong. Healthy. Because that's why you're here, isn't it?"

I look down at my scrawny body. "What gave it away?"

"So let me help you," he says.

He sure isn't deterred by my sarcasm or lack of enthusiasm so far, and his positive attitude is getting to me. Does he really believe I can benefit from his help? With anyone else, I would've accepted already, but this is Benoni. It's hard for me to separate Benoni, the trainer, from Benoni, my son's friend. My son's very, very sexy friend, whose body has only gotten more perfect over the years. No wonder, with him working in a gym every day.

I sigh. "What would you advise me?"

"Nothing until we've had a proper intake and I know what your starting point is in terms of health, diet, and exercise."

Jerry promised me this, an individual approach based on my needs and baseline, not some generic program that's supposed to be one size fits all. "Up until six months ago, I was a drug addict who lived on caffeine, opioids, and junk food, with the occasional alcohol mixed in. I was overweight, and my only exercise was being on my feet in the ER for twelve-hour shifts."

He blinks. Then his eyes roam my body, starting at my

face and slowly drifting down. "You're not overweight now. The opposite, I would say."

"Yes. Detox will do that to you. My body didn't appreciate being deprived of the only way it knew how to cope."

"How's your eating pattern now?" He nudges my shoulder and gestures toward a little sitting area in the corner of the room. Before I know it, we're sitting there and he's taking full inventory of my diet and my feeble attempts to get back in shape. He fires off question after question, and I answer as he scribbles notes on an iPad.

"Known injuries?" he asks.

I point at the scars on my knee. "Torn ACL. I had surgery, and it's supposedly all healed now, but I haven't put it to the test."

That knee was the whole reason I got addicted, but I leave that part out.

Finally, he looks up. "I think I have it all now."

"That's quite the thorough intake."

"I told you I'm good at my job."

"So what's your diagnosis, Dr. Healey?" I joke, but he's not laughing.

"We're gonna start slow. Very slow. I need to see how your body responds to being active again, especially your knee. So we'll kick things off with ten minutes on the bike at moderate speed and a light round of weights, followed by some stretching."

That actually sounds doable. "Okay."

"As for your diet, I don't need to tell you that if you want to get healthy, it starts with what you eat. So cut out the junk and load up on veggies and lean proteins. I'm sure you know the drill."

I like that he's not preaching but cuts straight to the chase. Of course I know what a healthy, balanced diet looks like. "I do. Just gotta get back on that particular horse."

"We have a dietitian if you should ever want specific advice, but for now, I think you should be good. How often do you think you can come here to train?"

"How often would I need to, to see some results?"

"Three times a week would be good, with a day of rest in between."

"I can do that." I sigh, averting my eyes. "It's not like I have any kind of social life."

"Why not?"

I look up, frowning. "What?"

"Why don't you have a social life?" he repeats, his eyes soft.

"Erm, because most people don't want to be friends with a drug addict? And the friends I had all dropped me like a hot potato when this whole shitshow started."

He leans back in his chair, crossing his hands behind his head. "Then you need better friends. We all fuck up at some point, and none of what you did was aimed at them."

Huh, I never thought of it that way. "They felt hurt that I had never been myself with them, that I hadn't been honest about my sexuality. And some of them preferred not to have a gay friend."

"Like I said, you need better friends. Your sexuality is your business and yours alone. You don't owe anyone an explanation whatsoever other than, in this case, your wife. Or your ex-wife now, I suppose. And people who don't like gay friends aren't the kind of friends you need in your life. That's toxicity you can do without. I'd ten times rather have a drug addict as a friend than someone who believes I'm an abomination for simply existing."

When did Benoni Healey get this wise? I've always

thought of him as a bit of a player, a fuckboy, but this is a whole new side to him.

"Anyway"—he checks his watch—"let's get started. I have an hour before my shift ends. On the bike, you go."

I'll never in a million years admit it out loud, but I find his bossy tone extremely hot.

4

BENONI

A day later, I still can't believe Kinsey Lindstrom walked into my gym and became my new client. He might have been hesitant at first—and for understandable reasons—but by the time he left, I had him convinced I'd be the best trainer for him. And I am. I will be. I understand him like no one else.

Kinsey has always been hot, though in a laid-back way. Crystal blue eyes that shine with intelligence, a strong face with a short beard that's gone partly silver now. He was sexy, but in a casual way, making it clear he had no idea how hot he was. To me, that made him all the more attractive.

He's changed. Physically, he's lost weight, and he looks pale and unhealthy. I don't have experience with drugs, but his appearance is a stark reminder of what that shit will do to you. Luckily, I never had the slightest inkling to even try them. Near the end, my mom used CBD oil and gummies to ease her pain, and I never even touched them for myself.

But Kinsey has changed in other ways as well, small things that are much harder to pinpoint. He's different from before. More open and real, less fake and about keeping up appearances—something Jonathan excels in too, by the way. And I don't know if Kinsey's sarcastic, self-deprecating humor is new, but I dig it. I admire people who can laugh at themselves, even in shitty situations.

Obviously, I never knew him that well. He was my friend's dad, not one of my friends. I will admit I've been fascinated by him for a number of years now. Ever since he caught me getting a blow job, and maybe even before that. But after meeting him at the gym, I'm more intrigued than ever, and I hope I'll get a chance to truly get to know him.

When I turn into my driveway, I shake my head in a mix of annoyance and exasperation. Leif, my roommate, has parked his car half on the grass again, proving that he legit is the worst driver in the world. He's cute as a button, which is why he gets away with so much. All he has to do is flash those baby blues, and everyone, regardless of gender, melts into a puddle. Even me. To a degree, that is.

I open the door quietly. If I remember correctly, Leif is in a session, but nope, the red light above his door is off. Was I wrong?

"Honey, I'm home!" I call out, a running joke between us by now.

"Welcome home, baby," he responds from the living room. "Dinner is ready."

I wince. If Leif has been cooking, he hasn't had a good day. He's an excellent cook, don't get me wrong, but he's also chaotic and forgetful as fuck, so him having dinner ready at six thirty on a weekday isn't a good sign. Is that why he wasn't working? "Be there in a minute!"

I quickly wash my face and upper body, then walk in my shorts and barefoot into the living room, where a steaming hot casserole is waiting for me. God, it smells delicious, and my stomach rumbles. "That looks amazing," I tell him, plopping down on the couch next to him.

"Thank you. It's a broccoli chicken casserole with extra chicken and extra cheese, so double the protein."

He knows that with as much as I work out, getting enough protein in is always a challenge. "You take good care of me, Bun."

I used to call him honey bun as a joke, but then it became a thing, and I shortened it to bun. The name fits him, somehow. We're Ben and Bun, and it works for us.

"My pleasure, as always."

Why was there only one plate? "Did you already eat?"

His mouth sets in a stubborn line. "I'm not hungry."

"Nah-uh, we've been over this. Grab a plate and eat." I make my voice stern.

He bites his lip. "I don't want to eat."

"It wasn't a question, Leif."

He sighs. "Okay. I'll eat a little."

"Good."

I load my plate full, then put a much smaller portion on his. The first taste already makes me moan in pleasure. As much as I hate to see him unhappy, it's got some undeniable benefits. The boy can cook, and while some people claim food made with love tastes better, I don't know about that. Leif makes the most scrumptious meals when he's either supremely pissed off or sad as fuck.

When I've eaten about a third of my portion and my stomach stops begging for food, I look at him sideways. He's picking at the casserole with his fork. "What happened, Bun?"

A dramatic sigh, though he probably doesn't even realize it. He rarely does. "Clark ended things."

Oh boy, here we go again. Poor Leif. He has the absolute

worst taste in men. "Let me guess. He has an issue with your job?"

He ducks his head, chin trembling. "I told him from the start, and he'd assured me it wouldn't be an issue, but..." He makes a helpless gesture with his hands.

"He became jealous," I fill in the rest.

It's a familiar story by now. Leif is a crossover between a porn star and a cam boy, inviting men over for sex that he films and then puts up on his lucrative OnlyFans channel. He's got a massive fan base and a long line of men all too happy to fuck him, even if he makes money off it and they don't. It's their proverbial fifteen minutes of fame—if they even last that long. He's good at what he does, and no one can make someone come faster than him...if that's what he wants.

"Yeah."

"Eat your food."

"I'm not—"

I pin him with a glare, and he swallows what he was about to say and obediently takes a bite. I stay silent until he's eaten a few more forkfuls. "Do you want me to give you a lecture, or are you good?"

He chews quickly. "I need the lecture." He peeks at me from between his lashes. Even before he speaks, I know what he's going to say. "And more."

Yeah, that's what I was expecting. I do a quick mental calculation. It's been about a month, so that makes sense. "If that's what you need. We'll have to wait a bit after dinner, though, or you'll throw up again."

A small nod. "True."

"Let's eat and watch TV, and then we'll tackle your problem, okay?"

He sits up straighter. "Yes. Thank you."

Clean Start at Forty-Seven

"No problem. *Leverage* okay?"

We recently started a rewatch. God, I love that show.

"Perfect."

I devour half the casserole, then wrap the rest and put it in the fridge for tomorrow. Dessert is Greek yogurt with raspberries. More protein and some extra fibers. Leif clears what I put on his plate, so at least he's eaten something. Meanwhile, we watch two episodes, enjoying the banter and antics. When the credits roll after the second episode, I turn the TV off.

"Ready?" I ask Leif, who nods.

I stand up, and so does he, stepping in front of me. "Tell me the rules," I say sternly. "Rule number one."

He takes a deep breath. "I can't stop eating just because I'm sad."

"Did you eat today?"

He shakes his head. "Not until now."

"That's one strike. What's the second rule?"

"I can't cancel work just because I'm sad."

"Did you have a session scheduled for today?"

"Yeah..."

"Did you cancel it?"

"Yes."

I click my tongue. "Two strikes. Rule number three."

"If I'm sad and it becomes too much, I need to text someone. I didn't," he says before I can even ask. "I feel like such a bother, Ben. You've heard this story a hundred times by now, and nothing ever changes because I can't keep expecting different results if I repeat the same mistakes. Rule number four."

"Thank you, that saves me the trouble." He looks so utterly forlorn that I pull him into my arms. He puts his cheek against my chest, rubbing my skin like a kitten who wants to be petted. "Bun, you've got to start making better decisions. You deserve better than these macho assholes who treat you like crap. Find someone who will cherish you and give you what you need at the same time. Stop settling for the crumbs. You're worth so much more."

"I know," he mumbles against my chest.

"Do you? Do you really? Because we've been over this."

"Are you getting tired of me?"

Am I? As always when he asks me that question, I take my time answering. I promised him eons ago that I would never lie to him, so he deserves an honest answer, even if he asks tough questions. "No, I'm not. You're nowhere near my boundaries, I promise. I love you, Bun, and I'll be here as long as you'll need me."

His half sob is muffled. "Tell me why I'm worth more. Please."

"You're way smarter than you give yourself credit for. You're kind and sweet, and you can cook and bake like no one else. I love your sense of humor and your weird habits. You're a fantastic fuck, a horny little animal in bed, and nobody sucks cock like you. Plus, you're adorably clingy and needy, which makes a man feel fantastic about himself."

As expected, he giggles, but then a sob rips out of him again, and a tear drops onto my naked skin. He needs more, and so I continue.

"You're super cute and pretty, with the most gorgeous blue eyes. Your body is amazing, all slender and sleek and with miles of perfect skin, and with a perfect bubble butt, like a soft, ripe peach."

I smile as I recall him from memory, which isn't that hard after being friends with him for five years and being roommates for just as long. He was my dorm roommate in college, and let's just say we hit it off instantly. We no longer have sex with each other, since our relationship evolved into something else, but we shared some memorable moments back in the day.

"I'm sorry," he whispers. "I want to do better. I want to *be* better, but it's hard."

"I know it is. But your man is out there, Bun. I promise. One day, you're gonna make a lucky man a fantastic partner."

"Thank you."

We stand like that until he's relaxed and breathing calmly again. "Time for your punishment," I say as I let him go.

"Yes, Ben."

He drops his shorts and underwear without me asking, and as soon as I've sat back down on the couch, he all but flings himself over my lap. I've spent a lot of time in college wondering why he needs this until I realized that question has no satisfactory answer. He just does. And since I'm the one he trusts, it's my job to dole out the discipline he craves.

I inhale deeply, getting into the right mind space for this, which comes almost automatically after this time. "Why am I disciplining you?"

"Because I broke the rules we set together, and breaking rules has consequences."

"Do you accept my discipline?"

"Yes, Ben. Thank you."

His gratitude always guts me, and at the same time, it makes it crystal clear how much he needs this. For him, domestic discipline isn't a kink or something that turns him on, though he does appreciate a sexual spanking as well. No, he needs this on a much deeper level. He requires it to forgive himself for fucking up so he can move on.

Without any more words, I hit him, and I don't hold

back. The slaps aren't intended to arouse him. He needs to feel this tomorrow and preferably the day after so he'll remember to do better next time. I pack a punch in my hand thanks to working out every day, and I deliver a rapid-fire series of sharp smacks that echo through our living room.

His ass is a work of art, and spanking him is almost as arousing as fucking him, since they both cause that incredibly sensual jiggle. God, the first time I fucked him, I must've gone on for at least half an hour, mesmerized by the sight of my cock disappearing between those luscious cheeks and the resulting tremble in his butt.

A red hue spreads out wider and wider over his ass as I rain down slaps all over his bottom. It makes it even more perfect. Leif is sobbing now, his arms wrapped around my leg for support as he's dripping tears and snot all over my skin. It's strangely satisfying.

I never count. I tried that the first few times, but it didn't work. No, I'll know when he's had enough because he'll surrender. He'll collapse, sagging onto my lap like a wrung-out dishrag, and when that happens, we're done.

He's needy tonight, and my hand burns before he gives in, wailing as he clings to me. My heart is so full as he throws himself at my mercy. I pick him up and carry him to his bedroom, where I deposit him onto his bed and grab the aloe lotion from his bedside table. I don't say a word as I take care of him, making sure every inch of his flaming skin is covered in cream. Meanwhile, he's grabbed some tissues and has cleaned himself up, hiccuping once more before settling down.

"Better?" I check.

"Mmm."

"Are you gonna get some sleep now, Bun?"

"Yesssss..."

He's already half-asleep, and I carefully tuck him in under the covers, then turn off the light.

"Ben?"

"Yeah?"

"Thank you."

I smile in the darkness. "Love you, Bun. Sleep well."

It's strange, but as I walk out, I have to think of Kinsey for some reason. Unconventional as our relationship may be, Leif and I have each other. I take care of Leif, and in his own way, he takes care of me. Who does Kinsey have? Does he have anyone left in his life who's willing to be there for him and take care of him?

5
KINSEY

I deliberated calling off the next session at the gym or at least book it with someone else, but here I am again. I couldn't bring myself to cancel, as if doing that I would disappoint Benoni, which is ridiculous. I'm a sucker for punishment, apparently, both emotionally and physically.

Benoni is waiting for me in the main room, dressed in a tight tank top that confirms that yes, he still has a six-pack, and shorts that show off his strong thighs. A man's thighs were never high on my list of sexy body parts, yet here we are, and I struggle to look away. It takes effort to focus on his face, but I manage.

"Hey, Kinsey," he greets me with a wide smile and maybe a little happy surprise as well. That makes two of us.

I sigh. "You're way too happy for someone who's about to torture me."

He chuckles, the sound warm and rich, and it draws my attention to his full lips. Like everything else on him, they're perfection.

"How are you feeling?" he asks.

"Sore. Everywhere, including in muscles I didn't even use. They're joining in on the misery because they don't want to be left out."

"We'll take it easy today, but for the first few weeks, this is what you should expect. Your body will need some time to adjust."

"Yay. Looking forward to it."

His smile widens. "I like that attitude, even if you were being sarcastic."

"Which I was, to be clear."

"I figured as much. Come on, let's get started. Bike or treadmill?"

I roll my eyes. "Considering I can barely sit from how much my ass hurts, let's choose the treadmill as our instrument of torture for today."

It only takes a few minutes for me to regret that. Benoni doesn't push the speed as high as I feared, but he adds a bit of an incline, and my legs and butt are killing me. Pathetic, at a walking speed of not even four miles per hour, but there you have it. It's going to be a mighty long road, this recovery. At least my knee is holding up, so there's that.

Fifteen minutes of absolute agony and then he finally tells me I'm done. With the cardio, that is. He leads me to a smaller room with mats on the floor, as well as a collection of foam rollers, stretching bands, and yoga blocks. It's just the two of us, and if I'm honest, I'm glad to leave the poppy, upbeat music of the main room behind.

"It's time to do some stretching," Benoni announces.

"Stretching? Isn't that what you're supposed to do at the end?"

"New research has made it clear how many benefits it has, so I always make it an integral part of anyone's training. Besides, your muscles are too sore to do much else, so stretching will help. I'm gonna teach you exercises that will help you work all major muscle groups. The more disciplined you are about this, the more you'll see the effects."

"What effects?"

"Decrease in muscle pain, prevention of issues like back- and neckache, and better mobility. Your muscles will become more supple, you'll recover quicker from intense workouts, and you'll prevent injuries. To name a few," he says, ticking them off on his fingers.

Before me stands a different Benoni than I've ever seen. He's always been flirty, oozing sexiness, but now he's all serious and professional. Though he's still sexy as fuck, and it's hot. "Okay, sold. What do I do?"

"We'll start with the legs." He sinks to his knees, then sits down on his feet and leans backward. Those thighs I was drawn to before? They're even more on display as his shorts ride up. "This is a great way to stretch your quads. Let me know if your knee can take this, okay? If not, I'll modify it for you."

I carefully lower myself to the ground as well, biting back a grunt as my sore muscles protest. The kneeling part is doable, even on my injured knee, but as soon as I try to lower my weight, my quads indicate that's far enough, thank you very much. "I can't go lower than this. This already hurts."

"Then don't force it. Go until you feel it pull without it hurting. And then hold it for at least thirty seconds. Every time you do this, it will stretch them a little more, and eventually, you'll be able to lie flat on your back...like this."

He drops back, his body almost flat on his back on the mat and his legs bending at an angle I didn't even know was humanly possible for nongymnasts. "Show off," I mutter as I clench my teeth and breathe through the discomfort.

Clean Start at Forty-Seven

He grins and sits back up. "I've always been bendy. My mom said I should've been a gymnast rather than play soccer. Okay, now sit like this."

He sits on his butt, then puts the soles of his feet against each other, dropping his knees sideways to the mat.

I eye it distrustfully. "That looks equally painful."

"That depends on how far I push your knees down."

"Let's get something clear right now. There will be no pushing anything down, okay? This body needs to take it slow."

He chuckles. "Yes, old man."

He did not just call me a... That little brat. I force my legs in the same position, though my knees don't even come close to the mat. It takes me a few seconds to be able to relax. "Why didn't you?"

"Why didn't I what?"

"Become a gymnast. I know you excelled at soccer, but I'm just curious."

My first hunch was the money, but would it have been more expensive than soccer at that age? Later on, Dory couldn't finance soccer on her meager income either. As far as I know, Benoni never found out who paid for his club fees, uniforms, and all the extra expenses that came with playing tournaments. I think his mom told him she'd gotten financial help or some kind of scholarship. That was all he needed to know.

He shrugs, but sadness clouds his eyes. "My mom wouldn't have been able to drive me to all the practices and, later, the tournaments. The soccer fields were close to our house, and I could ride my bike before I had my driver's license. But gym practice would've been too far from our house. I told her I wasn't interested, but..."

Right. That would've been a big problem. "Even as a kid,

you knew she'd never be able to pull that off. When was she diagnosed?"

"When I was eight, but she'd had issues for a while then. Even without the MS, it would've been a challenge. Single mom with a full-time job and irregular hours. How would she have ever managed that?"

She wouldn't have, and I'm not so privileged that I don't realize that. Sadness fills me. He gave up on something he could've been, could've achieved, to protect his mom...and she'd never known what he'd done for her. "You've been a good son to her," I say softly.

His smile is sweet. "She was the best mom I could ever have wished for. If I had to make sacrifices for her wellbeing, they were all worth it because she gave me so much more in return. Besides, I loved playing soccer, even if it was never my first choice. It helped me go to college."

Gah, he's gonna make me tear up. I look at the mat until I have myself under control again. Ever since I'm sober, I've become a sap. Seriously, I cry at everything. Those Facebook videos with puppies that save their owner from a snake or protect them from a bear or coyote? They have me bawling. Not kidding. And don't even get me started on military homecomings. Whenever I need a good cry, I put those on. Does the job every single time.

"Next one," Benoni says, and I refocus as he demonstrates another torturous position.

By the time we're done, my body is hurting less, which surprises me. "How is it possible that the muscle pain is less?"

"Stretching can help you recover better and quicker, though that's not even the primary goal. I'll be showing you a lot of different routines, and you can use the ones that benefit you the most."

"What else do you have planned for me for the next few weeks? A lot of cardio, I assume?"

"Actually, no. Yes, you'll be doing some cardio, but the main thing I want to focus on is strength training."

"Strength training? What, you want me to look like Arnold Schwarzenegger in his early years?"

He snorts. "Not really. Not that you could ever pull that off. First of all, you lack the natural build, and second, no offense, but aside from hard work, that usually also involved steroids. Few men can ever achieve muscles like that naturally."

"What's the idea behind the strength training, then?"

We're still on the mat across from each other, the room empty aside from us.

"I want you to grow stronger, to build muscles. That's not going to happen if we focus on cardio. Of course it's important, and we'll incorporate it as we get you back in shape, but it's not the main priority. We build muscles first to give you your strength back."

He's got a point there, though I don't quite agree with him on his wording. "I was never that strong, so I'm not sure if *back* is the right word here."

He assesses me, his head cocked. "You were never jacked, but you were definitely strong, Kinsey."

My belly tickles with the way he says my name, almost reverently. Maybe that's because he's not used to it after calling me Mr. Lindstrom for so long. "Why did you never call me Dr. Lindstrom, like all Jonathan's other friends?"

He quirks an eyebrow. "Don't tell me that's something that keeps you up at night."

"You called me Kinsey just now, and it made me wonder. All Jonathan's other friends always said Dr. Lindstrom, but you never did."

"I can't believe you remember that."

A muscle cramp shoots through my right calf. Damn, that one hurt.

"Cramps?" Benoni asks.

"Yeah, my calves. They've always been prone to cramping."

"All the more reason to be diligent about stretching, but for now, give me your leg."

"What?"

He taps my foot. "Give me your leg. Put it on my thigh."

I have no idea what he wants, but I obey almost automatically. It's hard not to when his voice gets all bossy.

Within seconds, he's untied my shoe and taken it off, the sock as well. "That's not gonna smell pretty," I warn him, but he laughs.

"I'm around sweaty people all day. Doesn't bother me one bit. Now, how does this feel?"

He digs his thumbs into the sole of my foot, and I shriek like a banshee. "Shit! Holy...."

"I'll take that as a 'Yes, Benoni, it's rather uncomfortable.'"

"That's not 'rather uncomfortable.' That *hurts*."

He grins. "I'm on the right track, then."

He keeps massaging my foot, and I let out a groan that's somewhere between a grunt of pain and a moan of pleasure. God, that feels good. He finds all these pressure points and puts his fingers and thumb into them, and it's awful and amazing at the same time. If it wasn't so painful, I'd be worried about growing hard, but there's no chance of that happening.

"I'd recommend getting sports massage." Benoni taps my other leg and takes off that shoe and sock as well when I put it in his lap. "Your muscles are tight, and while stretching will help with that, a massage can help you get rid of it even faster. You may also have some hot spots a good massage therapist could solve with myofascial work. I can recommend a few good therapists in the area."

"Okay, I'll look into that."

I have to close my eyes. The way he massages me is strangely intimate, even though it's not. His touch is clinical and professional, but I haven't been touched in so long, and I respond to it on an emotional level I wasn't expecting.

"So why did you never call me doctor?" I get back to our earlier discussion.

He's quiet for so long that I open my eyes. He's studying me while his hands continue their exploration of my muscle knots and pressure points. "I would've called you doctor if I had encountered you in your professional setting, but at home, it felt to me like it was unnecessary. Not that I don't respect you or the knowledge and experience you have, but...I don't know. Using a title also creates distance. It's a constant reminder of *what* you are, not *who* you are, and I guess I wasn't sure if that was what you wanted."

He's far more perceptive than I ever gave him credit for. "I appreciated it, just so you know. Made me feel like you saw me and not just my title and profession."

His smile is wide. "Then I'm glad I made that choice."

He lets go of my legs. "Let's take some pictures."

"Pictures?"

"Before pictures now that you're starting your health journey. We'll take new ones every month so you'll be able to track your progression."

I mentally groan. I can barely stand to look at myself in the mirror these days, let alone take pictures, but Benoni has a way of announcing something that makes it hard for me to say no. It would feel like disappointing him, which makes no sense at all. And so I dutifully pose for him. Shirtless. Front, back, sides, all both with my arms down and in positions that show the utter lack of definition in my biceps.

"Thanks for indulging me," he says when we're done.

"Indulging you?"

He grins. "It was clear you didn't want to do it, but you did it anyway. For me. So thank you for that."

Before I can respond, he walks off. "See you in two days, Kinsey!"

6

2014: BENONI

I'm pretty sure Mr. Lindstrom has been avoiding me ever since Jonathan's birthday party a few weeks ago. I've hung out with Jonathan three times since then, and for two of those, Mr. Lindstrom was home, but he went out of his way to evade me.

Not that I blame him. That must have been one of the more awkward experiences of his life. Now that some time has passed, I wonder if I misinterpreted his reaction. Wouldn't everyone get aroused from watching a scene like that, regardless of their sexual orientation? My ace and demi friends excluded, perhaps, but sex is sex. On some level, it's always arousing, isn't it? Maybe I came to the wrong conclusion about him. It doesn't matter anyway, since I never uttered a word about it to anyone, especially not to Jonathan. Fuck, no.

Jonathan and I are hanging around his pool. His parents' pool, I should say. And a very nice one it is, even for Floridian standards. Having a pool here isn't that exceptional, but few people have one this size and with such nice seating around it—all in the shade, should one so wish, courtesy of a set of sun sails that can be put up or taken down in a jiffy.

Usually, we're in the water a lot, but today, we're lounging in the shade. We're both tired as fuck after a party at Annika's. She's a girl Jonathan has fucked a few times, a cheerleader with legs for miles and great skills in bed, according to Jonathan. I'll take his word for it. They're not serious, he keeps telling me, but I'm not sure she knows that too. I overheard her mention something about maintaining a long-term relationship with him in college. Not my circus, though, and not my monkeys.

"Senior year is almost over," Jonathan laments. "I'll miss this."

I snort. "Yeah, your college dorm will be a definitive step down for you."

He got accepted into the University of South Florida in Tampa for Medical Sciences, a premed program. For as long as I've known him, it's been his dream to become a doctor, just like his dad. I'll never say it out loud, but I was a bit surprised he even got into this program. His grades weren't that good, and he's had to work hard to maintain a good GPA this year.

So have I, don't get me wrong, but I'm not setting out to be a doctor. I'm over the moon with my full scholarship to a small, private university in Buffalo, New York, to study sports science. Granted, that far north wasn't my first choice, but I'm not gonna say no to a full ride. For that much money, I can take the crazy amounts of snow Buffalo is known for.

"It will be." He's deadly serious, and I don't dare to make fun of him. I do like him, and we've been friends for years by now, but the dude is spoiled. Classic rich kid, full of privilege he's not even aware of.

"I'm sure you'll survive."

He opens the little poolside fridge. "Shit, we're out of soda again. Judith had friends over yesterday, and of course, they didn't restock. Stupid fucking teenage girls."

Judith is two years younger than him, and she's all legs with round hips and a pair of perfect boobs. If I were into girls, I'd definitely do her. She's dropped enough hints she'd be willing, but alas. One hundred percent gay here, always have been. Girls are amazing, and I love them to pieces, but they don't do anything for me. Besides, she's sixteen, and I'm not touching that with a ten-foot pole.

I push myself up on the lounge chair. "No worries, I'll grab some. You filled it last time, so it's my turn anyway."

I've been here often enough to know my way around the house. Sodas are kept in the garage, so they're already relatively cool when they enter the fridge.

"Thanks, Ben," Jonathan says, then stretches out on the lounge chair again and closes his eyes. "Fuck, I'm tired."

I head inside, where the cold blast of the AC makes my skin pebble. Jonathan's mom always prefers it at freezing temperature. No idea why. Seriously, it's like sixty-eight in there, and that while it's ninety outside. My fingers itch to crank it up, since she's not home anyway. She and Judith are shopping for a prom dress. But nah, I'd better not. Don't want to risk wearing out my welcome here.

Shivering, I continue down the hallway to the garage. A faint noise startles me. What the hell is that? I thought Jonathan and I were alone, but that sounds like a TV. I check the living room and the family room, but both are empty. Huh. Weird. I must've imagined it, then. But when I step back into the hallway, I hear it again. It's...moaning?

What the fuck? It's porn. Someone is watching porn. Or at least a sex scene because that sound is unmistakable. But who is watching it if Judith and her mom are gone?

Oh, shit. That leaves only one person—Jonathan's dad.

I shouldn't do this, and yet I move as if my feet have a will of their own until I'm right in front of his study. The grunts and groans are crystal clear. Yup, definitely porn. I slap my hand over my mouth to hold back a giggle. It shouldn't be funny that a grown-ass man is watching porn. I mean, we all do it. Or a lot of us anyway. Nothing weird about it as far as I'm concerned.

Still, the idea that Mr. Lindstrom is watching it, maybe stroking himself, has me fascinated. I press my ear against the door, but nothing else but the sounds of sex from the TV drift through. Obviously, I now need to know what kind of porn the man is into. He's a classy guy, so I'm betting he's got taste.

"Fuck, that feels good," a low, gravelly voice says. Definitely a man. "Mmm, yes, like that. Harder. Fuck me harder with that fat cock of yours."

Wait, what? Fuck me harder? If that's a man saying that, then...

He's watching gay porn. The sounds start again, loud and clear. Flesh slapping against flesh, grunts and moans... from two men. There's no woman in this scene.

Why the fuck is Mr. Lindstrom watching gay porn? Duh, what a stupid question is that. There can only be one reason, and it only confirms my earlier conclusion after that birthday party. Mr. Lindstrom is not straight.

An image fills my mind: Mr. Lindstrom in his underwear, his cock straining against the fabric. Only this time, he takes it out, fisting himself as he watches me get a blow job. His moan, low and sexy, shoots straight to my cock, which twitches in response. I shudder as I look down, my dick peeping out from under the Speedos I'm wearing. Fuck, I'm hard. I can't go back into the pool like this. Jonathan will have a conniption.

I press my hand against my dick and, after listening carefully and making sure no one is coming, slip it under my Speedos. It's not difficult to picture Mr. Lindstrom standing right in front of me, as hard and aroused as I am, biting his lip as he tries to hold back. "You're so sexy in those Speedos," he tells me in my fantasy.

I fuck into my hand. "So are you."

"Mmm, I get so hard watching you in the pool. You're like a young god, so sinfully sexy with your strong body, your round ass, and that perfect cock of yours. I've been watching you all afternoon. Didn't you see me? Behind the windows, like a pervert, a dirty stalker."

"You can watch me anytime."

"I want you to fuck me," he whispers, and I bite back a moan that threatens to spill from my lips.

"Yeah? You want this cock in your ass, Mr. Lindstrom?"

"I want you to fuck me hard. Make me feel every inch."

This time, I can't hold back the grunt that escapes me, and I freeze, my heart skipping a beat, my hand on my cock. A second later, the porn soundtrack stops, and I yank my hand so fast out of my Speedos that the elastic band snaps against my skin. Shit. I gotta get out of here.

Thank fuck I'm barefoot, and I race down the hallway and up the stairs, thanking my lucky stars it's carpeted so I barely make a sound. I reach the door to Jonathan's room just as the door downstairs opens. I rush inside, close the door as softly as I can, and dart into his en suite bathroom.

Only then do I stop, panting with my back against the closed door. Fuck, that was close. Way too close. I breathe in deeply and exhale, forcing my heartbeat to calm down.

Silence surrounds me. No running footsteps, no slamming of doors. I relax again. Damn, but that fantasy was sweet. Mmm, yes, it was. The chances of Mr. Lindstrom ever saying something like that to me in real life are nonexistent, but a boy can dream and then jack himself off to that dream. Twice.

7

KINSEY

I never thought one could get used to torture, but apparently, I was wrong. We're four weeks in, and I haven't missed a session yet despite my body doing its hardest to keep convincing me working out is a bad idea. A horrible one.

"It's time for our four-week evaluation." Benoni is as chipper as ever. No, chipper isn't the right word because it's never fake. He's not bubbly, over-the-top happy. He's just positive. Always encouraging, with kind words of comfort and inspiration, never pessimistic.

"Okay, which involves what?"

"Remember those pictures we took the second session?"

I nod.

"We're gonna take them again and compare."

I groan. "Seriously? I have to pose for you again?"

He puts his hands on his hips. "You're making it sound like I'm asking you to pose for nudes."

I snort. "With this body? Not bloody likely."

"You underestimate yourself."

I open my mouth to make light of that remark, but his

eyes show an honesty I wasn't expecting. And something else as well, something I can't quite put my finger on. Not quite teasing, but...I don't know what it is. "Nobody wants to see me naked, trust me."

He cocks his head, his eyes taking me in from top to bottom. "At the risk of repeating myself, you underestimate yourself."

I look away, tingles running over my body as if a colony of ants is having a day out. Why does his expression makes me so uncomfortable? "I appreciate you trying to be nice, I do, but we both know my prime days are way behind me. I can barely see them in the rearview mirror anymore."

"Kinsey."

His voice is clipped. Is he upset now? I meet his eyes. "Why is this so important to you?"

"You're putting yourself down. I don't like that."

I shift my weight from one foot to the other. It shouldn't matter at all what Benoni thinks of me or anything I say, and yet his displeasure sits heavy on my heart. "I'm just being realistic here. I'm forty-seven, Benoni. My body has been through a lot, even before I became an addict. Of course I want to get in better shape, and I do believe that's possible, but the idea of my body ever becoming attractive again isn't something I'm willing to entertain at this point. It would only lead to disappointment, and I've encountered enough of that from myself and those around me to last me a lifetime."

Benoni's eyes grow soft. "Come with me for a moment, would you?"

What is he up to? Still, I don't ask. Without even thinking about it, I follow him as he walks across the big room into the weight-lifting area. "Hey, Frank!" he calls out, and one of the men who are working out there looks up. "Can I steal you for a moment?"

Frank puts the dumbbells down and comes closer. I've seen him around, though I've never talked to him. "You? Anytime. How do you want me? Naked with a bow around me?"

Benoni laughs. "Quit it, you old flirt. Frank, this is Kinsey, a new client."

Frank extends his hand and gives me a firm handshake. "My apologies," Frank says, his chocolate-brown eyes serious and meeting mine dead on. "I hope my harmless flirting didn't make you feel uncomfortable."

"No, it's... No problem." Why is he even apologizing to me?

My confusion must've shown because he sends me a careful smile, his teeth white against his rich, olive skin. "Not everyone is comfortable with gay men flirting. Not that I mean anything by it, don't get me wrong. Ben is nothing but professional, and he knows I'm just yanking his chain. But if it made you uncomfortable..."

"Not at all. In fact, I'm..." I have to take a deep breath before I can finish my sentence. "I'm gay myself."

Frank gapes at me while Benoni sends me a look stuffed with pride. Jerry told me that coming out isn't a one-time thing but a constant in the life of someone who's not straight. I didn't grasp what he meant at first, but I've come to understand it. In situations like this, the choice to come out or not is mine. I could've kept my mouth shut, since nothing forced me to admit I'm gay, but I wanted to. I want to become so comfortable with who I am that I won't hesitate anymore.

"I'll be damned," Frank says. "My gaydar must've been malfunctioning."

I don't know how to respond to that, and I just smile. Please don't let me come across like a moron. Or should I admit I've only been out a short time? That seems too personal. I don't even know him, so I say nothing.

"Frank, can you show Kinsey your upper body?" Benoni picks the conversation back up.

Frank grins. "My pleasure."

"I figured, since you flaunt it for practically everyone who walks in here," Benoni teases him.

"If you'd told me he was gay, I would've had my shirt off already," Frank fires back. Their banter makes me smile. One day, I hope to be able to talk like that to someone as hot as Benoni, though Frank is good looking too. One day, I will get over my nerves and my self-consciousness and the frustrating voice inside my head that constantly judges me, and know what to say.

Frank lifts his shirt over his head and drops it on the floor, and holy shit, those are some serious abs. His shoulders are wide and well defined, and so is his chest, which tapers down in a perfect V-shape. Like Benoni, he's got multiple tattoos, and they look good on him, giving him a bit of a bad-boy vibe, even though his eyes are warm and kind. God, if only I could look like that.

"Now can I show Kinsey your before pics?" Benoni asks him.

"Absolutely. Do you still have them on your phone?"

Benoni already flips through his photos. He hands me his phone. "Look at this one. This was Frank a year ago."

I barely hold back a gasp. Is he kidding? That skinny, pale man can't be... I look from the pic to the real Frank and back. The face is the same, and so are some of the tattoos, though he's gotten a few more since that picture was taken. "That's an amazing transformation. Wow. I'm impressed."

"Frank is a cancer survivor, and in that pic, he had been declared cancer-free after two years of treatment. He came to me because he wanted to get in shape after losing a lot of weight due to his illness."

"Okay." I give the phone back to Benoni.

"Kinsey, he's three years older than you."

My mouth drops open. "You're shitting me. You're *fifty*?"

Frank laughs. "Turning fifty-one in two months."

I study him in more detail. His hair is much more silver than mine, and so is his beard, and he has lines around his eyes I'm only too familiar with. The evidence of his age never registered with me because I never glanced past how hot he was, how amazing his body was. To have a body like that at his age is just...

It sinks in. Frank is older than me. He looked like utter crap after his illness, and now he has this jaw-dropping physique. That means there's hope for me.

"Thank you," I say hoarsely, looking first at Frank and then at Benoni. "Message received."

"Good," Benoni says. "Mission accomplished."

"If you want some tips on how to get from where you are now to where I am, I'm always happy to talk to you," Frank says. "Ben can give you my phone number. Text me, and we can set up a coffee date or something."

"Okay. Thank you, I appreciate that."

A look passes from Frank to Benoni, the corners of Frank's mouth trembling. What am I missing?

"Thanks, Frank." Benoni gives him a slap on his shoulder. "Go back to your workout."

Frank sends me a smile and a wink, then walks off, putting his shirt back on. I follow Benoni into the smaller room, where it's just us. He stares at me as if he's debating with himself, then sighs. "He was asking you out."

"Come again?"

"Frank was asking you out. His offer to share his workout routine over coffee? That was him asking you out."

Fuck me sideways. How did I miss that? I groan, burying my head in my hands. "I feel like an idiot."

Benoni pets my shoulder. "You'll get the hang of it."

"Not spontaneously. God, the last time I dated was..." I let out a long, shuddering breath. "Twenty-eight years ago. That's how long it's been, and that was with a girl. A woman. And I'm not even sure if that could be called dating, but that's a whole different story. I have no idea how to do this."

Then I groan all over again. Way to go, blurting out all this. Can I make even more of a fool of myself? "I'm sorry, Benoni. That was unprofessional and way too personal, and I shouldn't have said that. This isn't your problem."

My cheeks heat up under his scrutinizing gaze. "Were you under the impression that I minded?"

In all fairness, I didn't even consider that. "No? I mean, maybe? I minded. I shouldn't discuss things like this with you."

"Why not?"

I blink. What does he mean? "Because I'm... You're... You're my trainer, not a friend, and you're twenty years younger than me, and..."

"And I'm your son's friend," he finishes softly. "Is that what this is about? Would you feel the same way with anyone else?"

"Honestly? Yes, I would. I'm not the type to share details of my personal life with everyone and certainly not with people I interact with professionally."

"Okay, but that implies you'll talk about this with someone else, right? So who will you ask for advice on dating a man and gay culture?"

I open my mouth and close it again. Damn, he's right. I've talked about some of it with Jerry, but we haven't gotten into details. Our relationship is good, but it's focused on my recovery. It would be all kinds of weird and awkward asking him for dating advice, aside from the fact that he doesn't want me to think about that yet. He doesn't feel I'm ready to date, and he's probably right.

"I don't know," I say finally. "You have to understand that this is... I'm not a talker in the first place, but this subject is... I don't know how to explain it."

"Try me. I promise I don't judge."

He wouldn't. I can't explain why I know that with such certainty, but I do. Still, that only makes it marginally easier. "I grew up conservative Christian." I mimic Benoni as he sits down on the mat. Good idea. This is a conversation I'd rather have sitting than standing. "My grandfather was a well-known preacher in his days, and my parents still are strict. Me coming out..."

I have to swallow before I can continue, the sting of their rejection so sharp it aches.

"They didn't take it well, let me put it that way, and neither did my two older sisters, who are both still involved in the church. Not that I expected anything else. I was raised in a culture that focused on holiness versus sin, the battle between good and evil, God and the devil, angels and demons. And above all, it emphasized the importance of purity, sexually speaking. No sex before marriage, no adultery, but nothing, absolutely nothing, was worse than being attracted to the same sex."

"You mean being gay."

I shake my head. "Being gay is using a modern term for it. That wasn't how the church worded it and how my family saw it, and they still don't. They deny being gay is a reality.

To them, it's not about identity. It's about a choice. They consider it being tempted by the devil by experiencing attraction to men. Something that needs to be battled, that can be prayed away. It's a test, so to speak, a trial you have to overcome to become more holy and Christlike. And in their eyes, I failed that test by choosing the homosexual lifestyle."

How come I have this conversation with Benoni, while I never talked about it with Jonathan and Judith? They never listened, weren't even willing to ask these questions in the first place. I don't want to blame Caroline because I understand she reacted from a place of intense hurt, but she played a big role in their attitude toward me.

"They deny being gay is something you're born with? That it's how you're wired?"

I nod. "And if you deny that, it all becomes a choice. In their eyes, I choose to be gay, to live in sin. Even though..."

No, I can't say that out loud. It's way too personal. Why do I keep wanting to tell Benoni much more than I should? He's a good listener who makes it easy to forget how young he is.

"Even though what?"

"It's not important."

He quirks an eyebrow. "Somehow, I doubt that."

I should've known he wouldn't let me off the hook that easily. He's tenacious. Is it the kindness in his eyes or the fact that he's listening to me and allowing me to share my side of the story that makes me respond to him? "It's hard to accept I'm living in sin when all I did was come out. I haven't... The divorce only became final mere weeks ago."

Understanding dawns in his eyes. "You haven't acted on it yet."

"No."

"Ever?"

"Ever. I was married, Benoni. I never violated my marriage vows, not even when she filed for divorce. My ex-wife was and is the only person I ever slept with. The only one I ever kissed. And yet I'm called a sinner and judged more harshly than pastors who slept with multiple women in their congregation."

"Because you're gay."

"Yes. In the list of sins, homosexuality ranks at the very top, above infidelity, sex before marriage, rape, and maybe even pedophilia."

He shakes his head, disgust painted all over his face. "Those opinions make me furious. I'm so sorry you had and have to deal with that, and from your own parents and sisters, of all people."

His compassion soothes my raw insides. Talking about this is hard. The only people I ever told were Jerry and Sosha, my therapist in rehab. Neither of them comes from a religious background, which makes it difficult to talk about this with them. Growing up as I did is like living in a foreign world, speaking a whole different language. Unless you've been a part of it, it's all but impossible to understand.

"But that's why talking about being gay and everything that comes with it is hard for me. Especially dating or"—I swallow—"sex. I have forty-seven years of internalized homophobia to overcome. That voice in my head that tells me I'm a sinner and I'm going to hell has grown much softer from a ferocious scream to a whisper, but it's still there."

We sit quietly, and I love that he's unafraid of the silence, that he allows it to hang so he can choose his words rather than say something quickly to avoid it.

"I want to say two things," he finally says. "The first is that your identity as a gay man isn't dependent on you acting on it. You're valid and authentic, even if you would decide never to date a man. And the second is this." He meets my eyes dead on. "Everyone's journey is different. There's no timeline for this, no schedule you have to follow. So walk this path at your own pace. Take as much time as you need to get healthy, physically and emotionally. And if you have questions about anything—dating, gay culture, sex, anything—I'm here. I may be a lot younger than you, but I've been living out as gay since I was thirteen. You can't shock me easily, and I'd love to be your safe place to ask questions and get answers."

My eyes grow stupidly misty, and it takes me a long time to speak, but Benoni just sits next to me, relaxed. "Thank you. That was... Thank you."

He bobs his head in acknowledgment. He doesn't get up but keeps me company, a silent and comfortable presence, while I process the conversation. His listening ear is both a gift and a curse, allowing me to realize how affirming it is when people listen...and how heartbreaking it is that those closest to me never even tried.

8

BENONI

Jonathan greets me with the standard bro hug, grinning widely. "Good to see you. It's been forever, man."

I hug him back. "I know. Sorry, life got crazy."

I wave at his roommate, Rip, who sits on the couch, playing Forza Horizon on the Xbox. He's got some kind of software programmer job that leaves him with too much time to play games half the day and get stoned, but whatever. Not my problem, since I don't have to live with him.

Jonathan grabs a couple of cold ones, and then we make our way outside to their tiny patio. When we both came back to Sarasota after getting our degrees, Jonathan suggested we share a house, but I kindly declined. I love him, but he's not as gay-friendly as he thinks he is. Even before his dad came out, he's made some questionable digs at my sexuality over the years, stuff like gay men being more promiscuous and less likely to end up in a long-term relationship, more prone to cheat, and crap like that.

In his defense, the reason may be that he was raised going to church until a few years ago and the strong conservative Christian influence of his grandparents, but still. I have zero desire to share a house with someone who has a problem with me taking advantage of the wide variety of available men in the area. Besides, Leif needs me, and I love rooming with him, even if he can be a pain in my ass.

The sun is setting, and it's still hot as fuck, but that's Florida for you, even at the beginning of September. My house is a little closer to the beach, so I often pick up a bit of a breeze, but Jonathan's is too far out to make that happen. We settle on the bright yellow Adirondack chairs, then clink our beer bottles. I take a big swig of the zero percent alcohol. I'm not in a hurry, but I have to drive back home, and I'm not doing that with alcohol in my system. Thank you, Mr. Lindstrom.

"How's work been?" I ask.

"Good. I mean, the usual craziness, but I still love it."

Jonathan is an ER nurse, following in his father's footsteps in a way. He wanted to become a doctor, but in college, he discovered he wasn't cut out for it. At least, that's what he told me. He dropped out of premed and switched to nursing school. He works for a different hospital than his father did, so the whole fallout of his father's coming out and addiction only caused minor ripples for him at work. News travels, of course, but it wasn't too bad from what I understand. "Any weird patients?"

He frowns. "You always asked my dad that, back when you used to come over a lot."

I shrug. "He often had funny stories to tell. I figured since you're in the same line of work, you might too."

"I'm not a doctor."

"Yes, Captain Obvious, I'm aware, but you're still seeing patients, no?"

Jesus, why is he so testy about this? I asked a simple question.

He holds up his hands. "Sorry. I overreacted. It's just... It reminded me of my dad, and that's not something I like at the moment."

Yeah, no shit. Ever since the news broke about Kinsey's addiction, followed by him entering rehab and the Lindstroms getting divorced, Jonathan has refused to talk about it. Whenever I bring it up, he shuts that shit down faster than the speed of light. "No worries."

He leans back in his chair, relaxing again. "But yes, we had the craziest woman come in yesterday. She brought her teenage kid in, fourteen years old. And the kid is as red as a tomato. Like, so red that I cringed when I saw his skin because holy crap, that had to hurt. So we ask her what happened, and she launches into this whole tirade about how she used sunscreen, but it didn't work. I'm thinking that she didn't put enough on, you know, like maybe forgot to reapply. But no, it turns out she thought the SPF factor on those bottles was the age range for that product."

"*What?*"

Jonathan nods, grinning. "Yup. She'd used SPF 15 on her son and SPF 50 on herself and then wondered why she was fine and he was sunburned within an inch of his life."

I groan. "Oh my god, that poor kid."

"Yeah, we kept him for a few hours in the ER, loading him up with fluids and helping his skin cool down. But he's gonna feel that for a good week or so."

"Only in Florida."

"Damn right. How about you? Still loving it at the sports studio?"

"Absolutely. I signed on a few interesting new clients, and I'm looking forward to seeing their transformation."

I'm not mentioning his dad is one of those new clients, obviously. Aside from taking confidentiality seriously, even if I'm not legally bound to anything, I don't want Jonathan to know. Not when he's still being such an asshole to Kinsey.

He smiles at me. "That's awesome. I'm glad you found a job you loved."

Is there a hint of condescension in Jonathan's tone, or am I imagining it? He never understood what fascinated me about sports science. Sure, he understood I loved sports, as I'd been playing soccer since I was a kid and made it to varsity in high school. It's how I got into a good college: on a full-ride soccer scholarship. Without that, I would never have been able to afford it. My mom busted her ass paying for my soccer, and I'm still not sure how she pulled it off. She said she got financial aid for me, but I think her brother, Tim, pitched in.

Jonathan never got that sports was more to me than a hobby, even knowing that I'd never be good enough to play professionally. I never wanted to. All I wanted was a job where I'd be involved in sports, as a coach, a trainer, or something similar. I think Jonathan didn't feel that was a college-level job, but I suspect he has a chip on his shoulder from not getting into med school. He never got any flak for it from his parents, that much he's been clear about, but he was disappointed in himself, I think.

We chat easily, like we always do, covering all kinds of topics and catching up on people we know. Finally, I drop the question I've been wanting to ask him all night. I haven't brought the relationship with his kids up with Kinsey because I don't want to pry. Even more since it seems to be such a painful topic to him. "How's your dad doing?"

His face tightens. "Don't know, don't care."

"Really?"

Clean Start at Forty-Seven   61

He scoffs. "What's so hard to understand about that? He ruined our family, our reputation."

I let that sink in for a moment. "I'm assuming you're referring to his addiction?"

"That, plus everything else. The way he left my mom, how he hurt us... Everything."

"I thought your mom was the one who filed for divorce?"

He waves his hand. "Semantics, at that point. He was in rehab, so it's not like she had much of a choice."

Way to stick it to a man when he's already down, but I don't say it. "She could've waited until he was out."

"Maybe, but we weren't even sure if he'd kick his habit, you know? Like, he's an addict who has lied to us for ages. We can't trust him."

"Mmm. So when you're saying he ruined your family, you're referring to his addiction."

Jonathan sits up a little straighter. "That first and foremost, but also... Him saying that he lived a lie for all those years hit us hard. If he's really gay, he should have realized that ages ago. In fact, he should never have married my mom. It was completely unfair to her."

I inhale, forcing down the irritation that bubbles to the surface. "Not everyone's journey to coming out is quite that easy and straightforward."

He cocks his head as he studies me. "You knew you were gay when you were thirteen. You told me."

"I did. I also had a very liberal, accepting mom who didn't give two shits about my sexuality. From what I understand, your father grew up in a conservative Christian family. Big difference. Plus, it was a long time ago in a different time."

"What do you mean?"

"Opinions have evolved over time. Thirty years ago, being

gay wasn't as accepted as it is now, especially not in conservative families." The conversation with Kinsey plays in my mind, what he told me, the emotion in his voice as he tried to explain what had been new to me. When I got back home that day, I spent hours online reading stories like his. I learned so much, and all of it was gut wrenching. "In fact, most of the time, it wasn't even called being gay. It was considered a lifestyle, a decision, a path you opted to go down. Not something you were, something you had no choice in."

He frowns. "I'm not sure I understand."

"It's a difference in how it's talked about, the terms we use. You told me I knew I was gay when I was thirteen. Being gay isn't an expression they used back then. They would've called it choosing the homosexual lifestyle or even a deviant lifestyle. All the language they used denoted choice, not identity."

He's quiet for a long time. "I never thought of it like that," he finally says. "My father's family, like my grandparents and aunts and uncles, are super strict Christian, and until I was fourteen, we went to church every Sunday as well. Youth group condemned homosexuality, but I never knew the church didn't see it as an identity."

"How did your father's family react when your dad came out?"

Jonathan cringes. "Not good. They told him he's no longer welcome unless he repents or something."

My heart breaks for Kinsey. Rejected by his parents, his siblings, and his kids. And they wonder why he waited so long to come out. The man lost everything. He knew he would, and he still chose to live authentically. That's some serious courage right there.

But I don't want to bash Jonathan over the head with it.

No, let me rephrase that. I *do* want to bash him over the head with it, but I refrain. All I can do is give him the facts, ask the right questions, and hope that he'll change his mind. He's smart, and despite the awful way he reacted to his dad coming out, he's not anti-gay or a bad person. He's just showing his privilege and his upbringing, is all. Kinsey managed to overcome it, though he still has demons to fight, from what I understand.

My guess is Jonathan got caught up in his mom's fury. Jonathan was always closer to his mom than his dad. He and Judith both were. Not that strange with the number of hours Kinsey worked. And of course I understand that Mrs. Lindstrom was heartbroken when Kinsey came out. Well, I can't understand, as I've never been in that position, but I can imagine. But I still don't think it's fair to poison your kids against their father, no matter what he's done. It's not like Kinsey is a rapist or a child molester.

"That's what I mean. He must've known they'd react that way," I say kindly.

"I suppose so. Never thought of it like that."

"And don't forget that your father was a teenager in the eighties and early nineties, at the height of the AIDS crisis, when gay men were dying left and right. The whole public opinion on that was judgmental toward, again, the homosexual lifestyle. Under those circumstances, coming out as gay is far from easy. He would've had to go against his family, his religion, his entire social circle, and even against society as a whole."

Another long silence. "How do you know all this? Is there some kind of Gay History 101 that's required when you come out?"

I bite back the sharp remark that's on the tip of my

tongue. "Nope, no required reading for being gay," I say instead, going for a light tone.

He sighs. "Yeah. Thank you anyway. It's been... I didn't know all that. It doesn't change that my dad is a dick, but I guess I never looked at it like that."

Small steps. Rome wasn't built in a day, and if I want Jonathan to see things from Kinsey's point of view, I have to be patient. Change is almost always gradual and the result of repeated exposure, rarely radical and spontaneous. "I know you were hurt," I say, leaving in the middle who did the hurting. "All I'm saying is that you might want to try to see your dad's point of view too."

The silence stretches between us, but I can tell he's thinking, his brows furrowed. "Did you hear Trevor is getting a divorce?" he asks. Not a subtle way to change the subject, but I let it slide. I've given him food for thought.

"Again? That's what, his third? What happened this time?"

Jonathan launches into a story about a guy we went to school with, and all I can do is hope that my words have had some impact on him. I don't know why it matters so much to me to see the relationship between Kinsey and his kids restored, but it does.

9
KINSEY

February 8, 2021

Kinsey,

We received your letter informing us you've chosen to divorce Caroline and live a life of sin. I can't tell you how disappointed and hurt we are that you would turn your back on Jesus like this, denying all that you were brought up with. We hope and pray that you will change your mind. It's not too late to return to God's family.

We will pray for your soul, but until you repent, you are not welcome in our home, and we no longer consider you our child. No son of ours will choose to be a homosexual. It's an abomination in the eyes of the Lord.

Our wills have been altered accordingly. We will not allow our money to be used for your indulgence in sin.

Samuel and Esther Lindstrom

10

KINSEY

"You look good," Jerry says as soon as he sees me. He gives me a warm hug before I settle down across from him in the Starbucks. "I take it the gym is working for you?"

"It is. Better than I expected, to be honest."

I hesitate. Shall I show him? For fuck's sake, this is Jerry. He knows all the bad stuff about me already, and he's never even blinked twice. I take out my phone and pull up the before and after pics Benoni sent me.

I hand him the phone. "This is the difference in four weeks."

He whistles between his teeth. "That's a remarkable difference, even in that short timeframe. How did you do it?"

"Followed my trainer's advice to a tee. We did lots of strength training and stretching, only a little cardio, and I started paying more attention to what I eat. I gained two pounds, which thrills me."

"It should." Jerry gives me my phone back. "That's great work, Kinsey. I'm proud of you."

As always, I choke up at those words. Jerry knows the

effect they have on me, how they remind me of the parental approval I miss so terribly. He's my age, so it's not even about him fulfilling some kind of father figure role. It's just a deep need inside me that we've identified together, and that I'm working on with his and Sosha's help.

Jerry sits back in silence, which gives me the time to recover, and I take a couple of deep breaths, then sip on my tea. I don't drink caffeine anymore these days. For the foreseeable future, I want to keep my body as clean as possible, including what I put in it.

"How are you otherwise?" Jerry asks when I've collected myself.

"Good. Better than I was last time."

Jerry and I meet in person every other week, but at my request, we text daily. When he became my sponsor, he told me he'd let me decide on the intensity and frequency of our contact, and I'm grateful he's been so flexible and accommodating. He's been sober for ten years now, and since he's gay as well, that makes him a perfect sponsor for me.

"Tell me three things that went great."

"I didn't skip a single session at the gym. I created a daily schedule I stuck to, getting up at six thirty and being in bed by ten." I check them off on my fingers. "And I've had three meals every day, with some snacks in between."

"Good job, Kinsey. I'm glad to see you're taking better care of yourself. It's so important on this journey. Now, what are you struggling with?"

On the drive over, I thought about this question, which always comes up. In the six months he's been my sponsor, Jerry has made it clear that he wants the truth from me, not a whitewashed version of it or whatever I think he wants to hear. So even if my struggle is the same week in, week out,

Clean Start at Forty-Seven 69

that's okay. And it is the same. It hasn't changed since the moment I left rehab.

"I miss my kids. I miss them so much."

Oh, the irony of the situation. For years and years, I hid in my work because spending time with my family made it too hard for me to keep my mask up, to keep pretending. Now that I've finally found the courage to ditch the facade, I don't have a family anymore...and I can't even blame them for it. I was never there for Jonathan and Judith, so for me to expect them to support me now is the highest level of hypocrisy. Yet the heart wants what it wants, and all I can do is hope. As long as I'm breathing, hope is still alive.

"I'm so sorry for you, Kinsey. I hope they'll find it in their hearts to forgive you," Jerry says, his voice kind and understanding.

Yeah. I don't see it happening anytime soon, but a man needs to cling to even the smallest sliver of hope to avoid losing what's left of his sanity.

"How are you doing on developing a new social network?"

I sigh. "Not so good. I never knew how hard it was to make new friends at my age. It's so complicated, especially because most men my age are married, and I'm single."

"Can you tell me what efforts you've made?"

Did I mention I love and hate Jerry in equal measure? He never lets me get away with anything. Come to think of it, I should introduce him to Benoni. Those two would get along just fine.

"None," I say. "I don't even know where to start."

"Kinsey."

I cringe. God, I hate the hint of disappointment in his voice. I may be forty-seven years old, but I feel like a child again, about to face my father's ire about something I did wrong.

"I'm sorry," he says softly. "I didn't mean to make you feel like you fucked up."

He can read me so well. It's one of the reasons why he's such a great sponsor. "I don't take disapproval and disappointment well," I admit.

"I know, and I should've been more sensitive toward you. That's not a button I meant to push."

"Thank you." We sit in silence, and my thoughts drift off to Benoni, like they do a lot. Probably because he's one of the few people I talk to other than Jerry and Sosha, who I still see every month. Oh, wait. I perk up. "I sort of became friends with my trainer."

"You did? Who are you working with?"

"Benoni. Ben."

"Benoni? I've never heard anyone call him that. I didn't even know that was his full name."

Right. I messed up there, didn't I? "I know him from... before. He was one of my son's best friends. Or he still is, I suppose."

Jerry's face grows serious. "You never mentioned that. Why? You know anyone from your past is a potential trigger for you, especially if they're in any way associated with you using."

"He's not. Absolutely not. I've barely seen him the last few years, as he was off to college in New York. Yes, he's from my past, but from before I was using."

Jerry studies me, then nods. "Okay. So you're saying you have become friends?"

"He's been helping me get back in shape, and we've talked quite a bit during sessions."

"There's a considerable age gap between you if he's the same age as your son."

I frown. "Are you saying I can't be friends with him?"

"He's gay, Kinsey. And attractive, I might add. *Very* attractive."

My mouth drops open. Is he seriously suggesting that...? "We're friends. I don't... What you're implying is ridiculous."

"Is it? Your face changed when you talked about him. As if you have feelings for him."

I fight hard to keep my features blank now. "Of course I have affection for him. He spent a lot of time at our house, and I liked having him around because he was polite and a good kid. That hasn't changed. He's determined to help me, and his support has already made a difference. But your suggestion there's more than that is just...absurd. He's over twenty years younger than me, not to mention the fact that I'm an addict in the worst shape of his life. Well, a little better shape than four weeks ago, but still. What could he want with an old fart like me? I'm sure he has his pick of men and that even if I were interested in him, which I'm not, I'd be dangling at the very bottom of his list."

Jerry leans back in his chair, crossing his arms. "That's a no, then."

Heat fills my cheeks. "A definitive no."

"Okay. Be careful, Kinsey. That's all I'm saying. You're not in a place to start a relationship right now."

I fight back the wave of irritation that swells up inside me. How do I throw Jerry off the trail? "I know, which is why I turned down an offer to go out with a guy my age."

"Someone asked you out?"

"Frank from the gym."

Jerry's mouth curls up in a smile. "Oh, I could see why he'd be interested in you. He's an old flirt, but it's all harmless, and he's a good guy. And he's your age and also attractive."

"He is, but since I'm not ready for anything yet, I said no."

"Smart. I'm glad to hear you're aware of the risks. You need to focus on you for a while, make sure you're strong enough to deal with whatever comes your way without having the urge to use."

"Hence my decision."

Jerry's expression softens. He puts his hand on mine and gently squeezes. "It must be hard for you, being out and still not being able to act on it. Though as I've said before, hooking up wouldn't be an issue at all as long as you're careful and keep it casual. That's sex. It's emotional entanglements I'm concerned about."

Jerry has brought the topic of casual sex up before, and while I appreciate him being so open and candid about it, it still makes me squirm. The idea of sex is enough to give me heart palpitations and make me break out in a sweat all over. How the hell would I ever be suave enough to get through a hookup? I'd be so nervous I'd throw up on the poor guy as soon as he touched me.

No, for now, porn will have to do, though that's not without its own issues, as I still get the occasional huge wave of guilt when I watch it. But I got myself a Ballsy Boys subscription, which, in combination with my right hand, is enough. It has to be.

11

BENONI

I check my watch. Kinsey should be here in fifteen minutes. Not that I'm counting down or anything.

Riiiight.

Of course I am, just like I have been for the six weeks we've been working together. He's always on time and hasn't missed a session once. He's an ideal client: dedicated, serious, someone who follows my advice to a tee. He's started working with a massage therapist to gain more flexibility in his knee, and he even booked a session with our dietitian to get some tips about his eating habits.

Like I said, ideal except for the pesky fact that I can't stop thinking about him. He shows up in my thoughts all the time and has even made an appearance in my dreams. Highly detailed and erotic dreams, I might add.

I'm not sure what's fueling this obsession with him. Sure, he's hella attractive, even if his body shows the effects of his addiction and lack of self-care. He's gained a little weight in all the right places, and he's getting some muscle definition, though he still has a long way to go. But I like him as a person too. I always have. He's kind and caring, and he has a wicked sense of humor, self-deprecating and sarcastic. Part of that is a defensive shield, but it still cracks me up.

That still doesn't explain my weird fascination with him, and neither does the fact that he's lonely. He hasn't said it in so many words, but it's become obvious from what he has shared about his life. He works, eats, comes to the gym, and has appointments with his sponsor, his therapist, and now with his massage therapist. That's it. He's never mentioned he sees anyone else.

He misses his kids. There's no doubt about that, even if he also communicated crystal clear that was a topic he didn't want to discuss. I've respected that, but knowing how much that hurts him has been gnawing at me. I want to help him, want to ease his loneliness, and reconnect him with his family, but that's impossible. I already pushed my luck by bringing it up with Jonathan in the first place. If I raise the subject with him again, he'll catch on for sure.

"He should be here in five minutes," Frank says, and I spin around. He stands behind me, observing me with sharp eyes that see far too much. He's always the joker, that one, hiding the real him behind a silver fox bad-boy exterior, but he doesn't fool me anymore.

"Who, Kinsey?" I try to make my voice sound neutral.

"Who else could you be waiting for?"

I shrug. "I have a lot of clients, Frank."

"You do, pretty boy, but none that you schedule three times a week at five thirty on the dot."

He's got me there. "I can't help but notice you're usually here around that time as well, whereas before, you used to come a little earlier."

Frank grins. "You're not the only one looking forward to seeing him, pretty boy."

I clench my jaw, fighting the urge to protest. It'll just rile

Frank up, and besides, it would be a bald lie. I *am* looking forward to seeing him, and apparently, so is Frank. "You still hoping he'll accept your coffee date?"

If it came out sharper than I had intended, Frank doesn't show it. "Hope springs eternal. We have a lot in common, including our age, so I'd like to think I have at least a shot with him."

They do have mutual interests. Frank is a former EMT who then became an ICU nurse, so they share that medical background.

"I don't think he's in the right place for a relationship, but you'll find out."

Frank cocks his head, studying me. "Why wouldn't he be?"

"You know I can't talk about what my clients tell me," I snap.

Frank holds up his hands. "Sorry, you're right. I didn't mean to pry and make you spill his secrets."

"I would never do that, and you know it."

"I know." He sighs. "But I can't help but be curious about him, Ben. He's closed off. I tried getting him to talk in the locker room last week, but all I got were polite short answers."

Warmth flares up inside me. Kinsey does talk to me. Not voluntarily and I know it costs him. He's always fighting his instinct to clam up, but he's shared some things with me, like the letter his parents sent him after he came out.

I'll never, ever understand how parents can reject their own children for their sexuality. If you ask me, it goes against every parental code, every maternal and paternal instinct, and even against the Bible—at least the way my mom and Uncle Tim interpreted it.

"He's got his reasons, Frank. Be patient with him." As

much as I hate to say it, I force the next words out. "He could use a friend."

Frank's eyes light up. "You think?"

I nod. "And that's all I'll say about it."

Frank puts his hand on my shoulder. "Thank you. I'll try to be his friend." He sighs as he lets go. "Let's face it. I've long since lost my taste for casual sex and hookups anyway."

From time to time, Frank and I run into each other in one of the two gay clubs in the area. After all, there are only so many places where gay men can score a hookup other than on Grindr. Although it's been a while since I went clubbing, and my last hookup was over a month ago. He and I gave each other a mutual blow job ages ago but then decided we'd rather stay friends.

"Are you sure? You've never had an issue finding some pretty twink to bounce on your cock."

"Sure, but I'm ready for more. I appreciate a good fuck as much as the next person, but that doesn't keep me warm at night or have breakfast with me in the morning. I'm fifty, Ben. I want someone to spend the rest of my life with, to grow old with. And none of those twinks, sexy as they may be, will ever want that role. They're not ready to settle down."

His words are surprisingly honest and serious, considering how flirty the man usually is. It's like he lets me see a different side to him, a deeper side. One that makes it easy to imagine him and Kinsey together. Frank has the life experience to help Kinsey find his way and show him how to live authentically, to introduce him to the wonders of gay sex and, ultimately, love. Isn't that what I want for him? Then why does it hurt so much to picture them together?

"I know how you feel." Huh, where did that come from?

"Yeah? You ready to settle down?"

I take a deep breath. "I think so. Like you, I love sex, but it's not enough in the long run. I want to come home to someone other than my roommate."

Frank chuckles. "I wouldn't mind coming home to that sexy thing at all."

He met Leif when we were clubbing once, recognizing him from his OnlyFans he's subscribed to. I try not to think about that too much. "He's not exactly a low-maintenance guy."

"I know he's got issues, but I'm pretty fucked up too, so who knows? Maybe our crazy will balance each other out."

I try to picture Frank disciplining Leif, and much to my surprise, it's easier to imagine than I expected. Huh. Not that I'll tell Frank that. Leif needs to get his shit together before he starts dating again, much like Kinsey, come to think of it. Or am I only telling myself that as an excuse to scare off Frank?

"Good luck with that," I say instead, and I'm spared further conversation when Kinsey walks in, dressed in a pair of black Nike shorts and a loose, blue Nike shirt. No formfitting clothes for him, and it drives home how insecure he still is about his body.

"Hello, Benoni," he says, and as always, his voice sinks deep inside me. "Hi, Frank."

"We were just talking about you," Frank says, and my heart skips a beat. What the hell will come out of his mouth next? With Frank, you never know.

"You were?" Kinsey looks from Frank to me and back. "Good things, I hope?"

His hopeful tone radiates vulnerability, and not for the first time, I fight the urge to wrap my arms around him and hug him, to tell him everything will be okay and that I'll protect him. Leif may appreciate that shit, but Kinsey won't. Although he might. He often manages to surprise me.

"Wonderful things," Frank assures him. "Like my hope that if I would ask you for a coffee date again, you'd accept. As friends," he adds quickly as Kinsey frowns. "I only want to be your friend."

He sounds sincere, and I guess Kinsey feels the same way because he nods. "Okay. I can do a friendly...meeting."

Frank fishes his phone out of his pocket. "Perfect. Can I have your phone number to set it up?"

Kinsey rattles off his number, and Frank enters it. "I'll send you a text so you have my number, and then we can make this happen."

"Okay."

"Let's go," I say curtly, and Kinsey hurries after me as I stalk out of the main room into one of the private rooms.

"Do you think I made a mistake accepting his invite?" Kinsey asks after a few minutes. I'm helping him stretch his quads, and he's leaning on my shoulder with one hand, my skin burning under his touch. Dammit, why do I react so strongly to him? Why can't I treat him like any other client? It's like I'm hyperaware of him, sensing his every mood, his every emotion.

"Why would you think that?" It comes out snappier than I intended, and I mentally wince.

Kinsey shrinks, his shoulders stooping. "You seemed irritated by it. Maybe you're right. I need to focus on my recovery, on getting healthier. I don't have time for complications."

Guilt sweeps through me. "Friendships are important, Kinsey. Especially when you've lost a lot of your old friends."

I release his leg, and he lets go of my shoulder. "But you did seem frustrated."

He picked up on that, huh? But how can I explain to him what I don't even understand myself? "Frank's flirting can get a little excessive."

"Hmm, I can see that. But he wasn't flirting this time, was he? His offer for friendship seemed sincere."

He sounds so vulnerable and insecure. Nothing like the self-confident doctor I knew in my youth. And why does my opinion even matter to him? "I think it was. Just make sure to communicate clear boundaries to him."

Kinsey's body jerks, and then his face contorts. "Oh, shit," he groans. He stumbles to the floor, clutching his calf and grunting in pain. Muscle cramps again, and they're bad this time.

"Let me. Lie down on your back." I squat next to him, gently lift his leg, and stand again. "Push against my hand and hold it." I make sure to keep his leg straight, stretching the calf muscle as much as possible, as he does what I say.

"I'm sorry." I rub the muscle down his leg, then back up again. "This one looks painful."

"It hurts like a mother," Kinsey says between clenched teeth.

I finally get the muscle to stop clinching, and he relaxes a little. Without asking, I take off his shoe and sock. If I don't massage him now, it'll cramp again within minutes.

With my right hand, I untie his other shoe and free his left foot. His left calf is tight as well, but nowhere near as bad as the right leg. Good, that means I can focus on that for now. I'll let him push against my hand later so it won't cramp up too.

Once the worst tightness has passed, I shift so his knee rests on my legs, offering me easy access to his calf. He's still on his back, his hands folded underneath his head. I grab some baby oil that I always have within reach and pour some onto my hands, then massage his calf.

Kinsey grunts. "Too painful?" I ask.

"No, but it's close."

"Okay. Let me know if it gets too much."

He's silent as I knead his tight muscles, which take their time relaxing until they become more pliant. He's closed his eyes, his chest rising and falling with the deep rhythm of his breaths. His shirt has ridden up, exposing a smattering of hair near his belly button. I'm not usually a fan of body hair, but I love it on him, all masculine and sexy. His chest hair is the same salt-and-pepper mix as his hair. Would his pubic hair be the same?

Shit, I have no business even thinking about that, and I turn my attention back to massaging his leg. I ease my grip, making it lighter and almost tender as I keep working his muscles until they're all soft and his body is relaxed. Ah, that's better, though I don't stop touching him. I should, but I indulge myself for a bit longer, my need to hold on to him too strong to ignore. I knead his legs, massaging until all traces of tension are gone. It's silly, but I love taking care of him like this. It's intimate and personal, and it somehow feels right.

He lets out a soft moan, which startles me, and I look up. His eyes are still closed, his mouth slightly open. Then he moans again, and he shifts his hips. Is he...? Oh my god, he's asleep or maybe halfway there, reacting to my touch but not fully aware. The fabric of his shorts flutters, and I gasp as his cock hardens until it's erect, perfectly outlined.

Shit. Now what? I can't leave him here on his own, but if he wakes up and discovers the state he's in, he'll be mortified. What should I do? How can I protect him from his own reaction?

"Oh..." The sound falls from his lips, soft as a whisper, and my body reacts. My cock stirs, and I clench my hands, digging into his flesh a bit too hard. His eyes fly open, and I freeze.

Time seems to stand still as he blinks, reconnecting with reality. Then he shoots up into a sitting position, pulling down his T-shirt.

"Kinsey," I say, but it's useless.

He pulls his leg from my lap and scrambles to his feet, his cheeks reddening. "I can't..." he stammers, and before I realize it, he's grabbed his shoes and is running out of the room as if someone is chasing him.

When I have enough control over myself to go looking for him in the main room, then the locker room, he's gone. Two days later, I wait for an hour for his next session, but he never shows up.

I lost him before I ever had him.

12

KINSEY

I've always been a man of my word, but for the first time since I kicked my drug habit, I cancel an appointment with Jerry, telling him I'm not feeling well. Technically, it's not a lie, but deep inside, I know better. I'm letting him think I'm physically unwell, whereas I'm fine. It's my mental state that's the issue.

I can't believe I fell asleep when Benoni massaged my legs. In my defense, I'm still not sleeping well, even months after being drug-free. Those opioids have messed up a lot of things in my brain, including my sleep pattern. Jerry keeps telling me it'll take time for that to get back to normal, but I'm not sure I ever had a normal pattern to begin with, what with working such crazy hours. By the time I made it to bed, I was usually so exhausted that sleep came instantly.

Then again, it wasn't me falling asleep on him that prevents me from going back to Fun & Fit, back to Benoni. It's how my body reacted. I'm so *aware* of him. Is this a consequence of me coming out and releasing the tight hold I've had on myself for years? An overreaction after decades of denying myself? I don't know what it is, but it's like he's the true north my inner compass turns to. Whenever he walks into the room, I feel it, even if I'm doing cardio and not even watching him. I just know, like my brain—and my body—registers he's close.

And when he's near me, my senses are overloaded. He smells amazing—a mix of subtle cologne and his body odor. Sweat shouldn't be sexy, but I've had a weird urge to stick my nose in his armpits and breathe him in. I know, I'm deranged. I'm too scared to ask Jerry if this is normal, especially after he already seemed suspicious about my friendship with Benoni.

No doubt Benoni has seen my erection. My completely inappropriate erection, courtesy of this intense physical reaction I still have to being touched. How the hell could I have let this happen? How could I betray his trust, the wonderfully supportive care he's shown me by reacting to him this way?

Even as I think about it now, a wave of nausea barrels into me, almost making me dry heave. I can't ever face him again, not after that. I'm sure he'd be nice enough to keep me on as his client, but how could he ever trust me again after what happened? He must think I'm some oversexed perv. The shame is so intense I hide my face in my hands, even though I'm home alone.

What do I do now? Find another gym? But what would I tell Jerry, who will most definitely ask after the reason for my switch? I can't lie to him. Well, technically, I can, and I bet I'd be able to pull it off. Not that I'm proud of it, but I've become skilled at lying over the last few years. But I swore to myself I'd be honest with him when I started my recovery journey. Lying is a downhill path that will lead me straight to reaching for the pills again.

And how I want to. How I ache to numb the shame and

pain inside, to stop these thoughts that jump around in my head like bouncing balls, returning with ferocity every time I manage to send them away. I would do anything to not feel like this, to not cringe from embarrassment and shame. It's been quiet, this voice in my head that says that the pills would make everything better, but now it's screaming at me. That I wouldn't be this depressed, this sad, this ashamed if I took them. All I need is some pills, and I'd be blissfully numb, no longer caring about the utter shitshow of my life.

My kids still don't want anything to do with me, and now I've managed to offend and alienate the one friend I had. Frank has texted me twice to set up a coffee date, but I've held it off, telling him I wasn't well. He seemed to buy it, but I don't know how long I can keep postponing.

I'm such a fuckup, such an utter disappointment to everyone, including myself. And even though rationally I know I shouldn't think like this, it's impossible to fight the thoughts. I don't want to sink back into that black hole, but how do I stay out of it? What can I hold on to now?

The doorbell rings, drawing me out of my downward spiral. It's past seven in the evening. Who could possibly come visit me? Maybe it's a salesman or some fundraiser. Whoever it is, I owe them my gratitude for preventing me from plummeting even deeper.

But when I open the door, Benoni is standing there, and shame fills me so quickly I can barely breathe.

"Kinsey," he says softly. "Can I come in?"

Manners triumph over embarrassment, and I step aside and let him into my house. It's small, much smaller than the one I shared with Caroline, but it has everything I need, including a room I use as my study, and I love the garden that surrounds my corner lot. Plus, I got to decorate it exactly the way I wanted, which was surprisingly empowering, as if I was staking my ground, my territory, claiming it as mine.

"I got your address from your file," Benoni says as we're standing across from each other in the narrow hallway.

I sigh. He might as well come in all the way, and I lead him into the living room. "Can I get you something to drink? Lemon-flavored seltzer? Water?"

"Seltzer, please, thank you."

I disappear into the kitchen, and when I come back with two cans of seltzer, Benoni is studying the pictures on the wall. "That's a great one of Jonathan and Judith you have there," he says. "Where was that taken?"

"My parents' fiftieth wedding anniversary. We did a glam photo shoot with both my sisters and all our families. There's also one of Caroline and me, but I couldn't stomach to hang that one. Besides, I was high as a kite at that shoot. Not that anyone ever noticed."

Why am I telling him all this? I'm gonna blame it on the nerves that have my heart racing and my palms all sweaty.

Benoni takes a can from me, then sits down on the couch, while I pick the love seat. "You can probably guess why I'm here," he says.

"I didn't show up yesterday."

"Right."

"I apologize. I should've canceled. I'm sorry for wasting your time. You can bill me for the session."

He leans forward, resting his forearms on his knees. "Kinsey, I don't give two shits about the money. What happened?"

I laugh humorlessly. "You have to ask? I thought that was obvious."

"You had an erection. So what?"

Leave it to Benoni to flat out address the elephant in the

room. "I'm deeply ashamed and embarrassed. Mortified. I behaved unprofessionally, and I can't even look you in the eyes anymore."

I peek at Benoni from between my lashes, and he frowns. "Unprofessional? I'm not following."

"You provided a service, and I responded inappropriately. It's inexcusable."

"Do you think you're the first one? Or the last one? It happens, and it's no big deal unless you make it one. I understand it's embarrassing, but it's not inappropriate at all. Not if you don't act on it."

I swallow. "You have more clients who *react*?"

"God, yes. I work with a lot of nonstraight men, and more than a few have responded to me, either to my body or my touch. It's a normal biological reaction, nothing to be ashamed of, and I would think you of all people would understand."

Huh. Why hadn't I thought of it that way? I have had patients respond as well, though mostly back when I was an intern or doing brief stints at other departments. Those who end up in the ER are often too sick or hurt to even think about sex.

But Benoni is right. It is a physical reaction, a biological response to a stimulus, and when I look at it that way... "I still feel like crap about it, but I see what you mean."

Benoni hesitates, then asks, "You don't have to answer this if you don't want to, but why does this trigger so much shame for you?"

I let out a deep sigh. "The long explanation would bore you to tears, but the short and quick of it is that I've always associated sex with something to be ashamed about. Not just gay sex, but all sexual acts, even sexual thoughts or attraction. It's sinful."

"I'm assuming that's something you were taught in church?"

"In church, at home, at youth group, everywhere in the culture I grew up in. From a young age, we learned that our bodies are sinful and need to be controlled at all times. And covered, in case you're a girl. Because if you show even a hint of cleavage to a boy, he may lust after you and fall into sin, and that's on you."

Benoni's eyes grow big. "They blame the girls for that?"

"Hell, yes. For example, whenever we went swimming with the youth group, the girls were forced to wear a one-piece bathing suit, as if the sight of a bare midriff would send all the guys into a sexual frenzy. Their skirts or dresses couldn't be too short, and they couldn't show bra straps or, god forbid, underwear. More than one girl was sent home for dressing inappropriately or forced to wear some guy's hoodie to cover herself up."

"Fuck, that's wrong on so many levels."

I rub the back of my neck. "It is, and it baffles me at times how long it took me to see that. But it's hard when that message is all you hear and anything that challenges that or contradicts it is considered sinful."

"It must've been a challenge for you to come to terms with the fact that what you'd been told was a lie."

"You have no idea. From the time I was twelve until I left for college, all I learned about sex is that you had to wait until you were married and that even masturbation was a sin."

Benoni holds up his hand. "Wait, seriously? Jacking off is a sin? Then what are teens supposed to do? And grown-ass adults, for that matter."

"Fight it. Pray and deny yourself. That was the message."

"You can't tell me everyone obeyed that command."

I scoff. "Of course not. If you're a teenager with a sex drive, it's damn near impossible. But the result was that you felt horrible and ashamed every time you touched yourself. Even now, I struggle with letting go of that guilt."

Why did I add that last bit? It's way too personal, but it feels good to admit it. And it's the truth. I don't jack off a lot, and it's gotten less, but at first, the guilt ate me alive every time I did it. Usually when I was watching porn, another major sin, so it's hard to tell which one made me more guilty out of those two.

Benoni's eyes are warm and kind. "If you internalized that message, I can imagine it'll take some time to overcome it."

"Yes."

"Is there anything I can say or do that would help you let go of that shame?"

He's so sweet. "This helps. You forcing me to talk about it and telling me straight up it's okay."

His mouth curls up in a smile. "So you're saying me being bossy did the trick?"

I laugh, my insides warming at his easy smile. "It totally did."

"Good, 'cause it's hard for me to turn the bossy off."

I like you bossy. I don't say it, but the truth of that statement lights up inside me. Why do I like it so much when Benoni tells me what to do? Surely, that's not normal. Not for a man. The man is supposed to be the head of the family, the one in charge, the person who makes all the final decisions. At least, that's what I've always been taught. But how would that work in a gay relationship? Not that Benoni and I are in a relationship, but it makes me wonder.

Then again, the church also taught me those traditional role patterns, which are old fashioned and outdated and probably complete bullshit. Yay, something else I need to get out of my system. At this rate, I'm gonna need years of therapy before I can function as a normal human being.

"You okay?" Benoni asks, concern in his eyes.

"Yeah. Sorry, lost in thoughts for a moment."

"No worries. So are we good now?"

"We are. Thank you."

"My pleasure." He rises from the couch. "I expect to see you tomorrow, Kinsey."

The words fly out of my mouth without me thinking about them. "Yes, Benoni."

13

1990: KINSEY

I hate the worship part. Not because I don't like music, although one guitar accompanying a bunch of teens singing doesn't really constitutes music to me. No, it's the awkwardness of it. My voice has dropped, but it still cracks occasionally and, as fate would have it, usually at the worst possible times. I've been the target of the girls' giggles, and I wanted to die of embarrassment.

And that's not all that's awkward about it. The whole thing is just...weird. Like, we're singing songs for God or to God—still not quite clear about the difference—because for some reason, God appreciates a bunch of teens singing off-key? I don't get it. The lyrics are all the same, telling God how awesome he is. You would think he'd know by now after two millennia of Christians singing the same songs to him.

But I seem to be the only one who feels that way, since most kids in my youth group have closed their eyes and are swaying to the music, their hands raised in what's understood as a sign of being swept up in worship.

One hand means you're into it. Two hands means you're

all in. Two hands and standing while everyone else is still sitting is, like, being overcome by the Spirit. I've never raised my hand. Maybe because I'm not the type to get swept up in anything, I don't know. I've always been calm and level-headed without much of a temper.

Even Daniel, my best friend, has been sucked into it tonight, and he's usually right there with me. Lately, he's been more into church, advocating the benefits of daily Bible reading and praying to me, which the church refer to as silent time. Before, he was a rebel. He's smoked weed, has been drunk a few times from the liquor he stole from his father's liquor cabinet, and he's even had sex. He told me more details than I cared for, trust me. I don't know what the deal is with breasts and why everyone is so obsessed with them. They're nice, I suppose, but I don't get why every boy is gushing about boobs.

But he's changed. He's much more into all the church stuff, showing up for youth group every week and even picking me up on the way, since he has a car, whereas I don't. Hell, he's even been talking about getting baptized, something our church doesn't do automatically. You have to be at least twelve to be baptized, but once you've reached that age, it's your own choice.

I'm sixteen now, and the urge to get baptized has never hit me, much to the disappointment of my parents and especially my grandparents. My grandfather is the famous Reverend Lindstrom, known far and wide for his passionate sermons. Sermons that last for freaking ever, I might add. His record during a church service is an hour and a half, and he boasted afterward he could've continued for another two hours if he'd had to. God help us all if he ever does.

Daniel is singing with his eyes closed, rocking back and forth, his hands high up in the air. He's beautiful, but even more so with his eyes closed. It gives him an angelic appearance, with his slightly too-long curly hair and his pale face. He still doesn't need to shave, while I have become good friends with my razor already. Not that I'm complaining, but he's super pretty. All the girls go dove-eyed over him, though he ignores them. He's serious about God and all that.

His body is perfect too. I'm six feet, and he's a full head shorter than me, with a much more delicate build. Not feminine, per se, but more like… I don't know how to describe it, and come to think of it, I shouldn't even try. All I know is that I have this weird urge to protect him, which is ridiculous. We're the same age, and he can hold his own, but there you have it. It will go away once he becomes more masculine.

I've been thinking about him a lot. We've been friends since we were in Sunday school together, so over eight years now. His parents and mine are in the same church small group that meets every Tuesday night for Bible study and prayer. We often hang out then, and I'm always looking forward to it. I've even dreamed about him, weird dreams that I can't remember but that make me uncomfortable when I wake up. No idea what that's about.

Worship is finally over, and with that, so is youth group. Thank goodness. But when I get up from my chair, Adam, one of the youth leaders, is almost in my face. "Hey, Kinsey."

"Erm, hi?"

"I just wanted to have a quick talk with you. Let's find a quiet place."

I don't even get the opportunity to respond. He already stalks away, expecting me to follow, which I do, of course. What on earth is his problem? I try my hardest not to get on anyone's radar at youth group. Nobody can ever accuse me of being disruptive. Okay, I'm not an enthusiastic participant either, but at least I attend every time, and I'm not being a pain in the butt.

He walks into an empty room and closes the door behind me, and my heart skips a beat. All the signals point toward me being in trouble, but for what? I can't think of anything I did, any area where I messed up. "Is something wrong?"

"Have a seat, Kinsey," he says. He drags two chairs to the middle of the room and sits down, waiting for me to take the other. All my alarm bells are blaring by now. What on earth did I do?

"Kinsey, I just wanted to tell you I'll be praying for you and that you shouldn't give up hope. God is testing you for reasons we don't comprehend, but he is faithful."

God is testing me? Am I in an alternate reality? I have no freaking clue what he's talking about. Not that Adam notices. He just drones on in this solemn, encouraging voice that gives me the heebie-jeebies.

"The Bible says in 1 Corinthians 10, verse 13, that God is faithful and that he will not allow you to be tempted beyond what you are able. With the temptation, he will also make the way of escape, that you may be able to bear it."

"Amen," I say automatically. I'm familiar with that verse, as it's one of my grandfather's favorites. Should I ask Adam for specifics on this temptation he's going on about? Or will that make me look stupid?

"You just have to keep praying that God will take away these urges from you," Adam says.

Urges?

"I promise you that if you marry a good Christian girl and pray for God to take these urges away, he will listen to your prayer. He wants you to be happy, get married, and have a family."

My heart stops beating for a moment as the meaning of his words sinks in. He thinks I'm... "I don't have homosexual urges," I blurt out, almost tripping over my words. If this gets back to my parents, I'm beyond screwed.

He frowns. "Kinsey, I see how you look at Daniel, and I'm not the only one who has noticed."

"I'm... You're getting it all wrong." My head is spinning so fast I'm dizzy as I try to come up with something, anything to get him off my back. And then my brain finds the right words. "I'm praying for him."

"You're praying for him?"

I nod vigorously. "After his brother got his girlfriend pregnant and moved in with her, I was worried Daniel would follow the same sinful path. You know he's run into some trouble himself. So I've been praying for him to grow closer to Jesus. That's why I've been looking at him so much because I was silently praying for him, bringing him before the throne of the Almighty."

He's buying it. His eyes light up, and joy and pride bloom on his face. "Of course. I'm so sorry, Kinsey. I should have known better. No grandson of Reverend Lindstrom will ever choose a homosexual lifestyle."

"I forgive you, Adam. It's all good. By the way, I think I'm ready to get baptized. Do you think we could talk about that sometime?"

As I drive home that night, my mind keeps going back to that conversation. I'm confident Adam believed me, but this can't happen again. Why did he think I'm struggling with homosexual urges? It doesn't matter. What matters is that I can't have people think that. If my grandfather ever found out, he'd disown me, and my parents would never talk to me again either. I'll do what Adam suggested. I'll find a good Christian girl and marry her, and then all this will be in the past. If I need to, I'll even get baptized. Anything to get them off my back.

I don't know what those weird feelings I have for Daniel are, but they need to stay where they belong.

In the dark.

Hidden.

Forever.

14

BENONI

I still can't believe what Kinsey told me a few days ago about what he was taught about sex. It's such a foreign concept to me. My mom was spiritual, though she resisted organized religion. God is love, was her message, and it was one that she lived out her whole life.

Even though money was tight for us, she never let a neighbor go hungry, and our house was always open to whoever needed a couch to sleep on or a safe place to stay for a few nights. Throughout the years, even when she was sick, friends and neighbors stayed with us, ate at our dinner table, and left with a full belly and a warm heart. No one was ever turned away. Isn't that what being a Christian is about, helping those in need?

But Kinsey was taught something else, and I still don't fully understand it. I don't want to keep asking him about it. Not during our training sessions, which aren't conducive to such serious conversations anyway, but is it something I should ask him in the first place? It sounded like he was suffering from a lot of pain and trauma, and do I want to stir that up?

No, I don't think I should bring it up with him unless he does it himself, but I know someone I can ask. My uncle Tim, my mom's brother. He's a pastor, but like my mom used to say, one of the good ones. And so on my day off, I make the drive in my rusty old Toyota to Tampa to meet up with him.

His bear hug damn near squishes me, no easy feat, and his smile is wide as he lets go. "It's so good to see you, Ben."

"You too, Uncle Tim. Thanks for seeing me."

He waves my words away. "We're family. You don't ever need to thank me for making time for you."

He leads me into his messy living room, where piles of books occupy every flat surface, including the floor and tables. He's always been single, and for as long as I've known him, he's been a slob. My mom once told me he has a cleaning lady who stops by every month, and he pays her a fortune to work in his mess. I have to admit, his house looks clean, even if it's like pure chaos. I would go crazy here.

He removes a few piles of books off the couch, then gestures, and I sit down. His favorite chair is easy to spot, right under a bright reading lamp, and he lowers his hefty frame into it, the chair creaking in protest.

"How have you been?" he asks.

"Good. Still working at the gym, and I love it."

He pats his belly. "I could use some gym time."

"I'd be happy to work with you, but it would be quite the drive."

He grins. "We both know that'll never happen. But I'm healthy, so I cling to that. Just had my physical last week, and all the blood work was according to the book."

"Glad to hear it. You still walk every day?"

"Ten a.m., rain or shine, I walk my 5k route. It's my daily

conversation with God, and by the time I'm done, my heart is ten pounds lighter, even if my body isn't."

We chat a little more, and then I raise the topic I came here to talk to him about. "Uncle Tim, can I ask you some questions about Christianity or more specifically, conservative Christianity?"

"Of course, but what brought this up?"

"A friend of mine mentioned some things from his past, and I'm trying to understand him better. He's forty-seven, and he grew up evangelical."

Uncle Tim cringes. "Let me guess. He's dealing with religious trauma?"

Religious trauma. I never thought of it like that, but it fits the bill. "Can you talk to me about how his church would feel about sex and relationships?"

Uncle Tim whistles between his teeth. "You had to jump right to the hottest topic, didn't you? Would this friend of yours happen to be nonstraight?"

Did I mention my uncle is part of a church that believes all people are welcome with God, including the ones on the rainbow? "That would be correct."

"He's had to walk a tough road, then. For someone coming from that background, the step to come out and live authentically is a huge one. One that has a lot of consequences."

"His parents cut off all contact. They said he wasn't their son anymore. And I think his siblings are shunning him as well."

His eyes spew fire. "It disgusts me when parents deny their own blood because of that. How they can defend that with their hand on the Bible is beyond me."

"So what was he taught?"

Uncle Tim leans back in his chair, his fingers laced on

his ample belly. "It all boils down to what we now refer to as the purity culture, this idea that sex was sinful and dirty and that the goal was to stay pure until marriage."

"No sex before marriage, that part I got, but my friend also mentioned masturbation was frowned upon."

"Oh, it sure was. It still is in those circles. Every sexual act is seen as sinful. Some churches even teach you shouldn't kiss before marriage and proudly hail couples who shared their first kiss during their wedding ceremony."

Kissing is already a sin? Holy shit, how did these people live? How much did they deny themselves? It boggles my mind. "That's almost creepy."

"I wouldn't call it creepy, but it's extreme. In the same way, they resist the dating culture and propose people stay friends until they are certain they're meant for each other, and then they get engaged and marry quickly."

"That sounds like a recipe for a lot of unhappy marriages. I mean, sexual compatibility plays an important role in a relationship, doesn't it?"

"They believe God will sort that. If you stay a virgin until your wedding night, everything will work out, and you'll have a spectacular sex life."

"Riiiiight. 'Cause two bumbling virgins are the perfect combination for amazing sex."

Uncle Tim grins. "Practice makes perfect? I don't know what else to tell you, son. It's not my belief system."

"So that purity culture, what else did that mean? No sex, I get that part, but what else?"

Uncle Tim sobers, sadness in his eyes. "Shame. To me, that's at the core of it. People were shamed if they weren't sexually pure, so every time they couldn't live up to that almost impossible standard, it made them feel dirty and sinful. And most of the time, they didn't mention exceptions where it had happened without consent, so they made even girls who had been sexually abused or raped feel like they'd been soiled and sullied forever."

I gape at him. "That's fucking awful."

"It's horrendous, and it has scarred many women for life. And of course, out of all the sexual sins, being gay was the worst. It was almost universally held up as the absolute worst you could be or do."

Didn't Kinsey mention the same, how it ranked above premarital sex or even adultery? "So what would happen if someone would come out as gay?" How did Kinsey word it? "Or confess they had same-sex urges?"

"I can tell you've talked to him about this because that's the language they would use. Urges, sinful thoughts, being tempted. Not an identity or who you were, how God had created and wired you, but the deliberate choice to be a sinner."

"Yeah, that's how he described it."

"If someone would confess to such a thing to a church leader, they'd be told to pray for it. They'd maybe set up some kind of accountability system where someone had to report to a leader and report back on how they had fought their urges. The expectation was that over time, you overcame it, that you became victorious over this temptation from the devil."

I close my eyes for a moment as I try to imagine Kinsey as a teenager, fighting the very thing that defined him, who he was to the very core. Being told time and again that who he was wrong and sinful. From the devil. How did you counter that? How could someone be strong enough to stand in their true identity?

"Did people ever come out? Walk away from the church?"

"It happened, but rarely. Now, it's far more common, but that's because people get such a different message through the media. TV shows, movies, books are so much more LGBT-accepting, and that's brought freedom to many people. But back then, that wasn't the case. If you were evangelical, you were most likely limited in what you were allowed to watch, which countered worldly influences, as they'd call it."

"So that was it? You'd either pray away the gay or come out and leave the church?"

"Sadly, yes. Though some people did come out but stayed in the church. They accepted their sexual orientation as something they couldn't change, but as a result, they vowed to stay celibate for the rest of their lives. So they acknowledged their identity, but the solution was to deny themselves."

My heart breaks. "Why would anyone pick such a life of loneliness? I mean, choosing not to be in a relationship is fine and valid, but if you do it because you believe who you are is wrong... It's so hard to imagine."

"It is." Uncle Tim sighs. "Many people in my church are survivors of that culture, and the wounds run deep. I don't use the expression lightly, but they need to be deprogrammed from what they've been taught before they can accept and love themselves. It's heartbreaking to see how much damage has been done in the name of Jesus."

We sit in silence. "Mom said God is love, and that's that. She refused to entertain any other interpretation of the Gospel 'cause what could be better news than that?"

Uncle Tim smiles. "She always had a way to get to the core of the message."

It's been ten months since she passed away, but sometimes, the pain is as fresh as it was back then. My eyes well up. "I miss her every day."

"Same. She was an amazing woman, and she loved you something fierce."

"She did. I couldn't have wished for a better mom."

"And she couldn't have wished for a better son. You took great care of her, Ben, even when it became such a heavy burden to carry."

A tear escapes from my eye, and it trickles down my cheek. "It never felt heavy to me. More like a privilege."

For a long time, we just sit, and I love that Uncle Tim allows my sadness and grief to exist without feeling the need to make me feel better. Mom was like that too, giving me space to feel whatever I was experiencing without pressure to label it or move on. It's a rare gift. The only other person I know who does this is Kinsey. Maybe because he knows a thing or two about pain and grief.

"Your friend, is he okay?" Uncle Tim finally asks.

"I have hope he will be, but he's got a journey ahead of him."

"If he ever needs to talk or has questions, you know I'm here."

"Thank you."

When it's time to leave, he walks me to the front door and puts a strong hand on my shoulder. "Be careful, Ben. You've got a big heart, but it's more fragile than you often realize. I don't want you to get hurt."

I think it may already be too late for that.

15

KINSEY

It's time for my two-month evaluation, and I dutifully take off my shirt so Benoni can take pictures again. He's beaming as he shows them to me. "Look at the difference."

He holds out his phone in such a way that I have to step close to him to see it, and as always, his smell envelops me. Don't ask me how I can even detect it amid the heavy scent of sweat, including my own, but he invades my senses. I swallow before I can focus, and then a small gasp flies from my lips.

He's right. The difference in the pictures from two months ago and today is more than obvious. I've gained weight, but in the right places. My face is fuller, and my shoulders are less bony and pointy. But I've also developed some definition, and I wasn't expecting that yet. I thought that would take months, maybe even a year.

"Congratulations, Kinsey." He bumps my shoulder. "You worked hard for this."

"Thank you." My eyes are still glued to the pictures until they grow moist. Benoni's gaze is fixed on me, shining with warmth and pride. My belly swirls, and my eyes tear up even more. Have I become that desperate for praise? Or maybe I always was. God knows I tried everything to get my father's approval and praise, though I received it so rarely.

"I'm still no Frank, though." I chuckle to cover my emotions.

Benoni lowers his phone but doesn't step away. "Is that your goal, to be like him?"

"I'm still not convinced I'll ever be able to get there, but even halfway between him and me now would be amazing."

"Maybe you should take him up on that offer for coffee, get him to share some tips on how he did it."

Something about Benoni's tone makes me uneasy, as if it has a deeper meaning I'm not privy to.

"I don't know. He seems nice, but also very..."

"Gay?"

I scoff. "That'd be hypocritical of me, don't you think?"

"You'd be surprised by how even within the gay or broader LGBT community, there can be a pecking order, with more feminine presenting men at the bottom and flamboyant, demonstratively gay men like Frank right above."

Is he serious? I'm gonna say yes, considering there's not even a hint of a smile on his face. "That's disturbing, to be honest."

"It is, and it shows that even among nonstraight men, misogyny still exists. The more masculine you are, the higher your proverbial rank."

"It reminds me of the church, and not in a good way. Not that I have that many pleasant memories there in general, but still."

"Oh, I have no trouble imagining that. But if it's not his level of gayness, so to speak, why are you hesitating to take Frank up on his offer?"

There's that tone again, that slight edge, though Benoni's face shows nothing. "I'm not ready to date yet."

"He said he wanted friendship."

"Yes, but watching how he flirts with you incessantly, I can't help but question how long that resolve will last."

Benoni drops his shoulders, though I hadn't even noticed how tense he was until he lets go of it. "You may have a point there."

"Even friendship is complicated right now. My sponsor is encouraging me to find new friends, but it's intimidating. How do people my age even make friends? Hell, how do you maintain friendships, period? I've always focused on my work, and what little time I had left was for my family. Now all that has fallen away, and I feel like I somehow missed that step and never developed that skill."

You know what I love about Benoni? He's such a good listener. With some people, impatience wafts off them whenever someone else is talking, but Benoni truly listens, his whole attention focused on me. He *sees* me, and that's equal parts satisfying and terrifying.

"You never had a close friend? Not even as a teen?" he asks.

My thoughts go to Daniel, as has happened often lately. Where is he now? Did he even survive? Or did his mother's worst fears become reality, and hasn't he survived the AIDS epidemic? I've never tried to find him, too scared of what I would discover and too scared of how I would react when I saw him again.

In hindsight, everything was so easy to recognize. I was in love with him, had been since we were young teens. "I did. His name was Daniel, and we were friends all throughout youth group. We lost contact even before I finished high school," I say.

Benoni's eyes soften. "You had a crush on him."

Why am I amazed that he can tell from two sentences what took me years and years to realize? Still, it's impressive. "I was in love with him."

"Did he know?"

Did he? I've been pondering that question a lot. Considering the path he took, he might've reciprocated my feelings if I'd given him a chance. Was that why he'd become serious about church, just so he could spend more time with me? I'll never know what could've happened. Instead, I met Caroline, and everything changed. What would have happened if I had come clean to him about my feelings? Would we have run away together? Would we have made it as a couple? It's such a foreign thought, so scary that I barely dare to entertain it. But how can I not, knowing what I know now?

"I don't know, but I think he was attracted to me. When I met Caroline, we grew apart, and I pulled away from him. In hindsight, I realized even then the danger he posed to me and my relationship with Caroline."

Benoni is so easy to talk to, and it strikes me once again that he's asking the questions I had hoped my kids would ask, my sisters, maybe even Caroline herself. Was it too much to expect that those closest to me would at least attempt to understand me, to grasp what I went through all these years? I hurt them, and I will never deny that, but why can't they see how much pain I was in?

Sadness washes over me, and the fierce sting of being alone pierces my soul. They've all abandoned me: my parents, my sisters, my wife, my kids. I'm a pariah to them, all because of who I am.

And yet even as my heart aches, I know beyond a shadow of a doubt that I prefer the truth over the lie, the light over the darkness, the freedom over the prison of living someone else's life. Being my authentic self came at a price, but I'd do it again. I'd rather be alone and live in truth than have my family but have to pretend and act for the rest of my life.

"Do you want a hug?"

Benoni's voice startles me, and maybe that's why I immediately nod. If I'd taken the time to think about it, I would've said no, but Benoni takes a step forward and wraps his strong arms around me.

I brace myself, ready to bolt from him at the first signal he's had enough, but he holds on, hugging me tighter. Nerve endings I never knew I had light up, my whole body glowing with it. It feels so good to be held, not to have to be the strong one but to let go.

And so I do.

I cling to him with all my might, burying my face against his neck, breathing in his smell. I sling my arms around him, loving the fact that he's an inch or two taller than me. My eyes drift shut, even as a few stray tears escape, but I don't even wipe them away.

His cheek rests on the top of my head, his breath drifting through my hair. He rubs my back soothingly, not speaking a word and yet saying all the words I need to hear.

You're safe.

You're valid.

You're loved.

No one ever told me that. Not my parents, not my grandparents, not my siblings, or any youth leader I ever encountered. All they said was that they'd accept me as long as I was the person they wanted me to be. If I was the good Kinsey, the Christian Kinsey, the straight Kinsey. Not once in my life have I ever felt as safe as I do now with Benoni, and then the tears come with an unstoppable force.

I don't know how long the hug lasts, but I revel in every minute of it. Even when my quiet sobs have subsided, Benoni still holds me. Touching me. Comforting me. Letting me know without words that it's all okay.

I have to let go of him now—not because I want to, but because I have to before it becomes weird and uncomfortable—but then he speaks. "I know things are messed up in your head and that you're adjusting to your new reality. And from what you told me, I understand that the concept of friendship is hard for you and maybe loaded with a lot of painful memories. But I need you to remember that I consider you a friend, Kinsey, and I'd be honored to be yours."

I inhale to answer him, but he squeezes my shoulder. "Hush, I wasn't done yet."

I hush.

"You're going to bring up Jonathan and our age gap and the fact that I'm your trainer, but none of that changes anything for me. I can be friends with more than one person, even if they are at odds with each other. Of course there's an age difference, but I have experience you don't, so there's that. And if I have to choose between being your friend or being your trainer, I'll gladly hand you over to someone else here at the gym and continue being your friend."

Words refuse to come, my brain a hot mess of emotions, but my throat is too tight to speak them anyway. And so I hold on to him, clinging even tighter, and he not only lets me but continues to caress my back.

"I've got you, Kinsey. I've got you."

Who knew that when I finally fell apart, it would be Benoni who'd catch me?

16

BENONI

"I'll see you next week, Sonja." I wave at the grandmotherly sixty-eight-year-old who's been my client for two years now. She's amazing, and I want to be as badass as she when I grow up.

My next session is with Kinsey, but not for fifteen minutes, which is enough time to call Leif and check in on him. He had a nasty encounter with a client who got way too rough with him yesterday, and he was all shook up when I got home, the poor thing.

"Hey, Bun," I say as he answers the phone. "How are you feeling?"

A deep sigh is the answer. "Words," I remind him. "I still can't read your mind."

"Still sad," he says softly. "But a little better than this morning, I guess?"

"Did you eat?"

"I was just about to."

"Bun, it's almost time for dinner. You didn't eat all day?"

Not that I'm surprised. I could've called this one just like I know what he needs.

"No."

The whispered word barely reaches my ears, but I know him so well I could have guessed.

"You know the rules." I make my voice low and stern. Leif always responds to that tone.

"I didn't cancel work."

The one time I would've let him get away with it, he chooses to be good. That's Leif for you. "Was it good?"

"Yeah. It was a guy I hooked up with before, and fans kept asking for a repeat. He's a nice guy and a good fuck, so I figured he'd be a safe choice."

"Okay. Glad to hear it went well."

"I promise I'll eat now."

"Leif..." How do I put this so he'll understand? "You don't need to be bad to deserve a spanking. You can ask me for it if you need it, and I'll happily give it, even without you breaking the rules."

He's quiet for a long time. "I know, but it wouldn't be the same. Even if it's something small I did wrong, I need to feel I deserve the punishment. Otherwise, it won't help me forgive myself."

He's never worded it like that, and I'm intrigued. "Is that what happens in your head when I discipline you, that you forgive yourself?"

"Yeah. It took me a while to figure that part out and to understand why I need it so much, but that's what I came up with my therapist. By allowing you to punish me for something I did wrong, I can forgive myself for everything else as well."

I'll be damned. Now that he explains it, it makes total sense. Why didn't I think of this before? Not that it matters. I did this for him before I understood why he needed it. He's my friend, my bun, and that's reason enough.

"Thanks for telling me. That helps in understanding better why you need the discipline. Not that I wasn't willing to spank your bare ass anyway, but still."

A throat clears behind me, and I swivel around. Kinsey is standing there, his hand covering his mouth, eyes wide as saucers. He must've overheard me. *Oops.*

"I gotta go. I'll see you tonight."

"Thank you, Ben. For everything."

I smile, even though Leif can't see me. "Always. Love you, Bun."

"Love you too."

I end the call. "Sorry, I didn't hear you come in," I say calmly.

Kinsey's cheeks are fiercely red. "I didn't mean to listen in on a private conversation with your boyfriend."

"He's not my boyfriend." My reaction is automatic by now after years of people thinking Leif and I are together.

"Oh! I thought... You said... Never mind. It's none of my business."

It's not, and yet I find myself curious how Kinsey will react if I share more. "You mean the discipline and the comment about spanking his bare ass?"

Kinsey stares at the ground as he mumbles a soft yes.

"Leif's not my boyfriend, but he is my roommate and my best friend. We met in college, and yes, we did hook up back then, but that evolved into a deep friendship. And I do discipline him."

Kinsey jerks up his head. "Why?"

"It's what he needs."

"I don't understand. Is this a BDSM thing?"

"Not really. It's domestic discipline, and while it's more common between partners, Leif doesn't have one, so I provide that service for him. We've set rules, and if he breaks them, I spank his bare ass."

"He *likes* that?"

The incredulity in Kinsey's voice makes me chuckle. "It's a punishment, Kinsey. He's not supposed to like it."

"Right." He rubs the back of his neck. "I thought it was... Never mind."

"You thought it was a sexual spanking, for pleasure."

"Yes. Not that I have experience with those." He rolls his eyes. "I don't have any experience other than plain vanilla straight sex, but at least I've heard of it. As an ER doctor, you learn a lot about people's sex lives, trust me."

"I bet. No, this isn't for pleasure." How much can I tell him? Leif has been pretty open on his OnlyFans channel about it, without mentioning my name of course, so I'm not spilling any secrets. "Leif sucks at taking care of himself, and he's prone to making bad decisions. The domestic discipline helps him with that. Every time he fucks up, he has to tell me, and I punish him."

"Is he younger than you? No, never mind. You said you were college roommates, so he's not."

"Leif is emotionally immature, I suppose, but above all, he's submissive, though not in a Dom/sub kind of way. He functions best when someone takes charge and tells him what to do. Trust me, he'd prefer for me to be much more involved in his day-to-day life, but I don't have the bandwidth for that. I would take such a commitment seriously, and it would require more time than I have available."

Kinsey nods, his forehead creased with what I've come to recognize as thinking lines. He's a good listener. I've always thought that about him. Too bad his kids didn't inherit that skill. "And you don't feel strange to do something so intimate to him when you're not in a relationship?"

"We *are* in a relationship," I correct him gently. "A close friendship, forged in years of sharing a room and an apartment. Sometimes, that's worth more."

Kinsey blinks, and then a slow smile spreads over his face. "You're right."

"But the answer is no, I don't feel weird about it, but I've had time to get used to it. This started back when we were still in college, so it's been going on for a good three years now. It's what he needs."

Kinsey cocks his head. "That, I believe, but it also has to be something you can provide, which you can, it seems. And that you have to like."

Oh, he's considering it from all angles. "I do like it. I've always been a caretaker, I suppose, what with my mom and everything, so that part comes naturally to me. And the discipline part is...satisfying. I like being able to do that for him, and..."

I hesitate. Should I say this to a man who's a baby gay and still struggling with his sexuality? I don't want to offend or shock him, but on the other hand, he did ask, and I don't like being dishonest with him.

"And what?" he asks. "Don't hold back on my account."

Well, if he puts it like that... "Doing this for him is hot. It turns me on."

"Oh." He swallows.

"More than you bargained for?"

"No, it's... I asked, didn't I?"

"You did, but you didn't know what I would answer."

He straightens his shoulders. "No, but it's okay. I'm not a prude, even if I may come across as such. It's not the sexual choices of others I have trouble with. It's my own, and only because of that judgmental voice inside my head."

"Mmm, I understand that. And I know you're not judging me. If you were, I wouldn't have told you all this."

"I envy you." He clamps his hand over his mouth as if he's taken aback by his admission.

"Envy me? How?"

"You've been out since you were a teenager, comfortable in your own skin. You're so confident and easy about it, and effortlessly, it seems. I wish I had that swagger you have. I'm twice your age, and..."

My heart aches for him. "You're not twice my age. I'm twenty-five. You're forty-seven."

"I rounded up, but my point stands. I feel so lost in all this, so lacking."

"You're not. You're never lacking, Kinsey. You're enough, you hear me?"

I can't help the tone of my voice, which is forceful and decisive. As always, he responds to it, his shoulders losing their tension as he lets out a breath. "Thank you."

"I'm sorry you feel lost. I know it may be hard for you to accept, but my offer to answer any questions still stands. I'm here for you, for whatever you need."

"Thank you. That means a lot to me, and someday, I hope I'll have the courage to ask you all the questions I have. I need to find a way to overcome my awkwardness and shame about it."

"Maybe it helps to approach it as a medical professional? You told me you've seen plenty of weird stuff as a doctor."

"God, yes. This is Florida after all."

Maybe I should distract him so he relaxes again. "Didn't you have an oddity cabinet where you saved all kinds of crazy things you've removed from patients? I remember you talking about that once."

He laughs, his face splitting open in a smile that's

genuine and free. "We did. And those are only nonperishable items. The number of cucumbers, zucchini, squashes, and various fruits I've pulled out of people's rectums and vaginas is too high to count."

I shudder. "God, I can't even imagine. Why don't people just use a dildo or a vibrator?"

"Beats me. Those are not only far safer but more hygienic as well. My favorite is the guy who came in wearing baggy sweatpants and a long overcoat...in the summer."

Kinsey's eyes sparkle as he scratches his beard. Oh god, I can tell this will be a good one. Kinsey was always a great storyteller. I loved his tales at the dinner table when I was a teen. I'm glad I made him smile again. It matters to me, though I don't understand why.

"It turned out he'd tried to enhance his sexual pleasure by using an industrial-sized nut as a cock ring. He'd put his penis in when it was still soft, but then he grew hard, and it filled, cutting off the blood flow and preventing him from removing it again. He'd tried everything, oil, butter, lube. Nothing worked. Desperate, he came to the ER, hoping we could get it off."

I'm fully invested in the story now, wincing as I imagine the poor guy's predicament. "That's not so easy. It's not like your cock is a muscle you can relax with drugs."

"Exactly. And the danger is that if you cut off the blood flow for too long, the penis will develop cyanosis and, eventually, become necrotic."

Ouch. "Yeah, that's something you want to avoid."

"We did everything, but we couldn't remove it either. In the end, we had to put him under and bring in someone with specialized equipment to carefully saw through the metal. It took about an hour before we could finally get the nut off his dick. Needless to say, we had a mortified but grateful patient who swore up and down he'd never try anything like that again."

He's so different now, almost like another person. I see some of the old Kinsey—or the old Mr. Lindstrom, I should say, since I didn't call him by his first name back then—with his self-confidence bordering on swagger.

"Do you miss it much?" I ask.

The light in his eyes gives way to sadness. Damn it, why did I have to ask that?

"Every day. It was so much more than a job for me. A dream, a purpose. A calling, if you will." He sighs. "But I can't blame them for firing me. I was high on the job, Benoni. Never so much that I couldn't function, but even a little bit was too much. I never hurt anyone, thank god, never made any medical errors, but I must've made some risky calls I wouldn't have made otherwise. I got lucky they turned out well, but at some point, my luck would've run out. I'm grateful I got caught before it did."

I put a hand on his shoulder, his sadness affecting me much more than it should. "I'm sorry for bringing it up, especially after that story. I didn't mean to bring you down."

His smile is sweet, but it doesn't reach his eyes, where his sorrow lingers. "I'll have to live with what I did. Pretending it never happened doesn't help me. I need to face it and forgive myself."

What has Leif said about needing punishment to be able to forgive himself? Would that work for Kinsey as well? The idea is too ludicrous to even consider, and yet an unbidden visual of a naked Kinsey spread over my lap fills my vision. Oh god, not the picture I want in my mind when he's standing right in front of me.

But it burns inside me, this need to give him what he craves. I can't explain how I know he wants it, but I do.

Maybe it's this whole discussion and how interested he is in the dynamic between Leif and me.

"Let's get moving," I say, hoping Kinsey doesn't realize my voice is hoarse.

And of course he says the two words that have me revved up all over again.

"Yes, Benoni."

17

KINSEY

Domestic discipline.
Those two words keep circling in my brain after the conversation with Benoni, and when I wake up the day after, they're the first that pop into my head. To say I was shocked by him oh-so-casually confessing he spanks his roommate is an understatement, though I'm still not sure if it was the discipline itself or the fact that he acted like it was the most normal thing in the world.

I grew up sheltered and didn't learn about BDSM and other sexual practices until after med school, and let me tell you, that was a steep learning curve. I did my internships in Atlanta, and I had to learn a whole lot really fast about how the world worked. In hindsight, that was when the first big crack in my Christian view of the world came. I saw too much to hold on to that naïve outlook.

And yes, domestic discipline was one of the things I encountered after a male patient who had cut himself came in. While chopping vegetables, he'd severed the tip of his finger, so that needed to be sutured. I numbed the area, of course, but as I threaded the needle through, he kept squirming. I asked him if he needed extra sedation, but he told me his boyfriend had spanked him hard that morning. Obviously, that still hurt, and the local numbing for his finger did nothing for his buttocks.

He was open and casual about it, almost proud, I would say, and I asked him a lot of questions, which he answered willingly. At first, I was concerned he was being abused, but he cured me of that notion. Besides, he showed no other injuries, nor did he have a history of showing up in the ER. No, he submitted himself to his boyfriend for domestic discipline, and he said it was the best thing that ever happened to him.

At the time, the thought crossed my mind that I should condemn it, if not to him, then at least in my head, but the way he described it, it was hard for me to find fault with it. He and his boyfriend had clear rules and guidelines, and both had agreed to them. He said the punishment helped him to change his behavior and work harder at not only being a good boyfriend but a good person.

When I was almost done, his boyfriend showed up, worried sick, and the love between them was palpable. Oh, it hurt to see them like that, so tender and caring. Jonathan had just turned two, and Caroline was due any moment with Judith, and I barely had time to eat and sleep, let alone be a father and husband.

Caroline wasn't complaining, but we rarely saw each other. Hell, I'm still amazed I even managed to get her pregnant, though that was because she kept meticulous track of her cycle and informed me when it was time to have sex. I wanted what those two men had, that intimacy, and at the same time, it scared me. How was my patient okay with submitting to his partner? Didn't that hurt his ego, his pride?

And now I know Benoni has a similar relationship with his roommate, though in his case, they aren't even boyfriends. I'm not sure if that makes it better or worse, to be honest. Why would he do this? Why would he offer this...this *service* to his roommate? Even if they're close friends, that's still one hell of an intimate step. Spanking someone's bare ass? The thought alone sends a shiver down my spine. I can't even imagine being in that position. Or maybe I can because an image fills my head as I close my eyes.

Benoni's strong hand, coming down. Slapping, swatting. His stern voice, admonishing yet kind and loving, telling me to be good for him so he doesn't have to do this again. And I lie over his knee like a child, my bare butt in the air, and even though it hurts when he punishes me, it also feels good. Cleansing. Like a new start, and this time, I'll do better.

I gasp, my eyes flying open. Where did *that* come from? Why did I put myself in that scenario, and moreover, why was *I* the one being spanked? I'm older than Benoni. Shouldn't I have been the one in charge? But that thought feels so wrong. He's bossy, Benoni, but I like it. I really like it. It's nice not to have the responsibility, not to have to make the decisions.

Then something else registers, and I freeze. Literally. I'm hard. I slide my hand down, circling the undeniable evidence of the effect my little fantasy of Benoni spanking me had on me. What the actual fuck? Why would that idea arouse me?

Something stirs deep inside me, but as soon as I let the thought in, guilt washes over me. I shouldn't feel that way. I'm a man. I'm supposed to be the strong one, the dominant one. That's what I've been taught my whole life: I'm the head of my family, and my wife should submit to me. So if I'm the one who wants to do the submitting, then...

But I'm gay. It can't work the same in a gay relationship, since both partners are male. No, this is another remnant of my old thinking, of my upbringing and my old viewpoints. Men and women are equal. All people are. No one should be dominant based on sex or gender.

Still, the idea that submitting is lesser and weaker is deeply rooted, and even though I know it's not true, it's hard to accept. I've never been that alpha male outside of work. And even in my job, I've always had a reputation of being reasonable and friendly, the least arrogant of all the doctors. It's not my style, and besides, I believe you get much more done with teamwork.

With Caroline, I've always struggled to be the man she wanted me to be, that she needed me to be. She had a great example in her father, who loved her mother until the very end but who was still very much in charge. His word was law, and Caroline and her sisters learned obedience from a young age. My father is like that as well. Hell, he still is.

That's never been how I'm wired, and yet it seemed she expected it of me. Or maybe the church did, I don't know. All I know is that I've always felt like a failure, like I wasn't manly enough. Too weak and feminine. A sissy, a guy once called me after I admitted I often cried during movies. Apparently, that wasn't acceptable behavior for a man. Lesson learned.

One Bible study leader said that if we, as fathers, were soft and emotional with our sons, they'd become gay. Even back then, I knew that was bullshit. All I had to do was look at my father and grandfather, who were both as strict as they came, and yet there I was. I may not have accepted it at the time, but I am gay. I've always been gay.

And I've always been submissive. Oh, that thought sits uncomfortably inside me, and I shift in my bed, my erection long gone. I force myself to experience it, the weight of my shame and my guilt, because deep down, I know I shouldn't feel this way. There's no need to. This is how I'm wired, how I was made, and if I follow my old way of thinking that God doesn't make mistakes, then that means God made me gay... and submissive.

Or is submissive too strong a term? In the church, it's such a common word, but in the real world, it has BDSM associations, and that's not what I mean. I don't understand why some people take pleasure from being humiliated or hurt or whatever it is they consent to, but I don't judge. It's just not me. I've watched some videos with BDSM, and while I'm sure they weren't the best examples, it only made me curious as to why people like it.

No, I don't want to kneel for a Dom or serve him or anything like that. I just want... I want to be taken care of. I want to not be the strong one, the one who's in charge and has to make all the decisions. God, how amazing would it be to let someone else take the reins of my life? I'd sign up for that in a heartbeat.

I don't know the specifics of Benoni's relationship with his roommate, but it sounds a lot like what I want. A groan escapes me. Not only am I gay, but now I want domestic discipline as well? 'Cause that will go over well if I ever find the balls to enter the scary world of gay dating. A forty-seven-year-old baby gay, as Jerry calls me, a virgin at this, who wants to be spanked, pretty please and thank you. I'm gonna be single for the rest of my life, aren't I?

As depressing as that thought is, I still arrive at the same conclusion I always come back to: it would still be better than living a lie. The longer I'm living as my authentic self, the more I realize I wouldn't have survived otherwise. If I had stayed in my marriage, with or without the addiction, I would've ended up dead at some point.

I had so little to live for. My kids, yes, but that relationship had gone south long before my addiction came to light. That was on me. I worked too much, hid too much, ran away from what I wasn't ready to face yet. They clung to their mom, and I can't and will never blame them for that. I failed as a dad, and that's something I'll have to live with for the rest of my life. All I hope for is a chance to do better, even if it's so much later than it should have been.

But will they ever give me that chance? It's been nine months since I've last seen them or spoken to them. Nine long months of being sad and lonely. When will it end?

This mood I'm in is dangerous, and my phone is in my hand before I can talk myself out of it. Asking for help is one of the hardest things to do, but I'm getting better at it.

Bad day. I'm missing my kids so much.

I send the text to Jerry, and not even a second later, a *beep* tells me he's read it.

Thank you for telling me. I'm proud of you. Wanna meet later today?

Tears fill my eyes. He's the best sponsor I could've asked for, always there for me when I need him.

Yes, please. Thank you.

My pleasure. See you at 7?

I send him a thumbs-up. Maybe he can help me out of this weird melancholy mood I'm in. And on that note, I need to get the hell out of bed because I have an anatomy class to teach in half an hour. Yay.

18

1991: KINSEY

Every year, the youth leaders in my church select a few lucky teens from our group who get to go to Fire Up, a massive Christian event where teens from youth groups from all over the country gather to worship and do Bible study but also to hang out and have fun. For years, I heard the raving stories from teens who'd been chosen, but they never made me jealous. I never put much energy into trying to get picked...until this year.

After that strange conversation with Adam, I realized I had to get serious about my faith. If being a better Christian was the key to cure me of my *temptations*, then I'd be the best Christian ever. Much to my parents' and grandparents' joy, I got baptized ten months ago, delivering a rousing personal testimony that had the whole church applauding me. Reverend Lindstrom's grandson, you know?

I expected to feel different after that experience. Holier. I figured it would make a difference to God, this clear sign I was serious about doing the right thing. But alas, I felt pretty much the same afterward.

I've been reading my Bible as much as I can motivate

myself to, and I try to pray every day as well. Some days, I manage to check off all the boxes my youth leaders taught me should be a part of our prayers, like worship, confession of sins, praying for others, and more. But other days, my prayer is a plea straight from my heart: *Lord, please take these feelings away from me. I'm begging you. I will do anything for you. Anything.*

I don't want to look at Daniel like this. I don't want to feel that way about him. I don't want to dream about him, fight the urge to fantasize about him. So far, God isn't listening. Maybe I'm not a good enough Christian yet. Resist the devil, and he shall flee, the Bible says, so I just have to be steadfast in this.

Maybe attending Fire Up will help, and so I put all my energy into a subtle campaign to get selected, even using my ultimate weapon: mentioning to my grandfather how much I want to attend. Two days later, Adam calls me to tell me I've been chosen...and so is Daniel. "We figured this would be a great opportunity for you to witness to him and be a positive role model," Adam tells me. "We're so proud of you for your dedication to making sure Daniel stays on the right path."

I bite back a groan. Having Daniel come as well is about the last thing I need. "I'll do my best," I promise Adam.

I finish my junior year of high school with perfect grades, and my parents are thrilled when I tell them I want to be a doctor. Even my grandfather is mollified enough by that lofty aspiration to forgive me for not following in his footsteps. I have a lot of extracurricular activities lined up for my senior year to make sure I stand a good chance of getting into premed, so Fire Up is my one opportunity to have some fun that summer.

This year, the event is held in Indianapolis, and we travel

there by bus, our group joining forces with teens from three other youth groups close to Sarasota. Daniel immediately sits down next to me, his smell enveloping me. Why does he need to make it so hard on me? He doesn't know, of course, so I can't really blame him, but I'm so *aware* of him. The way his arm brushes against mine, how his eyes light up when he smiles, his giggle that always makes my belly swirl.

I shouldn't have all these soft feelings for him, but I'm unable to stop them. When he falls asleep halfway the trip and his head drops sideways and comes to rest on my shoulder, I indulge myself for as long as I can. We're all the way in the back, so no one has noticed yet. But a few minutes later, a guy from another youth group looks at me funny, and I know my time is up. I gently push Daniel back into a sitting position, missing the sensation of his body against mine instantly.

We're staying in a hotel where we share rooms with four people. We have three girls plus Virginia, a youth leader, and then Adam with Daniel, me, and a kid named TJ who has just turned fourteen and hasn't hit his growth spurt yet, unlike Daniel and me.

"I'll share a bed with TJ." Adam pats his sizable belly. "That'll leave enough room for my delicate frame."

We all laugh, but my stomach clenches, and panic claws at me. I have to sleep in a queen with Daniel? What if he snuggles up to me the way he did on the bus? What if I get one of those strange dreams about him again and wake up with a boner? The only thing worse than Daniel picking up on it would be Adam noticing my reaction. It would ruin everything I've worked so hard for, all the energy I've invested in making sure no one can accuse me of having homosexual thoughts. But what choice do I have?

Then my eyes fall on the ratty couch in the room. "I'll take the couch so Daniel can be comfortable in the bed."

Daniel freezes, his eyes showing shock and something else I can't pinpoint that quickly, but Adam's whole face lights up. "That's a great idea, Kinsey. Thank you for volunteering to experience discomfort so Daniel will sleep better. I'm proud of you."

Phew, I dodged a bullet there, though Daniel doesn't seem to be happy about it. After that, he goes out of his way to avoid me, and as much as I hate the idea of upsetting him, I'm relieved. Having him close makes it much harder for me to be the kind of Christian my parents and grandparents expect me to be.

The next morning, the big conference hall is filled to the brim with teens, the sheer energy in the room powering me up. This is gonna be epic! Two rows have been reserved for us, and we shuffle to our seats. By coincidence, I'm the first, and I end up sitting next to a girl from another youth group. She turns to me with a big smile. "Hi! I'm Caroline. Where are y'all from?"

I clear my throat, temporarily stunned by her happiness. "We're from Sarasota, Florida. I'm Kinsey, by the way. And you? I mean, where are you from?"

"So nice to meet you! We're from Asheville, North Carolina."

My insides grow warm. "Oh, I love Asheville. I've been there a few times with my grandparents."

"How cool! Did you join them on vacation or...?"

She's so bubbly and joyful, and something heavy lifts from my heart. If I could find a girl like her, I could do this. I could fall in love and marry her and be the man I need to be. "My grandfather preaches there at least twice a year. He's Reverend Lindstrom."

Her mouth drops open. "Oh, my gosh, that's your granddad? He's amazing. My mom buys his cassette tapes all the time, and we listen to them together when she can't make it to the service."

Something in her tone alerts me there's more to this, and before I can overthink it, I ask, "Is your mom sick?"

Caroline nods, losing some of her cheerfulness. "She has cancer. She's been sick for three years now."

Everything I've ever learned from watching my grandfather minister to sick and hurting people rises to the surface, and I cover her hand with mine. "I'm so sorry, Caroline. What a heavy cross to bear for you and your mom."

Caroline blinks, then bows her head, leaning slightly toward me. "They... They don't think she'll make it. My dad won't give me a straight answer when I ask him, but I don't think she has long anymore."

I squeeze her hand. "I'll pray for her that the Lord may do a miracle."

Carline looks up at me, her eyes moist. "Thank you. That means the world to me."

I let go of her hand, allowing her to compose herself. "I'm going to be a doctor," I tell her when she's wiped off her tears.

"That's amazing, Kinsey. The world needs more Christian doctors who understand that healing comes from God."

We chat all morning between the program elements, and when service is done, we stay behind as long as we can. After lunch, we talk more, and my whole youth group teases me as they realize what's happening.

I don't even care because I'm over the moon. For the first time in months, I'm not worried about my future or the temptation I struggled with. God has answered my prayers. I'm cured of this affliction.

At the end of the weekend, I'm as heartbroken as Caroline when we have to go our separate ways. When I ask for her phone number, she gives it to me, as well as her address.

"Promise me you'll write me?" she says, her voice small.

"I promise."

And when the worship band sings Michael W. Smith's classic "Friends Are Friends Forever," we both sing along, our hands bumping against each other. My heart is filled to the brim with hope. That same night, I write her my first letter, and I get an answer within days. A month later, when we're on the phone, I ask her to be my girlfriend, and she says yes. My future is set. God has been good to me and has answered my prayers. He's rewarded my efforts to be a good Christian and has allowed me to overcome this temptation.

The only shadow over my happiness is the news that Daniel has left the youth group and doesn't attend church anymore. I call him, but his mom says he refuses to talk to me. Three months later, halfway through our senior year, he drops out of high school and vanishes from the face of the earth. Even his mom has no idea where he is.

I'm worried sick about him, praying for him daily, but as my relationship with Caroline grows more serious, I realize it's time to let go. I can't keep thinking about Daniel and then feel guilty every time I do. He's made his choices, and I pray for him one last time, putting him in God's hands so I can focus on my future.

19

BENONI

I expected Kinsey to bring the topic of domestic discipline back up, but he doesn't. In fact, ever since we talked about it two weeks ago, he tries to act as if we've never had that discussion, though he fails. He studies me when he thinks I'm not noticing, but I always know when his eyes are trained on me. It's like I have a sixth sense for him.

His three-month mark is coming up, and I couldn't be more proud of him. The guy with the gaunt, pale appearance is gone, and in its place is a healthy-looking man who's getting sexier by the day. The silver in his hair and beard is getting more pronounced, and it could be my imagination, but I think that holds true for his chest hair as well. It only adds to his appeal, which makes no sense at all, considering how much older he is, and yet here we are. I'm in serious trouble with him, and it's long past the point where I can delude myself into thinking it's fine. It's not. I'm not.

It's a Friday afternoon, and I'm counting the hours until Kinsey shows up. And when I say counting, I mean checking my watch every three minutes, then verifying it's the correct time by looking at the large clock on the wall, then glancing at my watch again. I'm pathetic. My stomach is all in knots, and I can't remember ever feeling this way.

I've had crushes, but they've been few and far between. Most of the time, I had a casual affection mixed with a solid dose of lust and sexual chemistry, but that's it. I don't know why I don't crush that easily, but it's never bothered me. Friends have wondered why I'd never been in a serious relationship. My answer has always been the same: I haven't met the right guy yet.

The truth was and is that I wasn't sure what I was looking for. Who I was looking for. On the surface, I may be an easygoing guy, and most of my friends would describe me as such. But I know myself. The guys I've met would've bored me to death within weeks. I need someone who can keep up with me, someone who is smart, who has seen his fair share of life, someone who wants more out of life than just existing.

And I need someone who will allow me to take care of him. My relationship with Leif has shown me how much I love that role, how much satisfaction it brings me. My mom saw it too and told me I needed to find a man who would let me take care of him. She's rarely been wrong, my mom.

God, I miss her. Every day.

"Waiting for Kinsey?" a male voice asks, and I spin around.

Jerry, Kinsey's sponsor. I've met him, but I don't work with him. "I am."

"I'm Jerry." He extends his hand.

"I know. We've met before." Then it registers why he's introducing himself. He's not sure how much I know and if Kinsey has told me about him. "You're Kinsey's sponsor."

His shoulders slump, and the worry lines disappear from his forehead. "I am. I wasn't sure if you knew."

"He hasn't told me any details, but I've known him for years, and I know he was an opioid addict. I'm friends with his son, Jonathan."

I'd better make it clear what I know so Jerry isn't put in a tough position. He plays an important role in Kinsey's life, and I don't want to do anything to hurt their relationship.

"He mentioned it." Jerry studies me. "I hope you know what you're doing."

"Excuse me?"

He huffs. "I'm not a fool. I know something is going on between you."

I quirk an eyebrow. "If by something you mean a friendship, then yes. Nothing else has happened."

With anyone else, I would've said it's none of their fucking business, but with Jerry, I can't. Technically, it is his business as Kinsey's sponsor. Doesn't mean I'm gonna tell him anything. That's up to Kinsey. Besides, I'm not lying. Nothing has happened between us. I want to change that, but that doesn't matter right now.

Jerry's expression softens. "Ben, I'm worried about him. He's doing so well, and I don't want to see that threatened."

"Neither do I."

"Then you know he can't be in a relationship right now."

I cross my arms. "That's up to him."

"He's not ready for that yet."

"With all due respect, but that's not your call to make or mine. Kinsey is the only one who can make that decision. I refuse to do it for him."

"But you can make sure it doesn't happen on your end. Just give him a reason."

"What are you asking me to do here? It sounds like

you're suggesting I lie to Kinsey and tell him nothing can happen between us, but give him another reason than him being in recovery. But you'd never ask me to lie, would you?"

Jerry flushes. "Yeah, you're right. It was wrong of me to suggest that."

"It was," I say coolly. "I understand and respect you're concerned for his well-being, but I won't go behind his back."

He puts a hand on my arm. "You shouldn't, and I'm sorry for encouraging you. Kinsey is..." He sighs as he removes his hand. "Look, I work with a lot of clients, and I know not all of them will make it. But Kinsey can. He's special. He's doing so well, and he's so determined, and I just can't bear the thought of something endangering that."

Kinsey is special. Isn't that the truth? Yet I don't detect any jealousy in Jerry's voice or his body language, even though I know he's gay. No idea if he has a partner, but it doesn't matter, not when he's not interested in anything more than being Kinsey's sponsor. That, at least, reassures me that his motives aren't selfish. "I understand. All I can promise you is I won't do anything that could lead him back to his addiction."

He slowly nods. "Thank you. Just know that even though he's doing well, he's not cured or healed. Addicts never are. They're always one setback away from sliding back in these first years."

Kinsey and I have never talked about his addiction. I don't even know what caused him to take that first pill. His knee injury, perhaps? Then again, I don't want to ask him either. The when and why have to be something he chooses to share. But what I can do is educate myself more about addiction. I know the basics, but maybe it's smart to learn more.

"Do you have some good resources for me that could help me understand addiction better?" I ask Jerry.

His face lights up. "Yes. Tons. Want me to email you a list?"

"Please. Lynn at the front desk has my business cards with my contact info."

"I'll shoot that right over when I'm home. Thank you, Ben. I'm encouraged by the fact that you take his recovery seriously."

"My pleasure, though I want to make it clear once again that we're just friends."

"For now." Jerry pins me with a harsh look. "Don't play me for a fool, Ben. The sparks between you two could power a small city."

I don't know whether to cringe or laugh at that, or maybe smile and take it as a compliment? God, I feel so much, but none of it is suitable to discuss with Jerry, not when Kinsey has no idea. Does he even recognize the attraction between us? Or does he think he'll feel that way about every gay man he meets because it's all so new to him?

I straighten my shoulders. "This is where I ask you to back off and let him set the pace," I say softly. "We can't decide this for him, neither you nor me. He needs to make his own discoveries and determine how fast or slow he wants to go. If you know him, you'll also know he doesn't do things on impulse. Trust in his decision-making process."

"You're right. My husband keeps telling me I get too invested in my sponsees."

He's married? Oh, I like the sound of that. "I don't think that's a bad thing. They're lucky to have you in their corner."

Jerry's mouth curls up in a smile. "I bet that's a hell of a lot easier to say now that you know I'm married, isn't it?"

Oops, he caught me there. "Yes, it is," I admit.

"Whatever reasons I have for meddling in Kinsey's life, jealousy isn't one of them."

"That's good to know. Thank you."

Kinsey walks in, and for a moment, he takes my breath away. What is it about him that captivates me? I drink him in, allowing myself a few seconds of indulgence. His cheeks are rosy, and his skin glows with a healthy tan. It looks good on him, as does the black shirt he's wearing with a pair of gray shorts, but then again, he's gorgeous in everything. I've never been attracted to older men, at least not specifically, but Kinsey pushes all my buttons.

"Hi." His gaze darts from me to Jerry, his gorgeous silver-blue eyes radiating insecurity. "Am I interrupting anything?"

"Nope." Jerry slaps him on his back. "Ben and I were just chatting."

At least he's not gonna rat on me. That's good to know, though considering what he does, it would've surprised me if he had.

"Oh, okay."

"Are you ready for the next round of torture?" I ask.

Kinsey winces. "You really know how to sell it, don't you?"

"You look amazing," Jerry says, his voice warm and encouraging. "The difference with two months ago is staggering."

"Thank you." Kinsey smiles shyly. "Benoni is a strict but wonderful trainer."

Jerry meets my eyes, then nods. "He is, but this is you, Kinsey. You've worked hard for this, and you've shown up without failure. Take the credit when you deserve it. I'm really proud of you."

"So am I," I add. "I don't have many clients who are as disciplined as you."

Kinsey's cheeks flush, and I didn't think it was possible for a forty-seven-year-old man to look adorable, but he pulls it off. "Thank you. That means a lot to me." Then he glares at me. "But it's still torture."

I grin. "Oh, I know, and I've got some fun stuff for you in store today."

"When he laughs like that, it's dangerous," Kinsey tells Jerry, but he's laughing too. "That smile hides a mean streak that's a mile deep and two miles long."

I slap a hand on my chest. "Mean? *Moi?*"

"Yeah, no, not buying your fake innocence there, Ben." Jerry bumps shoulders with Kinsey. "I'm with you on this one. You can always switch to my trainer. Guido is amazing, and he's not as harsh a taskmaster as Ben here."

I suck in a breath. He's not serious, is he? Kinsey wouldn't switch to someone else, would he?

Kinsey studies me, a finger on his lips. Then a slow smile spreads across his face. "Nah, I'll keep him. His fragile ego wouldn't be able to handle the rejection."

"Fragile ego, my ass," Jerry grumbles, but his eyes sparkle.

"Let's get to work," I tell Kinsey, and he nods.

"I'll go warm up on the treadmill."

"Five minutes, then ten on the StairMaster. That's my revenge for you calling me mean."

He rolls his eyes. "Yes, Benoni."

He walks off, and I watch him, then catch myself and turn my attention back to Jerry. He's staring at Kinsey too, his mouth open. "What?" I ask him, maybe a little sharper than I intended.

"He's submissive. Holy shit, how did I miss that? Kinsey is submissive."

A rush shoots through me. So I haven't been imagining

it, then. Jerry sees it too. "I think so, yes. Are you active in the D/s lifestyle?"

"No, but my brother-in-law, my husband's brother, is. I joined him a few times because I had a sponsee who was a Dom, and I wanted to know what I was dealing with. You?"

"Yes, though not in a club setting or anything. I'm..." How do I explain this without violating Leif's privacy? "I'm providing domestic discipline for a friend."

"Domestic discipline..." Jerry says it slowly. "You think that would work for Kinsey?"

"I don't know."

"But the thought has crossed your mind."

"Yes."

"Have you discussed it with him?"

"Not about him, but he overheard me talking to the friend I mentioned, and we discussed the concept. And yes, I noticed his interest."

Jerry scratches his chin "Yeah, I'm not surprised. Now that I see it, it fits." His eyes find mine again. "Please be careful with him, Ben. I know you don't need my permission or my blessing, but I understand better now why you're drawn to him. So just...be careful. He's vulnerable."

"I know. Trust me, I know."

With a last nod, Jerry walks off, and I turn back to Kinsey. He's watching me from the treadmill but looks away when I meet his eyes. What should I do? Ask him? Or do I wait until he brings it up? If only I had a manual for how to handle a baby gay yet grown-ass man with heaps of trauma, a history of addiction, submissive tendencies, and is interested in me disciplining him. And despite all that, I'm crazy attracted to him. Did I mention the age gap and the fact that I'm his son's friend? My guess is, that's too much to ask, so I have to figure it out myself. But how?

20

KINSEY

I wipe my brow off with my towel, mentally preparing myself for the next set of repetitions. As he announced in my take-in, Benoni has me doing a lot of strength training, and I like it much more than I expected.

Cardio is still a nuisance, even though my fitness level and endurance have improved. Running on the treadmill is boring. Yes, I've graduated from walking to running, though it's more an undignified, penguin-like jogging. And my absolute favorite is the StairMaster. Not. That machine is pure torture. Every time I've done my ten-minute workout, my legs and ass hurt for days.

No, I like weight training because I can see the results. My body is getting more defined, and while it's slow going, it's exhilarating to see the progress I've made in the last three months. Maybe if my kids see how hard I'm working at getting healthy, they'll believe I really am sober. I haven't lost hope my relationship with them can be repaired, even if they've given me no indication so far they're interested in that.

I do my next set of fifteen repetitions of biceps curls,

grunting at the last two. My muscles are protesting, but not too much. Benoni has warned me not to push myself too hard to avoid even microtears in my muscles. And of course, I do what he says. I don't know why I have this weird habit of wanting to please him, but I've given up on trying to figure it out. I just do, and since he doesn't seem to have an issue with it and hasn't shown any signs he's abusing it, I let it go.

Maybe it's part of that submissive streak I've become aware of ever since Benoni admitted to being into domestic discipline. I've read a lot about it and about being submissive or dominant, and I think that's what's happening between us. He's a dominant man, and with me being submissive, it's only logical that I gravitate toward him and want to obey him. As much as I struggle with the fact that I'm wired like that, I can't deny it.

The question is what I'm going to do about it, and I don't have an easy answer. Do I tell him and risk things getting awkward? It would give me the opportunity to ask him questions, but I'm not convinced I should risk it. But where else would I go? To Jerry? Frank? I have no idea if this is a topic either of them is even into and knowledgeable about. No, I'll need to figure this out myself.

I do a third round of repetitions, then put the dumbbell down and relax. Lynn has decorated the place with fun Halloween stuff, including spider webs, ghouls dangling from the ceiling, and little orange pumpkin-shaped lights. I can't believe tomorrow is Halloween. The time is flying by, and I'm surprised and saddened by it, as every day that passes is another day without seeing my kids. No. I shove those thoughts away. I don't want to think about that now, and so I look around the room.

Frank is on the treadmill, pounding away his usual 5k in

a steady cadence. He has AirPods in, probably listening to the classic rock he loves, his lips moving as he silently sings along to the lyrics. I still haven't taken him up on his offer for coffee, but it's just been too much for me. When I brought it up the other day, he waved my concerns away and told me he wasn't in a hurry and could wait until I was ready. He hasn't flirted with me again, and the only vibe I'm getting from him now is genuine friendship. Maybe it is time to start working on becoming friends.

One of the other regulars is Soren, his name betraying his Scandinavian descent. The man is massive, six foot three of solid muscles and a chest twice, maybe three times, the size of mine. Last week, he told me that years ago, he competed in Strongest Man competitions, where he pulled cars, threw tree logs, and carried heavy stuff like anvils and boulders. In the photos on his phone he was even bigger back then. More fat, he'd explained, because weight is important in those competitions. Kind of like defensive football players, who may look like they're way too heavy to play professional sports, but who need that extra mass to do their job.

I was pleasantly surprised by how kind and soft-spoken he was, proudly showing me pictures of his three kids. He's bench pressing an amount of weight I don't even want to know, his face contorting as he does another rep. His friend JJ—short for John Johnson, and it should be punishable by law to name your kid that—is spotting him. When he's not checking out the two women who are working out right next to them, that is. Not that I can blame him. Both of them are offering alluring curves in tight outfits.

Benoni is talking to a new client he's taken on, Ginger, aptly named, considering her gorgeous red hair. She's my age and incredibly nice. She and I had a fun conversation about a mutual love for eighties music.

I've gotten to know the people who are usually here at the same time as me. We don't talk much, but the short exchanges and friendly nods make me feel like I'm one of them, like I belong. Benoni says that because this gym is so small, people develop friendships with each other, and while I was skeptical at first, I'm starting to see he's right.

All right, enough daydreaming. Time for the next set.

I'm midway through my repetitions when a strangled groan interrupts my counting. It came from Soren, it seems, but why would he...?

Oh, shit.

It's as if time slows down. I jump up from my bench, dropping my dumbbell on the floor. JJ spins around from the woman he'd been flirting with, his face contorting in shock as he sees what's happening. He makes a mad grab, but he's too late, and the heavy bell bar lands on Soren's chest with a sickening noise. I'm halfway to him when it happens, and I swear, the sound reverberates in my entire body. Benoni swivels around, his face paling as he takes in what is happening. Soren opens his mouth, but nothing comes out but a choked-off grunt.

"Soren!" JJ cries out, pulling on the bar on Soren's chest.

"Call 911," I shout to Benoni, then kneel next to Soren. "Get that bar off," I snap at JJ. Thankfully, another guy has stormed toward us, and together, they lift it off.

I need to assess Soren's status. I haven't done this in months, but it comes back as if no time has passed. "Soren, I'm gonna take a look at your injuries, okay? I know your chest must hurt, but is there anything else?"

"It hurts..."

"Describe the pain for me."

"Stabs. Worst pain ever."

"Don't move your arms, but tell me where it hurts most. Your chest? Left? Right?"

"Chest. Right."

Thank God. If he's said left, I would've had to worry about his heart. This kind of impact could've easily ruptured his heart, causing cardiac tamponade and all kinds of nasty complications. Benoni has dropped a first aid bag next to me, and I find a pair of gloves and snap them on. With the scissors from the kit, I cut Soren's shirt from hem to neck so I have full access.

I lean my head near his mouth, checking his airway and listening for breath sounds. Little puffs of air tickle my cheek. He's breathing, but it's labored and rapid. His pulse is out of control, but at least he's still conscious. He's not bleeding anywhere that I can see, but he's bound to have fractured ribs, and he may have internal bleeding.

"What are you doing?" JJ asks, his voice panicky.

"Let him work. He's a doctor." Benoni sounds calm and steady. Thank god he's there.

Soren wheezes in air. "Can't...breathe..."

Soren's breaths become more labored, and panic rises in his eyes. Shit. With a blunt force trauma like this and the almost guaranteed fracture of multiple ribs, his lack of air can indicate a tension pneumothorax, but I can't diagnose that without more information. Hell, I don't even have a stethoscope.

"Do you have any heart issues?" I ask Soren.

"No..."

"Any known illnesses?"

"No..."

His heart rate is slowing down, and he's fighting for every breath now. It has to be a tension pneumothorax. I've seen it too many times not to recognize the symptoms, and I have no time to wait for the ambulance.

"Everybody quiet," I snap. I need silence for the next part. I bend close to his chest and percuss the right side of his thorax, then the left. I was right. The right side sounds tympanic, a sign of a tension pneumothorax.

"Soren, it looks like you have a collapsed lung. I'm gonna try to re-inflate it, so hang in there, okay?"

If only there's something I can do an emergency needle decompression with. The scissors are pointy and should be sharp enough to stab him with, but I need a hollow needle.

"I need a straw that's not paper. Metal, silicone, glass, anything." I've seen multiple people use them, a more environmentally friendly alternative to plastic or flimsy paper straws.

"On it," Benoni says and sprints away.

It's about the worst environment to do a procedure like this in, but if I don't, he'll die. Thank God the gym has a well-equipped first aid kit. I unscrew the bottle with cleaning alcohol and pour it over his chest. No time for subtleties now.

"Here." Benoni drops on his knees next to me and hands me a metal straw. It's thicker than I would prefer, so it may damage some blood vessels, but it's Soren's best shot. "The ambulance is four minutes out."

Soren doesn't have four minutes. His circulatory system has to be near collapse by now. He needs air, and he needs it now.

I dump alcohol over the scissors and the straw and turn to Soren, who is sweating and pale as a ghost. I probe his ribs until I've located the second intercostal space at the midclavicular line. It's an automatic process. Muscle memory, my fingers knowing what to look for. How many times have I performed this procedure? Must be at least a thousand times during my career. But I've never done it like this, with a pair of scissors and a metal straw, with the patient conscious and unsedated, and with a crowd of people around me, watching my every move.

I take a deep breath, then push it out. "This is gonna hurt. I'm sorry."

Without giving him any more warning, I stab him with the scissors. He screams, then passes out, thank god. Around me, people gasp and grunt in shock, but I ignore them as I work the scissors in deeper until I'm where I need to be.

I don't need to ask for silence, as the crowd around me is watching in quiet shock. I need to be able to hear the air release, or I won't know if what I did worked. Blood pours out, but it's at the expected rate, so I'm good. I pull the scissors out with my right hand, holding the hole open with my left, then gently manipulate the straw in. As soon as it's in, air hisses out, and I breathe out with relief. I did it.

Immediately, Soren's breathing pattern changes into something much deeper and steadier. He's not out of the woods yet, as he may have a crap ton of internal injuries I can't assess without scans, but at least he's stabilized.

I look sideways at Benoni. "He's stable for now."

A wave of excited gasps and murmurs travels through the room.

"You saved his life." Benoni's voice holds wonder.

I can't let it get to my head. This is what I've been trained to do. Despite everything that happened, this is still my calling. I'm a doctor. Saving lives is my job. "Make sure someone is at the door to guide the EMTs in," I say instead.

I dab the blood with some gauze. The kit has a roll of

medical tape, and I use that to affix the straw to Soren's skin so it won't come out.

"Lynn is ready for them," Benoni says.

"Do you know Soren's last name and age?"

"Anderson, and he's thirty-four. Lynn is pulling whatever medical information we have on him to give to the paramedics."

Quick thinking on his part. Part of the intake was filling out a medical form, disclosing any relevant medical information, which now, with Soren, comes in handy.

We wait in silence for the ambulance to arrive. Sirens are getting closer and closer, doors open and close. Then the paramedics come running in, and the crowd parts for them to get to us. The first one is a guy who can't be older than twenty-five, and I mentally wince at his inexperience. Behind him, a fortysomething Black woman strides in. She looks like someone who has seen her fair share of shit, and that always makes me feel better.

"What do we have?" she says, her eyes sharp.

"Soren Anderson, thirty-four, the victim of blunt force trauma after a bell bar dropped on his chest. He had labored, shallow breathing and decreasing cardiac function and complained of a stabbing pain in the right thorax. I diagnosed him with a tension pneumothorax and did a needle decompression in the field. He's stable, but I suspect multiple fractured ribs and possibly internal bleeding."

She blinks. "You a doctor?"

I've never met her before, but if I say my name, chances are she'll recognize it from gossip, and I don't want that.

"He's an ER doctor," Benoni says smoothly, preventing me from having to come up with an answer, and I want to kiss him with gratitude.

"Well, that's a fortunate coincidence for our friend here,

so thank you for your quick actions." She looks at Soren's chest while her coworker takes some vitals. "You used a metal straw? Goddamn, bro, you went all MacGyver on him."

"BP's 90 over 55," her coworker says.

That's low, which isn't uncommon after blunt force trauma with tension pneumothorax, but it can also indicate internal bleeding. Before I can say anything, the paramedic puts a hand on my shoulder. "We've got him now. All right, rookie, let's load him up and head out. Time is of the essence here."

"Can I ride with him?" JJ asks. He's as pale as a sheet himself. Once the shock has passed, he'll have to deal with the guilt for not paying attention.

"Are you family?" the paramedic asks.

"No, but we've been friends forever, and I have all his contact info, so I can call his wife."

She nods briskly. "All right. Let's go."

Two minutes later, they're out the door, the ambulance leaving with as much noise as it arrived. God, I've missed this. The adrenaline, the rush, the pressure of having to make a quick decision and having the courage to act on it. I love all of it, and I miss it so much my heart aches.

"I messed up your floor," I say to Benoni. What a ridiculous thing to say. The linoleum can be cleaned easily.

"No worries." His voice is soft as if he picks up on my emotions. He holds out a towel. "Dump all your garbage on this, and I'll chuck it into the trash."

I close the bottle of alcohol and put it on the towel together with the gauze, the scissors, the medical tape, which is all bloody, and last, my gloves. Benoni rolls everything up in the towel and hands it to Lynn, who has come over to check on us. He rises to his feet, then holds out a hand to pull me up. My knee buckles, but he steadies me until I've regained my footing.

"That was badass," Frank says. Why didn't he offer to assist me? Not that he could've done much, but it would've been nice to have someone to help me, and as a former EMT and now ICU nurse, he has the experience. But his face is tight, so I don't ask. I'm sure he has his reasons.

"Thanks."

More people come up to thank me until they all dissipate. Lynn has mopped up the floor, and it looks like nothing ever happened.

Benoni takes my arm and leads me to the locker room. "Get dressed," he says. "I'm taking you home."

21

BENONI

Something happened to Kinsey when he was taking care of Soren. I don't know what, but no way in hell am I letting him go home alone after this. He looks pale and shocked, and he shouldn't be, not when he's been an ER doc for god knows how long. Sure, doing a procedure like this in an ER differs from the way he had to do it here, but still. He shouldn't be as stricken as he is, and I intend to find out what's going on. I need to make sure he's okay before I trust him to be by himself.

I shoot off a quick text to Leif to let him know we're expecting visitors. Leif has a habit of walking around the house in various stages of undress, which doesn't bother me but may be a bit much for a first meeting with Kinsey. Besides, Leif is cute, and his body is damn near perfect, so sue me for not wanting him to show that off to Kinsey. The man isn't made of stone, and if he already got an erection from me massaging his calves, I hate to think how he'll react to Leif in a pink jockstrap and nothing else. I've lived with him for years now, and some days, *I* get hard watching him.

Kinsey is getting dressed, his movements slow, and I try

not to stare. He's come a long way already, his body so much healthier than it was when he first entered the gym. I'm so proud of him and grateful that I've been able to play a role in his recovery.

"Why are you taking me to your place?" Kinsey asks when he's ready, frowning in confusion.

"That was quite an intense experience," I say softly.

"Yeah, but nothing I couldn't handle or haven't seen a thousand times before."

Funny how factually he says it. Not bragging, but a statement of facts. He's so confident in his job but so vulnerable and insecure in his personal life. He must've been one hell of a doctor, and my heart aches for him that he lost all that.

"I know, but I think some debriefing might be in order."

"Debriefing? Were you under the impression this was traumatic for me?"

He's catching on. "Not so much traumatic, but... It did something to you, and I want to make sure you're okay before I let you go home."

I meet his eyes straight on, and oh, the battle in there is easy to spot. His pride is warring with shame, maybe with guilt, but also with the need to be taken care of. I've come to know him well, and I've never seen someone sink into care the way he does. He's much like Leif, who also soaks up my discipline like a dying plant takes in water and sunlight.

"*Let me* go home? I didn't know that was your decision to make." He tries to make it sound defiant and maybe even arrogant, but he fails spectacularly.

"It's not, but we both know you want it to be."

Oh, shit. I can't believe I said that out loud, and judging by the way Kinsey's eyes pop wide open, neither can he. He opens his mouth, and I expect a sharp response, but then his shoulders stoop, and he closes his mouth again. "I can't do this now," he whispers, avoiding my eyes.

Fair enough. "Forget I said that, but please, Kinsey, let me take you home and make sure you're okay."

He doesn't respond right away, and all I can do is wait. Ultimately, this has to be his choice. My mom always said that you can't help people until they're ready to accept help, and Kinsey struggles with that for reasons I can only guess at. It's gotta be a blow to his pride to listen to someone so much younger, that much is obvious, but I suspect there's more behind it. I can't quite put my finger on it, but it feels as if he's ashamed of needing help. Of needing me, specifically? I can't figure it out.

So I give him time, and finally, he nods. "Okay."

My heart leaps up with joy, and I put a hand on his shoulder. "Thank you."

I give him my address so he knows where to go in case he loses track of me, and then we drive home, Kinsey following me in his car. He parks on the driveway behind me, and I roll my eyes at Leif's car, which is parked in the middle of the driveway, taking up two spots. Again.

When we walk in, the smell of something delicious greets me. "Hey, Bun!" I call out.

Leif comes over, dressed in a pair of fuck-me jeans that are sculpted around his body and a white T-shirt that says Boy Toy in pink, glittery letters. It's better than half-naked, I suppose, though it may be a close call.

"This is my friend Kinsey. Kinsey, this is my roommate, Leif."

Kinsey blinks once, then holds out his hand to Leif, who giggles as he accepts it. "How old fashioned of you," he purrs.

Oh lordy, Leif is in baby boy mode, like he often is with

older men. He's *so* knocking on the wrong door there with Kinsey, but I won't even bother pointing that out. He'll find out soon enough.

"Old fashioned?" Kinsey lets go of Leif's hand and looks at me, an unspoken question for help in his gaze.

"That's Leif's code word for a man with manners. He usually hangs out with guys who wouldn't know how to behave like a decent human being in public."

Snappy? Yeah, I admit it. But for god's sake, why does Leif have to bat his baby blues at Kinsey? I love him to pieces, but his incessant flirting is hella annoying at times.

Leif shoots me a wounded look that slides right off me. I know damn well he's only being a drama queen. "What's that amazing smell?" I say to placate him.

He perks up. "My famous lasagna."

"Oh, yummy. You made enough for three, I hope?" His lasagna is incredible and exactly what I'm in the mood for.

Leif rolls his eyes. "Do I ever make lasagna in small portions?"

He doesn't because he knows I'll eat double portions of it any day and the leftovers for breakfast the next morning. "Awesome. How much time do we have until dinner?"

Leif checks his watch. "Five minutes."

"Let me set the table."

"Can I use your bathroom?" Kinsey asks me.

"Of course. Second door to the right in the hallway."

As soon as he's left the living room, Leif turns to me. "Who the hell is that? He's so fucking hot."

"I told you, he's a friend. A client who's become a friend."

Leif quirks an eyebrow. "A friend? Funny, you never mentioned him, and I know all your friends."

I avoid his all-too-perceptive gaze. "It's a new friendship, okay?"

"Is he gay?"

"Leif!"

He flutters his eyelashes. "Just asking. I wouldn't mind being the baby boy to his Daddy."

"He's not into that."

"And you would know, how? Seeing as how he's a client and a recent friend. Is that the kind of topic you discuss with all your clients?"

He's got me there. The toilet flushes, and I have only a few seconds left to get Leif off his quest. I need him to stop flirting with Kinsey. It'll make Kinsey uncomfortable, and I don't want that. He's not used to someone like Leif. And so I blurt out the only thing that will work. "I call dibs."

His eyes go wide as saucers. "Seriously?"

We live by this bro code. You can't flirt or approach someone if the other one has called dibs first. Not until they release that claim. So now I've claimed Kinsey, and it feels all kinds of wrong and yet wonderfully right at the same time. "Yes."

I make my voice firm, so Leif knows I mean it. He holds up his hands. "Okay, backing off."

"Thank you."

Kinsey walks back into the room, and Leif dashes into the kitchen. "Go sit," I tell Kinsey, and I smile when he obeys and finds a seat at the dinner table. "Leif's lasagna is the best thing ever. You'll love it."

"Anything with pasta is amazing," he counters, and he has a point.

Leif puts a steaming dish of lasagne on the table, and we all place a large serving on our plates. Kinsey takes his first bite and moans. "You weren't kidding. This is delicious."

Leif beams. "Thank you."

"Leif gave me the recipe, but when I tried it, it didn't

taste nearly as good, so he has some kind of secret ingredient he's not telling me," I tease him.

"So, Leif, what do you do for work?" Kinsey asks, and silence descends in the room.

Oops. In hindsight, I should've prepared him for this, but it's too late now.

Leif, bless his heart, looks at me, quietly asking me for permission. I nod. He should never have to hide who he is and what he does. That would imply he has something to be ashamed of, and he doesn't.

"I'm in adult entertainment through OnlyFans," he says, and I make a mental note to praise and reward him later for being so sweet about it. He's usually far blunter, but he's taking my dibs seriously and trying to make a good impression. I love him for it.

Kinsey frowns, but then he blushes. "That's... How did you... Do you like it?"

The man deserves major points for being casual about it, even when it's obvious how uncomfortable he is. Not judging but more flustered and uncertain how to handle this delicate topic.

"You don't have to answer this if you'd rather not talk about it," he says, and my heart does a funny jump in my chest. He's so sweet, even when he's out of his comfort zone.

Leif senses it too. His fake smile fades and gives way to something honest and vulnerable. "I like sex," he says. "I always have, and so I thought I might as well make money off it. And I know this isn't something I'll do forever, but for now, it works for me while I'm trying to figure out what I want to do with my life."

"As long as it's by choice and not because you're forced to do it," Kinsey says, and I love that he homes in on the consent part.

Leif nods. "It's very much by choice. I choose my partners, and I always ask for a copy of their driver's license so I know their real identity. Plus, they have to sign release forms to legally give me permission to use their videos."

"He's quite well known by now, so he has a long list of men willing to work with him," I add. "They do it for the fame while he gets the money, and it works."

"I'm glad it's working out for you," Kinsey says, and there goes that funny tingle in my chest again. Why do I even care how Kinsey reacts to Leif or him doing porn? It shouldn't matter, yet it does, and I don't understand why. What is this pull Kinsey has over me?

22

KINSEY

After the delicious dinner, Leif retreats to his room, and Benoni and I settle on the couch in the living room with coffee.

"You reacted well to him doing porn," Benoni says. My cheeks grow hot all over again.

"I didn't want him to feel uncomfortable or judged."

"He didn't. You did good."

I breathe out easier now. "Conversations like that are hard for me."

"Because they make you uncomfortable?"

"Yes, but also because..." How do I frame this in a way he'll understand? "I was raised to believe that sex was something negative. It was a sin unless it happened within marriage and then only between a man and a woman. So I have to overcome all those outdated ideas. But porn especially..." I sigh. "There's a crusade in the church against porn. Pastors preach how dangerous it is and how it's adultery."

Benoni frowns. "Adultery? I'm not following."

"If you're married and you're watching porn, that's

considered adultery because you're looking at another woman with lustful thoughts." I cringe. "Or in my case, a man."

Something flashes over Benoni's face, but then he leans forward. "I wasn't sure if I would ever tell you, but I don't feel like I should hide it from you any longer, not when we've grown so close. Remember when you watched me get a blow job in the basement?"

Do I remember? Is he kidding? "Yeah, I have a faint recollection."

He grins. "I figured. Well, about six months after that, I caught you watching porn in your study. Gay porn."

Oh god. I know exactly what time he refers to. I could've sworn I heard something, but when I looked into the hallway, no one was there. Yet a while later, footsteps came down the stairs. I told myself it had just been someone walking by, Jonathan most likely, but I never took that risk again and only watched if I knew no one else was around.

"That was you? I thought I heard something."

"In my defense, I heard a moan and was checking it out because I didn't know anyone else was home, but then I listened at the door, and it became obvious you were watching porn."

"Gay porn." I meet his eyes head on. "I was watching gay porn."

"I heard two men and some dialogue that made that crystal clear."

"You never said anything to anyone, even though you must've suspected I was gay or bi. Nonstraight at least."

"What?" Benoni glowers at me. "As if I would ever out someone."

No, he wouldn't. "You said nothing to me either."

"It didn't seem like a topic you'd want to discuss with me."

"God, no."

"Then I made the right choice, didn't I? I figured you'd come out when you were ready."

"I'm sorry you heard me."

"Why would you be sorry?"

"Because you caught me watching porn while I was still married. I shouldn't have. It was a betrayal of my vows to Caroline."

I lower my gaze, twisting my fingers in my lap as the all-too-familiar guilt sweeps through me.

"Kinsey, look at me."

Why do I find it so hard to resist his voice? Especially when it gets so low and deep, so effortlessly dominant. He's everything I should have been. Minus the gay part, of course. But maybe if I had been more like him, things would've worked out differently. *You'd still have been gay,* the voice inside me says. True, but would I have had the courage to come out sooner? I'll never know, but it's a thought that makes me sad.

I raise my head, meeting his kind, warm eyes. They gleam with so much understanding, so much acceptance. My soul sucks it up like I'm dying for it, and maybe I am. It's been too long since someone looked at me like that. Jerry does it at times, but that's it.

"I don't think you betrayed her," Benoni says softly. "Definitely not in the sense of adultery, which, if I'm honest, sounds farfetched to me. Adultery is having sex with someone else outside of a relationship that's supposed to be monogamous. That's it."

His words wash over me, and I cling to them, to the

warmth they bring to me inside. "I felt so awful every time I did it, but...I needed it."

"How?"

He asks the questions no one else would dare to ask, and it's both refreshing and scary. "If I wanted to... If Caroline wanted sex, I needed something to get me in the mood. I know it sounds awful, but—"

"It's not awful. You're gay."

He says it as if it's the most normal thing in the world, and it probably is to him. "Yeah, but that doesn't make it okay."

"Kinsey, I couldn't get it up for a woman unless I close my eyes and pretend she was a man. I love women, and I have close female friends, but I'm not attracted to them sexually at all. That's not how I'm wired."

"I know, but it's different for you. I *married* her, Benoni. I made her a promise to be faithful to her, and I wasn't."

He studies me. "I'm not sure I agree, but I respect you feel that way. But let me ask you this. Did she know you were attracted to men? Did you ever discuss it with her?"

I love how he worded it. Attracted to men. He's been paying attention, using my own expressions rather than talking about being gay. Of course I understand and accept that I've always been gay, but those words to describe past Kinsey is an anachronism to me.

But his question isn't quite so easy to answer, not without adding a lot of context. "Yes, I did, but she didn't understand what it meant at the time any more than I did. We were both still convinced God would take it away. When I say that now, it sounds so stupid and naïve, but we really believed that."

"Not stupid," Benoni says softly. "Not stupid at all. When did you lose that hope?"

I scratch my beard. "I don't know. Our marriage wasn't good, but I blamed it on my job, the odd and long hours. In hindsight, it's easy to recognize I found an escape in my job, which I loved. Every hour I spent there, feeling useful and validated, meant an hour less with Caroline, an hour less of feeling not good enough, of knowing that I was failing her as a husband...and yet being powerless to do anything about it."

"I can't imagine how hard that must've been for you."

Why has no one ever listened to me the way Benoni does? With him, I don't feel like I'm defending myself, like I have to explain my actions. He wants to understand but without judgment, and it makes all the difference.

"It was, and I think it played a role in us stepping away from the church. I had the excuse of often working on the weekends as to why I couldn't go or be active. At first, Caroline would go to church with the kids, but then she started skipping and eventually stopped going altogether. We talked about it, and we both felt the same way that we didn't connect with the church anymore. Caroline struggled with the constant pressure to be perfect, and we both had major issues with a lot of stuff that was surfacing about what leaders in the church had done. Not just our church, but the church in general. Embezzlement, using tithes for personal enrichment, sexual abuse, preaching against homosexuality while in secret sleeping with male prostitutes... It made us and many others angry and contributed to our decision to leave the church, though that was more of a slow process than a one-time conscious decision."

Benoni sighs. "Yeah, those people have a lot to answer for. My uncle Tim is a pastor, and nothing makes him angrier than hypocrisy and the clergy abusing their positions."

"It should make everyone furious, but sadly, it doesn't."

"True."

We sit quietly, but it's a comfortable silence. How easy is he to talk to. I'm telling him things I haven't even discussed with Sosha or Jerry. It's the way he listens, but above all, how he accepts me just as I am. He doesn't have some ulterior agenda, isn't trying to change me. He wants to understand me and get to know me. I can't get over the fact that he's doing what no one else in my family or even my friends has done. It makes my fascination with him so much more dangerous. What may have started with a physical attraction now has so many more layers, and I spend too much time every day thinking about him.

"I may have left the church, but those teachings, that judgment and condemnation still live in my head," I finally say. "The voices are getting quieter, but they're not gone."

"That will take time, I'd imagine."

"That's what my therapist keeps telling me. Though she doesn't have a religious background, so she doesn't understand all of it, and she never will."

"I asked my uncle some questions about it. He knew what you were talking about with the purity culture and everything."

He asked his uncle? "Why'd you ask him? Not that I mind, but..."

"I wanted to understand you better. There's a generation between us, but we also grew up in very different families. My mom was spiritual, but not religious, and my uncle is a pastor in an accepting, affirmative church where everyone is welcome. I wanted to get a better idea of how you were raised and the messages you heard every day."

I have no words for the emotions brewing inside me. They're too big, too confusing. Too confronting because

Clean Start at Forty-Seven

they all boil down to the same thing: Benoni's care for me. His kindness, his interest, his listening ear. But also the way he bosses me around, takes charge when he needs to, cares for me when I don't even want to admit I need it. Like today.

"Thank you."

It's all I can say without revealing too much, but Benoni watches me with those sharp green eyes, seeing so much more than anyone else.

"Kinsey, can we talk about what happened earlier?" he asks.

"You mean with Soren?"

He shakes his head. "Sorry, I didn't word that specific enough. I meant my remark about you wanting me to make the decisions for you...to tell you what to do. You said you couldn't do that then, but can you now? Are you ready to talk about it?"

Now would be a perfect time for the ground to open and swallow me whole. If only I could be anywhere else but here, with the one man who sees the real me that no one else has ever discovered. Does he realize the power he holds over me? What he could do to me if he chose to? God, he could break me into a million pieces with one careless word, and I don't even think he knows it. "I don't know," I whisper. "I'm scared."

"There's nothing to be scared of." His voice is equally soft. "I promise you, Kinsey."

I love how he says my name, always with warmth and affection. And he makes me believe him because he's never lied to me, and unlike many others in my life, he has never let me down. "Okay."

"Talk to me, Kinsey. What's going through your mind?"

Of course he puts the ball right back in my court. Should have seen that one coming. But how do I tell him? I don't even know where to start. Maybe with the most fundamental truth I've discovered about myself.

I take a deep breath. "I think I'm submissive."

There, I got the words out. I deserve an award for that.

But Benoni's face is a reward all in itself, so proud. He's beaming. "Thank you for sharing that with me. I feel honored you'd trust me with this."

"It's really hard for me to understand and even harder to accept."

"I gathered as much. Is this because of your religious background?"

"Yes. In many ways, toxic masculinity finds its core support in the church. I was taught to be a manly man, to be masculine. That meant being dominant, in charge, the head of my family. If you weren't like that, if it even looked like your wife was wearing the pants... And by the way, what a stupid, misogynistic expression that is, but that's beside the point."

"What was the reaction to men who didn't conform to that norm?"

How do I explain the power of disapproval? How heavy it weighed on me whenever my parents or church leaders showed they were disappointed in me? Or was that also only because of my innate need to please people, my natural desire to be obedient? I've never looked at it like that, but now that the thought has come up, I can't let it go. Maybe this whole submissive thing has had more influence than I thought.

"Do you think being submissive and having a need to please are connected?" I ask.

Benoni looks surprised for a moment but then nods. "They can be. Some subs have a deep need to please, and that's at the core of their kink."

Kink. The word almost makes me recoil, but that's what this is, isn't it? A kink. "That's a hard word for me to process."

"I can imagine, since all this is new to you."

"Yeah, apparently, it wasn't enough of a challenge to be gay. I had to add some more stuff to make it even more difficult and complicated."

Benoni is silent for so long I frown. Did I say something wrong?

"I understand why you word it like that," he finally says. "But I don't like that you think of yourself as difficult. You're not. Your identity doesn't change that. Not the gay aspect, but neither does the submissive aspect or anything else you discover about yourself. You're valid and good the way you are."

God, he's gonna make me cry again.

23

BENONI

I want to hold Kinsey, hug him until that wounded, haunted look has faded from his eyes. He's hurting, and I'm unable to stop it and take it away, no matter how much I want to.

His eyes are watery when they meet mine. "Sorry, I need a moment to process that."

"Take all the time you need."

Without thinking about it, I hold out my hand, and when he takes it, I curl my fingers around his. His heart rate speeds up, and arousal flares up deep inside me. He's so fucking responsive. If he already reacts like that to me holding his hand, how will he respond when I touch him for real? When I kiss him, run my hands through his salt-and-pepper hair, when I explore every inch of his body?

I don't think I've ever had it this bad for anyone, not even in high school. It's a little embarrassing, yet it feels wonderfully right, even if I can't act on it. And I can't. He's not ready for this, and if I force the issue, it could break his fragile mental state. He's so much more vulnerable than he looks, and I didn't need Jerry to point that out to me.

"The church has a strong culture of conforming, of peer pressure to fall in line with the opinions of the majority."

It takes me a moment to realize Kinsey is answering my earlier question about the reaction to nonconforming.

"In some areas, having an alternate opinion was accepted, but with most matters, you had to walk the party line. And the need to be strong and masculine was one of those. Even as a teen, I knew this. Acting feminine in any way was judged harshly, and that only got worse as we grew older. The church organized men retreats where they went back to nature. You know, chopping wood, catching fish with your bare hands, building shelters, stuff like that, with lots of Bible study in between. It was supposed to foster team spirit, help you become more masculine, and build character. Not participating was suspicious, and the only reason I got away with it was my job, which held a lot of standing."

Kinsey's religious upbringing has truly influenced every part of his life not only on Sundays or what he did in church but everything. It has shaped his entire way of thinking. I don't want to call it programming, not in front of him, but that's what it feels like to me. "That doesn't sound like fun at all to me."

Kinsey snorts. "It's not, trust me. A friend of mine went to one in the Smoky Mountains, and he was miserable the whole weekend. Cold, hungry, and forced to be cheerful and happy, he said he was glad to make it out alive and without falling ill."

"That must've made it impossible for you to be yourself."

"Yes, both the gay and the submissive part, though I didn't label them as such back then. All I knew was that I was different." His voice breaks. "You don't know how hard I prayed to be like everyone else, to not feel like I didn't belong...but God never answered that prayer."

"Maybe because he thought you were perfect the way you were."

He wipes away a tear. "You mean that?"

"My mom always said that God doesn't make mistakes."

"Funny, my church said the same thing, except they used that to defend their position that being gay was a choice. Homosexuality was against God's will, so God couldn't have made you gay. That would imply he'd made something imperfect."

"Well, I'm not the right person for a theological discussion, but I call bullshit, even according to their own theory. Don't they believe all men are sinful? Well, God created all of them, didn't he? He made some jealous or having a temper and others with a silver tongue. Those traits are imperfect too."

Kinsey blinks a few times. "I've never looked at it like that, but you're right."

"Don't get me wrong. I'm only following their line of reasoning that being gay is a sin, which I don't agree with. But you're good the way you are, Kinsey, gay *and* submissive."

Every time I say the word, his reaction is a little less intense.

"Is it a negative thing in the world, being submissive?" he asks.

"In the world?"

"Sorry, church language. I mean, how do non-Christians see being submissive? And how does it rank, for lack of a better word, in the gay community?"

Of course, he's asking the hard questions. "I wish I could

Clean Start at Forty-Seven

tell you it's seen as equal to being dominant, but it's not. Too many people still consider it as somehow less and for all the wrong reasons. It's getting better, I think, with BDSM knowledge spreading outside of the community. Believe it or not, but books like *Fifty Shades of Grey* have contributed to that. Even though I am critical of them, they sparked an interest in D/s play, and as a result, people went searching for information, so that's been a positive effect."

Kinsey sighs. "Yeah, it was too much to hope it would be different there."

His shoulders stoop, and my whole heart goes out to him. I squeeze his hand, which is still wrapped in mine. He's made no attempt to remove it, and neither have I. "I'm sorry."

"How do you see it?" he asks softly, his voice wavering a little. He's not afraid of my answer, is he?

"As a gift, an incredibly valuable, precious gift. I'm not a Dom, Kinsey. Doms have received formal training and should initially do their scenes under the supervision of an experienced mentor. That's all different for me. Yes, I did research when Leif and I started with domestic discipline, and I booked two sessions with a Dom so I knew what I was doing, but that's it. When Leif submits to me for his punishment, all I feel is gratitude that I get to do this for him. A sense of awe for that level of trust."

"He's lucky to have you."

I have to ask, and this is the best opening I'll ever get. "Kinsey, is this something you're interested in? Something you'd like to experiment with?"

He freezes and pulls his hand out of mine. Fidgeting with his fingers, he looks at the floor. "I can't..."

"Why not?"

"I'm forty-seven years old. It's ridiculous I would want this. I shouldn't even consider it."

"Why? What does your age have to do with anything? Being submissive isn't something that changes as you grow older. It's who you are, how you're wired."

He looks up, tears in his eyes. "You don't understand. My family doesn't even accept me being gay. How do you think they'll react when they find out about me being submissive? It'll only be another reason for them to reject me. I can't do it. I can't. I need them more than I need to have this."

How can I argue with that? He's using the one argument I can't refute, no matter how much I want to. He's right. Any chance of reconciliation with Jonathan and Judith will be a hundred times smaller when they find out about this. "I'm sorry, Kinsey. I understand, but I'm so sorry for you."

He buries his face in his hands, his shoulders shaking with quiet sobs. "I'll never be able to be myself, will I? I'll always have to hide a part of who I am."

My heart breaks, and I do the only thing I can do. I pull on his arm until he lets go and crashes into my arms, and then I hug him to me and hold him as he cries. It's so unfair, so utterly unfair. After everything he's been through, he deserves to be happy and be himself, and yet he's right. He will still have to hide because people won't understand his needs.

It takes a long time for him to calm down, and all that time, I hold him, whispering encouragements in his ear about him being stronger than he thinks and that he'll get through this. I don't know if there's anything I could say that would be both true and would make him feel better, so I don't even try.

When he lets go, the emptiness in his eyes, which I've

never seen before, scares me. "I'm not gonna ask you if you're okay because you're clearly not, but I need to know if you're well enough to go home."

His eyebrows squish together. "What do you mean?"

"I'm worried about your mental health. Please tell me I have no reason for it."

"Oh. *Oh.*" His face lights up with understanding, but he doesn't answer, and my concern for him increases. "I think I'm okay," he finally says.

"Kinsey, no offense, but you *thinking* you're okay isn't exactly reassuring."

"I know, but it's all I have."

"Thank you for being honest. That means a lot to me."

He sighs. "Lying is how I got into trouble with opioids. When I was in rehab, I promised myself I wouldn't lie anymore."

What about lying to his family about who he is, about his character and needs? I don't say that out loud, but it pains me to know he'll still have to live with that lie. "Maybe you should reach out to Jerry."

Kinsey winces. Did I hurt him with that statement? Maybe because I expressed a lack of confidence in his ability to stay sober? "I'm sorry if I hurt you," I say.

He shakes his head. "No, I understand why you said it. It's just... It's painful to be reminded that my weaknesses and failures are so public. Others get to hide theirs, but mine are out there for everyone to see, and it's humiliating. I deserve it, I know that, but..."

"I won't pretend I know what that's like, but I do have some idea from growing up poor. In elementary school, they made us kids on subsidized or free lunches stand in a separate line, did you know? Everyone could see you were poor."

"That's awful! I can't believe schools would do that."

"It's more common than you think. And that was just elementary school. I've experienced a fair share of prejudice and judgment over being poor."

"As if that was your fault. People can be so cruel."

"Remember in junior year when we made that trip to Germany? When Mr. Kaufman gave me the sign-up form, he told me he knew I wouldn't be able to go. He was such a dick."

"He was. I went a few rounds with him once over a ridiculously low grade for Jonathan."

"Yeah, I remember that. I still don't know how my mom got the money for that trip, but she did."

Kinsey looks away, but not before something flickers in his eyes. He knows more about that. Then it sinks in. "Oh my god..." I whisper. "You paid for that, didn't you?"

I'd always wondered how my mom paid for the trip, but I figured she'd saved up for it or had maybe asked Uncle Tim, even though he didn't make much as a pastor. But I never expected her to have accepted Kinsey's money.

"You weren't ever supposed to know," he mumbles, still not meeting my eyes. "I told your mom I didn't want you to because it shouldn't feel like charity to you, like you owed me. All I wanted was for you to have the same opportunity as Jonathan had."

"That trip meant the world to me." I drag a hand through my hair, my head spinning as the implications sink in. "Was that the only time you paid something for me?"

"You weren't supposed to know..." he says again.

"Kinsey..." I can't help the edge that's crept into my voice. I need to know.

He looks up. "A few times. We upped Jonathan's allowance and lunch money so he could pay for you if needed if you guys hung out or wanted to go to the movies or whatever. We figured it would be easier for you to accept if it came from him. And I paid for some extracurricular activities, like your soccer uniforms, cleats, and club fees. They charged an arm and a leg for that advanced program you were in when you turned fourteen, and your mom didn't want you to be forced to drop out."

I can't believe my ears. All these years, my mom said nothing, and neither did Jonathan or his family. "Did Jonathan know?"

"Just about the lunch money and his allowance. He understood he wasn't ever to mention it to you."

"He hasn't." Maybe Jonathan wasn't as spoiled as I thought. He never lorded this over me, and he could have. "Thank you. I don't know what else to say. I'm shocked."

"Please don't thank me. It was the least I could do. I could afford it, and I couldn't bear the thought you'd miss out on things because you didn't have the money."

God, can my heart be any fuller with gratitude and admiration for this man? He never wanted his generosity to be known and would've been content had this never come to light, not even now that he and I have grown close. He's got such a big, selfless heart. I lean in and press a kiss on his cheek. "Thank you nonetheless. You'll never know what a difference you've made."

His hand flies to his cheek, his eyes wide in shock as he stares at me. Oops. For a second, I forgot he's not used to those easy displays of affection. But a much bigger problem is that my lips are still tingling from that all-too-brief contact. And if he keeps looking at me like that, I'll have to kiss him again.

"I have to go." He jumps up from the couch, panic edged in his face.

"Kinsey..."

"It's getting late, and I have an early class to give tomorrow. Thanks for...for having me."

He darts out the door, leaving me empty and really, really stupid. What have I done?

24

2020: BENONI

My mom's breathing is labored, even as she's sleeping, and I rub my temples as I watch her. She's deteriorating fast. Her MS has always been aggressive, taking more and more from her. She's fifty-three now, and her body is giving up.

She's in a wheelchair, not being strong enough to walk other than a few steps to the toilet or the shower. Luckily, she lives in a bungalow that was easy to adapt to her needs. Throughout the house, I installed grips she can hold on to, and I made the bathroom as accessible and safe as possible, including a shower chair, and built a ramp to the front door.

Because her physical mobility has been so limited, her muscles have atrophied. I'm doing what I can to help her with exercises, but we both know we're fighting against the clock. We're trying to stop the inevitable, but what else can we do? Giving up isn't in our nature, hers or mine, and so we fight on.

Swallowing has become difficult for her, and she's on a diet with soft foods that are easy to swallow. I make lots of smoothies and shakes with added protein and vitamins. She may have to get a feeding tube in the future, but until now, she's been resisting it. She's losing weight fast, and we may not be able to postpone it for much longer. But that, too, will be a stopgap measure. We can't turn back this disease, and at some point, we'll have no choice but to accept that.

But the worst is the pain, which has progressed fast. She has muscle spasms and nerve pain, and as much as I try to help her with massages and exercises, it only goes so far. At her last checkup, her doctor upped her pain medications again but with the warning she was closing in on a maximum dosage.

I've moved back in with her, against her fierce protests, though I'm still paying rent on my place with Leif. He understands and is supportive, but he misses me. I wish I could be there for him, but I can't. Taking care of my mom takes up all the energy I've left outside of my job—and I've even cut back on hours there.

"Benoni..." my mom whispers, and her eyes flutter open.

I kneel next to her bed. "I'm here, Mom."

Even now, she gives me her special smile, the one that communicates love and pride, even when the words are difficult.

"How are you feeling, Mom? Is there anything I can do for you?"

"Help me sit up," she says, and I press the button to bring her up into a sitting position. The bed I bought for her cost a pretty penny, but it was worth it. So far, she hasn't developed bedsores, and that's a major accomplishment for someone who spends as much time in bed as she does.

I help her drink some water, then sit down next to her again.

"Benoni... It's time."

My heart stops for a moment before it resumes but in a

frantic beat. I know what she means, but it can't be time yet. "Mom… I'm not ready."

She lifts her hand and, with endless tenderness, takes mine. "But I am, and I need you to let me go."

Tears drip down my cheeks, my throat so tight I can barely get the words out. "Is it the pain? Do we need to increase your meds?"

"It's everything. My body is done. I am done."

"I can call Dr. Morales and see if she'll put you on a higher dose."

"Yes, I need you to, and I'm sure she will, but you know what that means."

I do. During her last visit, Dr. Morales was clear about what a higher dosage of morphine would do. There's no going back from it, and it could cause a lower heart rate and slow down respiration, both of which could start the final process for my mom.

I surrender to the inevitable. "If that's what you want, Mom… I'm here. You know that."

Another one of her sweet smiles. "You've been my biggest joy and the single best thing I've ever done in my life. A mom couldn't wish for a better son than you, Benoni."

Oh god, she is saying good-bye. I want to stop her, tell her she shouldn't do this, that she needs to keep fighting, but I can't. My wish to have her with me longer is selfish. She's ready, and she was right. I need to let her go, and I need to do it with love.

I kiss her hand. "You've been the best mom I could ever have wanted."

"Your father…" She swallows with difficulty. "He's a fool for not wanting to be a part of your life, but it's his loss."

"It is. I never missed him, Mom. You were enough."

"I thought I loved him." Her face tightens. "Don't make that mistake. Love and lust aren't the same."

Funny that she brings that up because I've been wondering about it. I have no trouble scoring hookups, but I've never wanted more than sex with a guy. "I know."

"Hold out for the real thing. Some day, you'll find a man who's worthy of your love."

"I will, Mom."

If only every kid in the world would have a mom like mine, so accepting and loving. My sexuality has never been an issue for her, and she's never made me feel different for it. All she wants is my happiness.

"Thank you..." She wheezes, her breath coming out in raspy pants.

"Stop talking, Mom. It's okay."

"No... No, I need to say this before I can't anymore. Words matter."

They do, and I know I will remember this conversation always. And so I wait until she's caught her breath and can continue.

"Thank you for taking care of me all these years."

Tears drip down my cheeks again. "Oh, Mom, you don't need to thank me for that. That's always been my pleasure, my honor."

With effort, she reaches up and cups my cheek. "You're a caretaker, honey. Find a man who will let you take care of him. You need that."

The image of Leif pops up in my mind, and I smile. She doesn't know about that part of my life, though it wouldn't surprise me if she suspects our roommate situation isn't exactly standard. She's always seen much more than people give her credit for. "I will, Mom."

"Don't settle. Don't ever settle. You deserve love, the kind that lasts forever."

I lean into her touch. "I promise."

I give her some CBD drops. They help with the pain, and I've found a good supplier who doesn't overcharge. Funnily enough, he's an old classmate of mine who got all entrepreneurial with that shit. Hey, whatever pays his bills.

Once she's settled and breathing more easily, I call the doctor, then contact Uncle Tim and tell him to come say good-bye. He stops by every day. We're both there when my mom passes away three weeks later, a week before Thanksgiving.

She's finally free.

25

KINSEY

His text comes out of nowhere. I haven't seen him in a year, but two days after I hightailed it out of Benoni's house like a man possessed, my phone buzzes with an incoming message. Jonathan. My heart skips a beat.

Can we talk?

Joy flares up inside me. He wants contact! This is the step I have been waiting and hoping for. I immediately reply.

I'd love to. Pick a time and place, and I'll be there.

He takes a while to respond, and all that time, I sit with my phone in my hand, watching the bubbles pop up and disappear again. Please don't let him change his mind. Please.

Tomorrow evening at 8? I can come to you.

Thank God he's suggesting to come to my place. The last thing I want is for Rip to be there. I'm sure he's a nice guy, but he's stoned most of the time and a bit of an idiot, and that's not what I need right now. Especially not for what could be an emotional conversation with Jonathan.

Perfect. I'll be here.

I send my address, in case he doesn't have it. He's never been here in the six months that I've lived here, and I'm not even sure if he ever wrote it down. I type how much I miss him but delete it just as quickly. I don't want to get off on the wrong foot, and he may not be ready to hear that yet.

Great, now I have one more thing to worry about other than what happened at Benoni's. I can't believe I just stormed out. All he did was thank me. So I'm not used to men kissing me. I'm sure it's a normal thing to do between gay men, right? Or nonstraight men. I always have to remind myself to be inclusive. Why did I run away after such an innocent gesture? Now I look like an idiot. As if Benoni needed another reminder of just how clueless I am.

He meant nothing by it. It's not like he wanted to kiss me. Like, *really* kiss me. That thought is too ridiculous to entertain, even if it heat flares up in my belly. No, he was shocked that I paid for some things for him when he was a teenager.

I'd never meant for him to find out, so I wasn't prepared for it. If I had been, maybe I would've reacted better. Now he caught me with my proverbial pants down. Come to think of it, it wasn't the first time. He overheard me watching porn. I bury my face in my hands. And I have my own memories of him. The image of him sinking his cock into the mouth of that kid is burned onto my brain. It was and still is the single hottest thing I've ever seen in my life.

I have a session with him tonight, so now I have two men to obsess over: Benoni and Jonathan. Sigh. I can get so tired of myself, I swear. If only I could get the fuck over myself and stop that crazy cycle of worrying over every little thing. Alas, it's been my normal since I was a kid, always anxious to be good enough, smart enough, devoted enough to earn my parents' approval. Look how that turned out.

I distract myself with work. The deadline for the next chapter for my textbook on emergency medicine is tomorrow, and I spend the day going over it again and again, triple-checking every line until I'm convinced it's the best it can be. With a whoosh, the email leaves my outbox, on its way to my editor, and it's time for my training. God help me.

Benoni is waiting for me. "Hey, Kinsey."

He greets me as if nothing happened. Huh. He even looks like he always does, his expression soft, his eyes warm. "Hi."

"You ready?"

He often asks that, and I usually try to come up with something sarcastic, but I don't have it in me today. "Yeah."

He quirks his eyebrow but leaves it at that, and once we start my training, he's his usual cheerful self. Maybe he's not upset about my abrupt exit? Or has he decided to pretend I didn't run out on him as if my ass were on fire? Whatever the reason, I'm grateful, and I let it go as best I can. Of course, the whole meet-up with Jonathan is still spinning around in my head, and I fumble through my exercises.

"Where's your head at?" Benoni asks me when I keep doing the calf stretches wrong.

I drop my leg back to the floor. "Jonathan is stopping by tomorrow."

"Oh my god, Kinsey, that's amazing. I'm so happy for you."

His genuine joy spreads warmth through my chest. We really are okay. Thank God. I don't know what I would've done if I had somehow ruined our friendship. "I have no idea what he wants, but he reached out to me. I haven't seen him and Judith since I entered rehab, so it's been a while."

"When was that?"

I love that he's unafraid to ask me things like that.

"January of this year. I stayed for four weeks."

"January? It's been *nine* months since you've seen him?"

I rub my chest as if I could eradicate the pain stabbing my heart. "He and Judith wanted nothing to do with me after that."

"Kinsey..."

"No, I understand. I do. I let them down and betrayed their trust. I can't blame them for needing time to recover from that."

He crosses his arms. "I hear what you're saying, but hell or high water could've kept me away from my mom had she been in that situation. People fuck up. Doesn't mean you get to abandon them when they need you most."

I love him for his loyalty. "I know, but your mom was always there for you. This isn't merely about my addiction and me coming out. This is about years of neglecting them, and that's on me."

"We'll have to agree to disagree on that, but either way, I hope you'll have a good talk with him."

"Thank you." I bite my lip. "I'm nervous. Really nervous. I don't want to say or do the wrong thing and run him off for another nine months."

He puts a hand on my shoulder, and I move toward his touch. I don't mean to, but I love it when he touches me. Does he realize it? I'm not sure, but he leaves his hand where it is, stepping closer until I'd only have to sway a little to lean into him. "Be yourself, Kinsey."

I close my eyes, and my head drops against his shoulder as his hand moves from my shoulder to my neck in a firm grip. "I'll try, but what if he still has an issue with me being gay?"

"He's been friends with me his whole life, and it's not like I was subtle about it."

"Mmm, true, but I'm his dad, not his friend."

"I'm sure it'll be an adjustment for him, but he can handle it. He needs to understand this is who you are, not something you choose."

His hand is strong on my nape, the contact steadying me. Funny how with one hand, one touch, he can support me so much. "I wish you could be there."

The words are out before I realize it, and I hold my breath. Shit. I never meant to say that out loud. What will Benoni think of me after that weird and strangely needy admission? Especially after my dramatic exit. I hope he doesn't think I'm attaching any meaning to that.

But his firm grip transforms into a caress, tender and sweet. "I wish I could be there for you too, but it would be hard to explain to Jonathan."

I let the air out of my lungs. Thank god. He didn't take it the wrong way. It would've crushed me to ruin the friendship between us that matters so much to me.

When I look up, his green eyes are way closer than I expected. My stomach does a little flip. He's so hot and strong and sexy. And far too young for me. If only we were closer in age. Not that he'd ever go for someone like me. He's probably looking for someone as outgoing and energetic as he is, not some old baby gay with a ton of baggage.

But oh, how I want him to choose me. He'd be perfectly bossy, telling me what to do, just like he does when we're training. With him, I'd never have to worry about messing up because he would be there to correct me and help me get it right. If only I could find someone like him to help me navigate being gay...and especially living out the fantasies in my head. How I long for my first kiss, my first touch, my first sexual act with a man.

"Kinsey," he says hoarsely, and I can't drag my eyes away from his lips.

"Yeah?"

"If you keep looking at me like that, I'm gonna have to kiss you again. For real, this time."

I freeze, my eyes darting away as my cheeks burn. He caught me staring at him. Did he realize in which direction my thoughts had gone? Oh, no, my cock is half-hard, and I didn't even notice it. Shit, shit, shit. I try to step away, but his grip on my neck becomes iron as he holds me back. "No. You're not running again."

His voice is so low and deep, the timbre settling deep inside me. Whenever he says something, I have this urge to obey him. Weird maybe, but why does it feel so natural, then? "I'm... I didn't mean to..."

I clench my eyes shut. I can't face him, not after this.

He brings his face close to mine, and his warm breath caresses my ear. "Did you hear me say what I wanted to do to you?"

Wait. What? He said... He said he would kiss me again. For real. That means he *wants* to kiss me, that my presence isn't leaving him unaffected either. No, that can't be. I must be misunderstanding him.

"Kinsey, look at me."

I can't disobey. I'm the weakest man on the planet, I know, but I'm powerless, and so I lift my eyes. His gaze is intense, burning with a fire I find hard to place. He's not upset or angry, that much I know, but then what does his expression mean?

"Did you think I was upset?" he asks, his voice barely above a whisper.

"Yeah."

"I wasn't."

"Oh."

"Aren't you gonna ask me what I was?"

I shake my head, and his soft chuckle dances down my spine. "Oh, Kinsey, what am I gonna do with you?"

A hand lands on my shoulder, and I startle. "What's up, boys?" Frank asks, breaking the tension between Benoni and me.

Benoni lets go of me, and I step back. Frank moves between us. What the heck?

"What's the problem, Frank?" Benoni snaps. At least I'm not the only one who doesn't understand his behavior.

Frank leans in. "Walk away, Ben." His voice is soft but commanding. "You can't do this. You're at your workplace, and you're drawing attention."

Benoni stumbles back as if Frank slapped him. "Shit. I'm sorry."

Before I can say anything, he rushes out of the room. What just happened?

"I'm gonna stand right here until you have yourself under control," Frank says. What does he mean? *Oh.* Heat spreads from my neck to my ears. He's noticed my arousal.

"No worries, no one else has seen it. But I was watching you two, so that's why I picked up on it."

"I'm sorry." I don't even know what I'm apologizing for, but it's all I have.

Frank chuckles. "What are you saying sorry for?"

"For feeling like an idiot? I don't know."

Frank squeezes my shoulder. "You're not an idiot. But at least I understand now why you still haven't taken me up on my offer for coffee."

"There's nothing going on between Benoni and me."

It sounds weak even to my own ears.

"Nice try. What I just saw had the potential to set this whole place on fire."

Groaning, I rub the back of my neck. "I don't know what I'm doing. I swear I didn't mean anything by it. Did I get Benoni into trouble?"

"Oh, Ben did that all on his own, no worries. That's not on you. But what do you mean, you don't know what you're doing?"

I boxed myself into a corner there, didn't I? Frank knows nothing about me other than that I only recently came out. He has no idea just how new I am to all this. "If I accepted your offer for coffee after all, would you think me selfish?"

"I've already concluded nothing will ever happen between us, Kinsey, and I'm okay with that. But Ben said you could use a friend, so the offer still stands."

I finally dare to meet his eyes, which are soft with understanding. "In that case, I'd love to take you up on it. Benoni was right. I do need a friend, and if you're willing to be the recipient of the most basic and embarrassing questions..."

"It would be my privilege."

Benoni offered to lend an ear, but how can I ask him when a lot of those questions are about him? I need to know more, but I can't ask him, not everything. My mortification would be through the roof. "I'll text you after," I say. "Thank you."

Frank nods. "My pleasure. You good?"

"Yeah."

He gives my shoulder a last squeeze. "Let Ben be for now, Kinsey. And if you want to talk to him about your relationship, I suggest you do it in private."

26

BENONI

I can't believe I almost kissed him. In public. At my work, of all places.

If Frank hadn't stepped in, I would have. I would've taken Kinsey's blushing cheeks in my hands and kissed the wounded look off his lips until they were swollen and burning under mine. And that would've only been the beginning. I got lucky Frank interrupted us. It could've cost me my job. What the hell is wrong with me that I would take such a risk?

Kinsey was my last client for the day, and so I leave, feeling like a massive hypocrite as I wave good-bye to Lynn and head home as if nothing happened. Something *did* happen. Everything has changed now, and I don't know if we can go back to the way things were. I also don't know if I even want that.

What I do know is that this can't ruin our friendship. It's too precious, too valuable for that. And with me walking away the way I did, it would be easy for him to jump to the conclusion that he did something wrong. He's prone to blaming himself. Every time I see it happen, it breaks my heart. His vulnerability tugs on all my heartstrings and then some.

With a muttered curse, I change course and head for Kinsey's house, the address still in my phone from the last time I visited him. He lives in a modest ranch on a quiet street. The baby-blue-painted house is tucked away in a corner, surrounded by a garden that's adapted to the Floridian climate. Palm trees, cacti, various decorative grasses that look to be drought-proof, and two sitting areas with Adirondack chairs on pavers. It's small but homey and sweet and cozy. Not at all what I expected from Kinsey. Such a contrast to his previous house, which was big, luxurious, and grandiose.

I park in his driveway, which is empty. He has a garage, so he could be inside already, but somehow, I doubt it. Frank wouldn't have let him leave in his aroused state. And I'm an asshole for walking away from him like that, but that's a whole 'nother discussion. To make sure, I ring his doorbell, but like I thought, no one answers. I'll wait for him, then, and I park myself in a rocking chair next to his front door.

Only a few minutes have passed when a dark blue BMW pulls into the driveway. It stops for a moment, and I raise my hand when I recognize Kinsey behind the wheel. The garage opens, and he pulls up inside. I get up from the chair. Do I follow him? Or do I wait here? He answers that question for me by walking out of the garage, closing it behind him with a fob.

"Hi," I say. This couldn't be more awkward if I tried.

"Hi."

At least it makes two of us. "I figured we needed to talk."

He sighs, avoiding my eyes. "Yeah."

"Can I come in? This isn't a conversation I want to have outside where people could overhear us."

Another sigh. "Yeah."

Hmm, he's not exactly generous with his words, is he? Then again, he's never been an easy talker. I always have to get him to relax first, and after what happened at the gym, my guess is he's anything but relaxed right now.

His hallway is painted in a gorgeous color between green and blue, and various sea-themed photographs decorate the walls. His whole house is in colors I associate with water, with the ocean. Did he pick these himself, or are they from the previous owner? Not that it matters now.

I sit down on the love seat while he grabs us cold seltzers, then lowers himself on the couch across from me, as if he wants to create distance between us. Did I fuck up that badly? "I'm sorry for what happened," I say.

His eyes flash, but then he shuts down, his face transitioning into a blank, emotionless look. "I see."

What just happened? Didn't he want me to apologize? For the first time, I can't get a read on him, and I have no idea what he's thinking. "What I did was stupid and unprofessional," I try again.

"I understand."

Same reaction. What's going on? "Talk to me, Kinsey."

He shrugs. "What more is there to say? You regret it. It's okay. Let's move on."

Ouch, I never knew he could be this cold and dismissive. It's a new side of him and one I'm not particularly fond of. "You're shutting me out. What's going on?"

If nothing else works, maybe being more direct will get me answers.

"There's nothing going on. Wasn't that what you said just now?"

It clicks. I get up from the love seat and sit down next to him. Ah, that gets a reaction from him. He's not as indifferent as he acts. I take his hand, lacing our fingers together, and he lets me. "That's not what I said, Kinsey. And if that's what you heard, then I didn't say it right."

"Then what are you saying? I'm so confused..." His voice cracks, and I squeeze his hand.

"Sometimes, I forget how new all this is to you and that you're not experienced in picking up and interpreting signals like most gay men I know. That's on me, not on you. I should've realized you'd jump to the wrong conclusion."

He's peeking at me through his lashes, and I suppress a smile. He's so goddamn adorable when he does that, evoking all these soft feelings inside me.

"What I was trying to say was that I was sorry because of the circumstances, because I put both of us in an awkward position by saying that in public. I shouldn't have. But I'm not sorry for what I said, nor do I retract it. I wanted to kiss you, Kinsey, and that's the truth."

"B-but why? I don't understand."

Oh, how naïve and clueless he is. He doesn't see himself the way I do. His words from when he first worked with me come back. How he found his body lacking, how he didn't want to stand in front of the mirror. "You have no idea how sexy you are, do you?"

His mouth drops open before he catches himself. "Sexy? I'm forty-seven, Benoni. I'm way past that stage...if I ever was sexy in the first place, which I doubt."

I shake my head, chuckling. "Oh, sweet summer child... Haven't you ever heard of a silver fox?"

He blinks. "I swear I need a dictionary with you sometimes. What the hell is a sweet summer child?"

Oh Lordy. "Someone who is naïve and hasn't seen anything bad yet. Does that mean you do know what a silver fox is?"

He blushes deliciously. "I've heard the nurses use that enough times to know what it means, yes."

"Well, that's what you are. The epitome of a silver fox."

"I...I just don't see it."

Inspiration strikes. "Do you have a full-size mirror somewhere?"

He frowns. "In my bedroom, why?"

"I need to show you something. Do you trust me?"

"Always."

He didn't even hesitate. My poor heart. How much mushier can it get before it completely melts? "Lead the way."

His bedroom is as neat and tidy as the rest of his house, with one dark blue wall and the rest a light, misty blue. He has a queen-size bed, made of course, and more ocean photographs on the wall. "You really like the beach, don't you?"

"I've always loved the water. It steadies me, somehow. On a bad day, I just sit on the beach or walk along the shoreline, and my troubles wash away with the waves of the surf."

"Is that why you chose the theme for your home?"

"I wanted a constant encouragement to find inner peace, to let go of whatever was bugging me."

"Is it working?"

His lips curl up. "Not always, but I'm a work in progress."

I guide him in front of the large mirror on one wall. "Take off your shirt." He obeys without even asking why. He's so fucking hot in just a pair of shorts and nothing else. Though I wouldn't mind him taking those off as well. A guy can hope and dream, right? "I want you to look at yourself in the mirror and tell me what you see."

He hesitates, but he is studying himself, his stomach pulled in and his posture straight. "Lots of gray is what I'm seeing. Scars from my knee surgery. Crow lines and wrinkles on my face." He turns sideways, silent now, and so I wait. He pats his abdomen. "I look much better than I did a few months ago. I've gained weight, and my muscles have more definition."

"Mmm, true."

He eyes me in the mirror. "What's your point?"

"My point is this." I hold up my phone with the pictures posted on the Hot Silver Daddy handle, the first one I found on Twitter when I did a quick search. "Tell me what you see when you look at these guys."

He takes the phone from me and examines the first picture. "He's..." He frowns. "He doesn't look like he's much younger than me."

"Oh, my guess is he's closing in on sixty."

"Really? Wow, he looks good for his age."

I swipe to the next picture.

More frowning. "He's my age too. And he's...hot, I guess?"

"He is, but why do you think so?"

He points at the screen. "That pic has almost a thousand likes."

"It does. Now look at this one and compare his body to yours."

I hold up another picture, and he squints as he takes it in. "He's... He doesn't look that different from me."

"Nope, he doesn't. And his picture has well over three thousand likes...in less than forty-eight hours. You're sexy, Kinsey, and I'm not the only one who will think so."

He turns back to the mirror, studying his body again. "I guess we're always our own worst critics, huh?"

"We are."

"It's hard for me to stop seeing myself as I was before. I

hated myself so much, you know? Every time I'd look in the mirror, it was a reminder of how badly I was failing my wife, my family, and, above all, myself. It got to the point where I avoided mirrors."

I put a hand on his shoulder, and he shivers at the contact. "I get that, but you've changed, Kinsey. You've come so far, and I hope you'll be able to see yourself more realistically."

My hand moves as if on its own accord, caressing his shoulder rather than squeezing it in the friendly, neutral way I planned to. His soft gasp makes it impossible to stop, and I trail my fingers over his neck, then down his spine until I reach the waistband of his shorts. Another shiver. "You're so sexy," I whisper. "Do you know how hard it is for me not to touch you?"

"Benoni..."

Does he realize he's practically begging me, the plea in his voice irresistible?

I step behind him, meeting his eyes in the mirror as I look over his shoulder. My hand slips around his waist, teasing his chest, stroking his pecs, then down to his belly button. Then I stop, putting my hand flat on his abdomen. With anyone else, I would've teased them much more, would've traveled further south and rubbed their cock, which would've been hard like Kinsey's is. But I can't, not with him. Not with Kinsey, who's never even been touched by another man—and what a thrill it is to know that I'm the first.

"You're beautiful, inside and out," I say softly in his ear, resisting the urge to nibble on it. Gotta go slow here.

"I thought you were just humoring me." His voice is low and deep and oh-so hot.

I step a little closer to him, then press my hard cock

against him, reveling in his gasp. "That's not something I can fake."

"Oh..." His eyes burn into mine in the mirror. "I didn't know."

With him, I need to be direct. He's not picking up subtler signals yet, not used to having to look for them. I step back and nudge him to turn around. "That's what I realized today. I'm crazy attracted to you, Kinsey, both for your character and your body."

"Oh." He swallows "I...I don't know what to say. I wasn't expecting this. You're..." He gestures at my body with a broad downward swipe. "You're so much younger and obviously hot, and...I never thought you would...*like* me."

"You think I'm hot?"

Ah, there's that gorgeous blush again, which I'm becoming addicted to. "You know you're hot. You knew it when you were eighteen at that party, and you still do."

I have to admit it's a brilliant answer, which puts the ball back in my court. "Mmm, yes, that party... That was the first time I suspected you weren't straight."

"Yeah, 'cause I was sporting an erection...much like I am now."

Okay, so he's using a somewhat clinical term for it, but at least he's brave enough to acknowledge it...and not run away. "I noticed."

"What does this all mean, Benoni? I wish I could play this all suave and cool, but I have no clue what I'm doing."

"I hate to turn the question around, but what do you want it to mean? I've told you how I feel. I like you, and I'm attracted to you. What about you? You find me hot, but is that it?"

His eyes bulge. He doesn't think I can read his mind,

does he? "Right. I, erm..." He shuffles his feet. "I do like you. A lot."

He's courageous for admitting that, which can't have been easy. "I'm thrilled to hear that, but the question remains. What do you want it to mean? I'd be happy to take this further, but the choice is yours."

"Take it further? You mean, like...sex?"

"I was thinking of a few dates first, but sure, that would be a tempting end goal."

He groans, hiding his face in his hands. "I'm such a moron about this."

I pull on his arm until he drops his hands. "No, you're *new* to this. And you're trying hard, and that accounts for something."

"You mean I get pity points? That's what Judith called it back when she did gymnastics and she'd get points, even though she fell off the balancing beam. Pity points."

Sometimes it's so easy to forget that Kinsey has grown kids, his son the same age as me. That alone makes this different from any other man I've been involved with. "I wouldn't call it pity points. More like a medal for effort?"

"Potaytoes, potahtoes."

I tip his chin up and meet his eyes. "I need to say something, and I need you to listen to me, okay?"

He nods.

"I'm glad we've both been honest with each other and that we know where we stand. That's important because we both come with baggage and a history. My usual MO is to go full steam ahead, but you matter too much to me to do that."

"You matter to me too," he whispers.

"I want to kiss you, Kinsey. I want to kiss you bad. Hell, I want to do much more than that. But I won't. We need time to figure out what this between us is and if we can act on it."

"You mean me. I have to figure this out..."

"Mostly, but it wouldn't be without consequences for me either. Jonathan has been my friend for a long time. That's not something I take lightly."

"I know." His eyes are pleading. "I can't believe you'd even consider being with me, so I'll have to wrap my mind around that first. But thank you for not rushing me. I think..." He hesitates. "If you had kissed me, I wouldn't have been able to think."

He's so heartbreakingly honest. "Neither would I." I put my hand against his cheek. "As much as I want to be your first, my sexy silver fox, it needs to be your informed choice. So we'll take it slow and take our time to consider our relationship, and when we both agree...that's when I'll kiss you."

27

KINSEY

It doesn't register with me until the next day what Benoni said. *When* we both agree, not *if* we both agree. As if it was a certainty, not a possibility, and the thought is wonderfully exhilarating and incredibly scary at the same time. Benoni *likes* me. Me, a recovering addict, twenty-two years his senior, a man with two grown kids, an ex-wife, and a hell of a lot of baggage. He must be a sucker for punishment to be willing to take all that on.

He was genuine, though. No matter my doubts and reservations—and trust me, I have a plethora of both—I don't question his sincerity. For some reason, he's taken a liking to me. Watching myself in the mirror through his eyes was strange and embarrassing at first, but after browsing the pictures in that group some more, I couldn't help but agree with him. Those men do look like me. They're even older in some cases, which still baffles me.

So I guess I'm a silver fox. Who knew? I'd counted on coming out being a learning experience, but I never considered me being attractive to others. I'll take it, though. And so what if I walk a little straighter, hold my head a little higher? This discovery is definitely a boost for my self-confidence.

Sadly it doesn't last through the day. Once the morning high after reminiscing yesterday evening's events has passed, reality sinks in. Jonathan is stopping by tonight, and I'm sick with nerves. He hasn't said why he wanted to come over, and the worst-case scenarios keep playing through my mind. Not helpful.

Just before eight, my phone buzzes with an incoming text. My heart skips a beat. Did Jonathan cancel? But no, it's from Benoni.

I hope it goes well. Thinking of you.

My chest warms at how sweet and attentive he is, but I don't have time to answer because the doorbell rings. Five to eight. Jonathan's early.

He stands outside with his hands in the pockets of his shorts. "Hi."

My eyes grow moist at the sight of my son. Shit. I can't cry. It'll chase him away. And so I swallow the lump in my throat away. "I'm really happy to see you," I manage. I don't hug him. His body language makes it clear he's not there yet, and I respect that. "Come on in."

I grab him a beer and take a seltzer out of the fridge for myself. "You don't drink anymore?" he asks when he sees my drink.

"I thought it smart not to tempt myself by switching one addiction for another."

"Oh. So you'll never drink again?"

"I don't know. I probably will because it's never been an issue for me, but for now, I just want to be cautious and not take any risks."

Silence descends.

"How have you been?" I ask. Can I even be more

pathetic? For fuck's sake, he's my son, not a neighbor I haven't seen in years.

He shrugs. "Okay. Work's been the same, nothing special."

"How's April?"

He sends me a pained look. "We broke up five months ago, Dad."

Warmth spreads through me that he's still calling me Dad. I half expected him to call me by my first name. "Sorry. I missed that."

Another long silence.

I don't know what to say without offending or upsetting him. I'm walking on eggshells because I can't do anything that will risk the fragile relationship we have.

"You look good," he finally says. "Better than I expected."

"Thank you." Was that a compliment? I'm gonna take it as one. "I've been working with a personal trainer to get back in shape."

For obvious reasons, I leave out the detail that my personal trainer is one of his best friends.

Surprise flickers in his eyes. "Oh, so you're serious about it?"

"About getting healthy? Yes. I've never been more serious about anything in my life."

"You're still clean, then."

I'm a little surprised he uses that word. As a nurse, he should know better. But maybe he's testing my boundaries? "Most addicts prefer the term *sober* or *in recovery*, since *clean* sounds like an addiction makes you dirty, but yes, I am. I have been since I entered rehab."

He shifts in his chair. "Sorry, didn't mean to use an offensive term."

"No harm done."

"The term addict is okay? There isn't another word like former addict or something?"

"I'm an addict. Not a former addict. I'm not there yet, considering how recent my recovery is. Maybe one day, I'll be comfortable using that, but for now, I prefer to face reality. A more clinical term for addiction is substance use disorder, which I'm sure you've come across in your work, but it's not something I use for myself."

He cocks his head as he studies me. "I wasn't sure if it would last, your will to break your addiction. I read up on it, and everything said that it's really hard to break an opioid addiction."

He read up on it? The thought stirs up hope in me. "It is, but I got lucky in several ways. I wasn't addicted that long, which makes a huge difference. And I was able to afford a quality rehab, which most addicts are not. There's a massive scam industry going on where addicts and their insurance companies are being ripped off for shitty facilities."

"I read about that in one of the books I got. People who paid thousands of dollars or their family did, only to be stuck in a room and left on their own. It made me furious."

He really did do research. Should I mention it? Nothing ventured, nothing gained. "It means a lot to me that you tried to understand it."

"I've had a lot of addicted patients, especially the last few years. It's a huge problem and not just in Florida."

"It is throughout the country, both in big cities and suburban or even rural areas. One of the biggest health challenges our country is facing right now, and people are dying left and right from unintentional overdoses."

"I always felt sorry for those patients...and I judged them too. How did they let it get that far? How did they do that to themselves? But I never thought it could happen to someone like you. You were successful, Dad. You were a doctor, for fuck's sake. I thought you were happy. How did this happen?"

I never intended to talk about this on our first meeting since forever, but I promised to be honest, and so I will. "Try to look at the past with fresh eyes. What made you think I was happy?"

Jonathan frowns. "But..." Then he's quiet, and I can practically see his mind at work. "When I was little, you smiled a lot more. You stopped smiling over the years."

"I did."

"I never realized it until now. And you always worked a lot, but the last few years I lived at home, we barely saw you. You always worked extra shifts, even on the weekends."

"True."

"Why?"

At least he's asking the right questions. "Because it was better than being home and having to face the reality that I was letting your mother down day after day. She deserved so much better, but she got me."

"Damn right she deserved better. You should have told her you were gay," he snaps, fire in his eyes now.

I hate doing this, hate putting Caroline in this position, but I refuse to lie, even for her. "She knew, Jonathan. I've been honest with her from the start."

His mouth drops open. "What?"

"Before I asked her to marry me, I told her I was struggling with same-sex attraction but that I was praying for it and that I trusted God to take it away."

"She never mentioned that." He studies me, and I meet his gaze head on without hiding anything, letting him see I'm not lying. "Why wouldn't she say that?"

Oh, I have to tread so carefully here. "You'd have to ask

your mother that, but my guess is because she was devastated and hurt. But she knew before we married, though neither of us understood what it meant at the time."

His anger deflates as quickly as it rose. "Ben said I was using the wrong terms."

I swallow. "Benoni?"

"He and I talked about you and how mad I was at you for what happened. He said that you didn't know you were gay, that they thought of it as a sin back then. It was a different time, and I couldn't judge the past you from what we know now."

A wave of gratitude rolls over me. Benoni never mentioned this. "He's right. We believed this was a temptation, a sin, one we could resist by praying. And I prayed. God, how I prayed. But you can't pray away the gay, Jonathan, no matter what people tell you."

"Like Grandpa and Grandma."

"I know they blame me, but they're wrong."

"Are you saying you don't blame yourself for any of it?"

I square my shoulders. "I take full responsibility for my addiction and for being a shitty dad to you and your sister. That's all on me. But I'm not at fault for being gay. I didn't choose that. If it was something that could be prayed away, don't you think I would've done whatever I could? I did. I prayed every day for years and years, begging and pleading with God to take this away from me..." My voice breaks. "But he didn't...because it's who I am. He made me like this, and I shouldn't be made feel guilty for that."

He stares at me for a long time. "You know I've never had an issue with Ben being gay. He's been one of my best friends for a long time, and I've always known he was gay. Never bothered me. But with you..."

My heart hurts. "It's different because I'm your dad."

"It shouldn't be, but it is. You hurt Mom, Dad. You hurt her so bad."

"I know." There's so much I could say about that, about the many ways in which Caroline hurt me, but I won't. I refuse to paint a bad picture of her to our kids. She was and is an amazing woman, and she's a fantastic mother. Despite everything, she deserves better. "And I can't tell you how sorry I am, but not about being gay. I won't apologize for that because I've felt guilty and ashamed long enough."

"I was so mad at you." His voice is soft now, and he's not looking at me. "For breaking up our family, for ruining what I thought was a good thing."

"It was never good, kiddo. It was decent at best, and I'm sorry if that's painful for you to hear, but it's the truth. I was never happy, not truly, no matter how hard I tried. I couldn't and won't ever be the man your mom and your grandparents want me to be."

He buries his face in his hands, and I let him, allowing him to gather his thoughts in silence. "I just feel like everything has been a lie, like my whole life, my childhood has been a farce," he mumbles.

"As much as I want to tell you that's not true, I can't. I love you and Judith more than anything, Jonathan. Please know that no matter what has changed, that hasn't. I may have done a shitty job at being your dad, but you and your sister are the one reason I'm still alive."

He looks up with a sharp move. "Dad?"

"For a while there, I didn't see any reason to live. Not like that. It was so hard and destructive to always have to watch my words, my actions, even my thoughts. This is the first time in my life that I've been able to be myself."

And I'm still not showing all of me. That thought hurts more than it should. I should be grateful I'm out as gay, that

I can at least live out that part of my identity, but I still won't fully be *me*. And that hurts.

"I'm...I'm sorry you felt that way, Dad. I wish I'd known."

"No one knew, including your mother. That was a battle I had to fight on my own."

Yes, because every time I even broached the topic with Caroline, she shut me down. She made it crystal clear that my homosexual tendencies were not something she wanted to discuss. Even now, even after everything that happened, we still haven't talked about it.

"A-are you, like, dating?"

"No. I'm not ready for that yet."

"Hooking up?"

My first instinct is to answer, but I hold it back. I love my son, but that doesn't mean he gets to ask questions like that. He needs to understand my boundaries and respect them. "When's the last time you hooked up?"

"Dad!" He gapes. "I don't wanna talk about that with you."

"Well, neither do I, but that goes in both directions. You're an adult, Jonathan, and you know I've never interfered in your sex life or who you were dating. All I ask is that you extend me the same courtesy."

He sighs. "Point taken." He takes a long swig from his beer. "What are you doing now for work?"

He's right. It's time to change the subject into less heavy topics. We've covered enough ground for one day. We chat for another half hour, catching up on all the mundane aspects of both our lives. When he leaves, he gives me a brief hug, which I count as a major victory.

I close the door behind him, then let out a long exhale. That went much, much better than I had dared to hope. He said he'd stop by again soon, and I can't wait. Hopefully, he'll talk to Judith and maybe influence her to meet with me.

I send a quick text to Jerry, knowing that he's waiting for me to let him know how it went.

Everything's good. Better than expected. Massive relief.

His reply comes instantly.

I'm so happy for you! Small steps forward, Kinsey.

Jittery, happy energy bubbles inside me. I need to tell someone. My thumb hovers over Benoni's name in my phone. Is it weird to call him? Jonathan is his friend after all. But I'm his friend too, and he'll want to know. Even more after yesterday. Before I can convince myself not to, I hit the Call button, and of course, my stomach does a somersault.

I shouldn't have called. He'll think it's strange. I've never called him before, just texted, and most of that was to schedule training sessions. Should I hang up?

"Kinsey," his warm voice says. Too late now. "How did it go?"

Ah, he understands why I'm calling. I settle on the couch with a happy sigh. "Really well. Much better than I hoped."

"Tell me everything."

And so I do.

28

1993: KINSEY

"Welcome, everyone, to this dating course," Adam says. "We're so excited to have you all here!"

I look around the room. Other than Caroline and me, I count seven couples. Most of them are around our age, but there are two people in their thirties as well.

"As you know, my wife and I have been hosting this course for five years now, so please give a warm welcome to my wife, Patricia."

We all clap obediently as Patricia sends us a beaming smile. "I'm always happy to do this because we've seen so much fruit from this course, couples who have dedicated themselves and their relationship to God, staying pure and holy until their wedding day."

I shift in my seat. They don't have to worry there on our account. Caroline has been crystal clear from the start that she doesn't want to sin and wants to stay a virgin until our wedding day, and I've been all too happy to agree with her. It's not like I've even been tempted, probably because I'm too tired to have sex anyway, what with my studies and the number of hours I work to save for our wedding.

"Our goal is to help you prepare for the next step in your relationship by showing you what a healthy marriage looks like, and then you decide together if you're ready for that," Adam takes over again.

They make some more general announcements, and then we're split into two groups. The men go with Adam to his basement while the women stay with Patricia in the living room.

"Today's topic is the role of the husband in a marriage," Adam says. We read through an all-too-familiar part of Scripture. "Wives, submit yourselves to your own husbands as you do to the Lord. For the husband is the head of the wife as Christ is the head of the church, his body, of which he is the Savior. Now as the church submits to Christ, so also wives should submit to their husbands in everything," Adam reads from Ephesians 5.

I must've heard that passage at least a hundred times. It's my grandfather's favorite to read when he officiates weddings, and I have to admit it seems appropriate, though it always makes me feel uncomfortable. It sounds like a warning for the wives, but not for the husbands.

"What does this mean?" Adam asks, and I try to pay attention.

"That as men, we're in charge?" one of the other guys says.

"I wouldn't use those words in your future wife's presence, but that's the gist of it," Adam says with a big smile. "God has put us in charge of our wives, and that's both an amazing privilege and a heavy responsibility."

He drones on about our biblical responsibilities as men, but I tune him out. It's nothing new. Both my father and my grandfather have made it clear who's the head of the family in their house. My mom doesn't spend a dime without my father's permission, and every decision she makes has to be approved by him. Caroline will expect the same from me, so I'll have to step up, be the man she deserves.

She's so sweet and kind, and I can already tell she'll be a great mother. Caroline's mom passed away within months of us dating, and her funeral was actually the first time Caroline and I saw each other again. I was so grateful my grandfather offered to drive me to Asheville. He even spoke at the service, and Caroline and her father were thankful for him ministering to them.

Ever since she's been helping take care of her siblings, and it's wonderful to see her nurturing nature. My parents love her too. The other day, my mom said Caroline would make me a fine wife and that it was time to make it official. I want to do right by her and be the husband she needs, but it won't be easy.

I still think of Daniel. I think of him a lot.

I thought that after meeting her, everything would be fine. And it was...for a while. She became my girlfriend, and I was so hyped about it I didn't even think about anything or anyone else. But I couldn't stop thinking about Daniel, worrying if he was okay. Even after I decided to let go of him and focus on my future, my thoughts still kept going back to him.

I finally gather the courage to stop by his house, and his mom bursts into tears as she tells me she heard from him and that he's moved in with friends in Miami.

"He's lost to us, Kinsey," she says between sobs. "Those so-called friends are all into drugs...and worse."

"Worse?"

She avoids my eyes. "Two of them are homosexuals... It's

only a matter of time before he has AIDS." I reel back, but she must contribute my reaction to shock because she only cries harder. "I know! I feel the same repulsion. How can he do this to himself and us? He'll be dead within months."

If he indeed has sex with these men, he will get AIDS... and he will die. We've had two lectures about it so far in med school, and this gay disease is the worst epidemic ever. Gay men are still dying by the thousands, and there's no cure, not even for those with money, like Freddie Mercury.

"I will pray for him," I tell her.

She looks at me with pleading eyes. "If I give you his address, would you talk to him? Maybe he'll listen to you."

I can't. How can I talk to him about the one thing that's my biggest struggle? Plus, seeing him again may stir up all those weird feelings. I can't afford that, not when Caroline and I are getting serious. And so I flat out lie.

"I'm so sorry, Mrs. Drummond, but I can't. My schedule at the university doesn't leave me with much free time, and you know I volunteer in church and help out with my girlfriend's siblings. I can't take this on."

She lets out a deep sigh, filled with resignation. "I understand. I wish he was more like you, Kinsey. Your parents must be so proud of you."

I hightail it out of there like someone's chasing me, and that's the last time I so much as mention Daniel to anyone. But not the last time I think about him because no matter how hard I try, his image keeps popping up in my head. Is he okay? Could he be gay? Is that why I was...tempted by him? Did I subconsciously pick up on that?

Whatever the reason, it needs to stop. I need to put Daniel in a box and close it, never to open it again. And so I pray once again with all my might, hoping that this time God will answer me, that he will take these feelings away.

29

BENONI

We became close friends in middle school, Jonathan, Bricks, Dash, and I, and our friendship has survived high school and college. We don't see each other as often as we used to, of course, but we still hang out, like today, on Dash's birthday.

"Twenty-six." I greet him with a firm handshake and a bro hug that lasts long enough not to break the straight guy code. Dash is sensitive to being seen as straight after he fooled around with me a few times. He's anything but, but that's on him to figure out. "Congrats, man."

He grins as he accepts my present: a gift card from Bass Pro. Cliché for certain, but the guy loves fishing, something I know jack shit about. "Thank you! I've been saving up for a sweet new reel, so this will contribute to that fund."

"Awesome." What's a reel? Isn't that what you use to bring the line in? I'm not certain, but he looks happy, so all good.

Dash lives in a house with his two brothers, the three of them all single, but unlike what you'd expect, it's not party central. They're all adorably nerdy and serious and not interested at all in partying hard. Sure, Dash likes his booze as much as the next guy, but he's pretty chill, and he loves his job as a Geek Squad guy, working for Best Buy.

The house has a nice fenced-in yard that offers privacy, and we all love hanging out here. As usual, he's set up the fire pit to keep us warm, and he even has two patio heaters on. It's a luxury, with temps expected to only drop to the high fifties this second week of November, but we Floridians aren't used to the cold, and my few years in Buffalo haven't changed that. I'm still a wimp when it comes to low temperatures.

Conversation is flowing smoothly throughout the evening. Dash has invited a small group, just us and a few more friends, but the others, including his brothers, all take off around ten, leaving us four. I'm sipping from my beer—I'm Ubering tonight—and munching on the mini pretzels Dash put out. Those things are damn addictive.

"Rose broke up with me," Bricks says, and we all make the appropriate sounds of empathy, even though none of us liked her. He sighs. "Cut the hypocrisy, guys. I know you all hated her."

"And with reason," Jonathan says. "I know you have a type, but really, could she have been any more of an airhead? The girl couldn't string two coherent sentences together if her life depended on it."

Bricks rolls his eyes. "I didn't pick her for her brain, you know."

Jonathan snorts. "Yeah, no shit, Sherlock. She had, what, a double D cup?"

"So I like big boobs. Sue me."

"All we're saying is that you could raise your standards a little," I bring in, and Bricks lets out another sigh.

"I know, I know. She excelled at sucking dick, though."

"So did Marc Hobson. Didn't mean I wanted to date him."

"Name rings a bell, but…"

"Cute nerd at Jonathan's eighteenth birthday bash. Sucked my dick like a champ in the basement."

"Right. With a description like that, I can't believe I didn't remember him," Bricks says dryly.

"He's doing well," Jonathan says. "He and I text on occasion. He started his own business, some kind of shopping app, and he's raking in the big money."

"Good for him," I say, and I mean it. Marc was super sweet, and I availed myself of his skills on several occasions.

"If he's that rich, maybe you should reconsider dating him," Dash says to me.

"He's taken," Jonathan says. "He got married last year to a guy who works as a park ranger in Yellowstone. I don't have a clue what those two have in common, but they looked cute in the wedding picture he sent me."

I put a hand on my heart, faking being in pain. "There goes my chance for happiness. If only I had known."

Dash snorts. "I can tell you're heartbroken about it."

"He hides it so well," Bricks piles on, and I laugh. "Though I may have good news for you. Rose's brother is gay, and he's hot. Just your type."

"If he's as dumb as his sister, Imma pass, but thank you."

"No, he's in college, finishing his degree." Bricks frowns. "Something in accounting, I think? Not sure."

"Still, I'll decline. I've lost my taste for the hookups and one-night stands."

"Oh my god, you're becoming an adult. We're so proud of you." Bricks pats my hand, and I slap his playfully.

"Fuck off, asshole. Find a girlfriend who has brains and beauty, and we'll talk."

I love these guys. It's not that common for a gay man to have such close straight friends, and I thank my lucky stars to have them in my life.

"I talked to my dad last week," Jonathan says out of nowhere, and I almost spit out my beer. I didn't expect him to bring him up.

"Oh, that's good," Bricks says. "How is he?"

Jonathan rolls his beer bottle between his hands. "Better than I expected."

Bricks frowns. "How come?"

"I wasn't sure if he'd stick with it, you know. With staying sober, I mean."

"Kicking an opioid addiction is no joke." For a guy who dances through life, Dash is surprisingly serious. "My cousin almost died from an overdose, and if the EMTs hadn't had Narcan on them, he would've."

"Wow," Bricks says. "How old is he?"

"He's thirty-four, married, two kids. Not someone you'd expect it from, but he has some high-powered corporate job, and he started taking pills to deal with the stress. But then he accidentally overdosed in his car, and luckily, someone called 911. They found him just in time."

I've never seen him so serious, and it seems we all feel we should tread lightly. "How is he doing now?" I ask.

"Better, but he's struggling to stay sober. Turns out he's been addicted for five years, and no one ever knew."

"With my dad, it was shorter," Jonathan says, shocking me again. He's never spoken a word about it. Never wanted to. If one of us brought it up, he made it clear it wasn't up for discussion. "He was addicted for a year. It happened because of the pain meds he got when he tore his ACL."

I suspected that, but I didn't want to ask, and Kinsey

never said anything. I figured he'd tell me when he was ready—whenever that was.

Bricks, the only one of us who played football, winces. "That shirt hurts, man. It happened to a wide receiver on my team during a game. Dude cried like a baby. Never played again."

"But your dad's doing well?" Dash asks, and I could kiss him for bringing the topic back to Kinsey.

"Yeah, he is. He looked much healthier, said he was on some kind of fitness routine."

"Good for him." Dash lifts his beer bottle in salute.

"He looked...happy. I wasn't expecting that."

"Why?"

Again, Dash saves me from asking.

"I thought he'd be struggling on his own, without my mom and us. I mean, here's a guy who lost his job, his family, and a lot of friends, but he seemed to be happier than before. Lighter."

Does he realize why that is? Does he understand that despite missing his kids something fierce, Kinsey still feels it was the right choice to come out? "I can understand why," I say.

Jonathan meets my eyes. "It's the gay thing, isn't it?" His voice is soft, not accusatory.

"Yeah."

"C-can you explain it to me?"

"Maybe you should ask your dad."

He shakes his head. "No, not now. We're not ready for that yet. Or maybe I'm not ready to hear it from him. But you understand, don't you? You understand what he's feeling?"

I take a deep breath. "I don't think anyone can understand what it's been like for him, Jon. To carry that around for all those years. Having to hide who you are is exhausting. He had to put on a mask every day, every hour, every minute. Like playing a role, only twenty-four seven. Not once in all those years was he able to relax and be himself. Everyone who sees me for more than a few seconds knows I'm gay, even the straightest man on the planet. Can you imagine me having to act as if I'm straight? Try to picture what that would look like."

Dash clears his throat. "You mean, like wearing different clothes?"

I nod. "I would have to be careful not to wear Speedos, to name one stupid example. Unless you're a competitive swimmer, straight men don't often wear those. I'd have to adapt the way I talk, my mannerisms, even the way I walk and move. I'd have to change and hide all that to pass as straight."

Jonathan has been listening quietly. "But why did he have to marry my mom? It's so hurtful to her."

"You'd have to ask him, but my guess is that he did what he was taught, what everyone was told who was in the church and gay back then. You prayed for it, hid it, married a woman, and pretended it never happened. He wanted it to go away, but you can't change who you are. And after all those years, Kinsey chose to live his authentic life."

"*Kinsey?*" Jonathan asks, his voice sharp.

Shit. I've never called Kinsey by his first name to Jonathan. It's always been *your dad* or *Mr. Lindstrom*. I could lie my way out of this, but I'm already uncomfortable enough as it is, pretending I barely know his father. But before I can say anything, he says, "He goes to your gym, doesn't he?"

Well, the truth is out. Or at least part of it. "Yeah."

"I figured. It's closest to his house, and the small scale

and personal approach would appeal to him. Are you working with him?"

With a silent apology to Kinsey, I nod. "I'm his trainer. I didn't want to tell you before because..." Should I tell the truth or lie? No, no more lies. I'm taking a page from Kinsey's book. "You were being a complete dick about it, and I didn't trust you with this information."

"He's right. You didn't want to talk about it, and when you did, you were just ranting about your dad," Bricks comes to my aid.

Jonathan doesn't react the way I expected. He doesn't fly up or shoot daggers at us. Instead, he sighs. "Yeah, I figured. I can understand."

"What made you change your mind about him?" What caused this transformation?

"At first, I just missed him. He hasn't been the best dad, because he was absent so much, but I never doubted he loved me. Not seeing him for so long didn't sit well with me, but I felt forgiving him would be a betrayal toward my mom. She was so hurt and lost, and I wanted to support her. But then..."

He looks at Dash instead of me. Why? What's going on here?

"I told him he was wrong," Dash says softly. He and Jonathan talked? The surprises keep coming tonight. "He ranted to me about it, and I set him straight. Told him that his anger over his father waiting so long to come out was unfair and unjust. People come out at their own pace, and you can't force them. Everyone walks their own path."

Is Dash coming out now? He's never said a word, and I never asked because, like he stated, I figured he'd come out when he was ready.

"He was right," Jonathan says.

"I also told him I was bisexual and that if he had an issue with that, I'd be happy to meet him outside and beat the shit out of him."

And with that, Dash is out. I snort. Classic Dash remark. He would've done it too, never one to walk away from a fight or a challenge.

"You got something to say about that?" Dash asks Bricks, but Bricks shrugs.

"I'd seen you suck Ben off, so I figured you weren't straight. Other than that, it wasn't my business."

This is why we've been friends for so long. We accept each other without question.

"Dash told me I'd made some rude remarks to you over the years," Jonathan says. "Homophobic remarks. I just wanted you to know that I didn't mean them. It's hard to explain, but I think it was the remnant from when we used to go to church and all. My grandparents spewed so much homophobic shit about my dad after he came out, you have no idea. Whole rants about what a sinner he was and that he would go to hell. Even my mom would say things like that, but I think those came from a place of deep hurt and betrayal. I guess it influenced me more than I realized. Anyway, I'm sorry."

And he wonders why his father didn't come out sooner. Sheesh. "I understand, and I always have. You can't help how you were raised and what others close to you tell you. But you can become aware of your internalized prejudices and attitudes and change them."

"Yeah, I'm trying."

"That's all anyone can ask."

"So your dad, is he, like, dating someone?" Dash asks.

"He said he wasn't. I asked if he was hooking up, and he

told me to mind my own business." Jonathan laughs sheepishly.

"No offense, Jon, but your dad is hot. Always has been," Dash says. "I haven't seen him recently, but he's definitely a DILF."

Damn, guess I'm not the only one who has noticed.

Jonathan almost chokes on a pretzel. "You can't just say shit like that. Just because you're out now doesn't mean you can perv on my dad."

Dash quirks an eyebrow. "Why not?"

"Because...because he's my dad!"

"Yeah, and? I distinctly remember you telling me how hot my stepmom was."

Oh, he's got him there. Granted, Dash's stepmom *was* hot. When we were teens, she was only twenty-two, a bombshell, especially when she paraded around in just a bikini, as she liked to do. Even I could see she was a MILF. But he's right about parents being fair game.

Jonathan groans. "I hate you so much right now."

Dash pats his shoulder. "That's okay. I just want you to be prepared that your dad won't have any trouble finding a date. Or a hookup. Or a boyfriend."

"As long as it's not you."

Dash shrugs. "You could do much worse for a stepdad than me."

Oh. My. God. The thought never even crossed my mind, but he's right. If Kinsey and I ever got together, if the crazy attraction between us ever grows into something more, that will be my relation to Jonathan. His stepdad.

Kill. Me. Now.

30

KINSEY

"I want to start by saying I'm sorry for not taking you up on your offer sooner," I say as Frank and I are seated across from each other in the same Starbucks Jerry and I always meet. "I feel bad about it, especially because now that I do, it's as if I'm using you."

"Oh, you can use me anytime." Frank winks at me, laughter in his brown eyes, but then he grows serious. "No worries, Kinsey. I understand now that I know a bit more about you and your background. You needed time to take this step."

I nod. Relief rolls through me that he's so nice about it. "I did. It's all been a long journey for me."

Frank sips his coffee. "Religious background?"

"Yeah. Conservative evangelical."

He winces. "You've walked a tough road."

"It's not been easy, but I'm relieved I've come to a point where I'm out as a gay man."

"I was lucky. My parents were the classic flower power couple, very liberal, loving, and understanding. When I came out, they were normal and accepting about it, and it's made a world of difference." He smiles. "They're still together, by the way, and nauseatingly happy."

What I wouldn't have given for parents like that. My life would have been so different. Then again, I also wouldn't have had Jonathan and Judith, and how could I ever regret them? "No boyfriend for you?"

He sighs. "I won't bore you with my history, but I had a serious relationship in the past. We met in 1991, when we were just twenty. We were together for four years when he died. AIDS."

"Oh, Frank, I'm so sorry."

He relaxes his shoulders, his face losing some of its tightness. "I don't broadcast this, for obvious reasons, but I'm HIV positive. I'm on all the meds, and I've been strict as fuck about my regiment, so my viral load is undetectable. But as you can understand, it makes dating complicated."

"I can see that, though an undetectable viral load means you can't infect someone else." I'm so glad for my medical training so he doesn't need to explain or defend himself. Then something occurs to me. "Is that why you didn't assist me when Soren had that accident?"

"Yes. At work, they know, and I always double-glove, just to be sure. But here, in a situation so chaotic with you doing a procedure in the field, I got scared. I didn't want to accidentally infect him."

I put my hand on top of his and squeeze. "I understand. What a worry that must always be for you."

"It is. You grow somewhat used to it, but you can never let your guard down. Kinda like you having to pretend you were straight for all those years."

He's spot on about that comparison, and it's a comforting thought that he understands what it must've been like for me. I let go of his hand. "I said the same to

Benoni, but I have years of internalized homophobia to overcome, even though I'm out."

"You know, I've always hated that word. Homophobia. It's not a phobia, a fear. It's hate, pure and simple. And like all hate, it poisons people."

He couldn't be more right. "It does, and even when you recognize that, it takes a long time to overcome it."

"How long have you been out?"

"Less than a year. Actually, it was about a year ago I told my wife." I hesitate. Can I be honest with him as well? Yes, no more lies or half truths. "But I spent a month in rehab for an opioid addiction earlier this year, so it's been a rocky road."

"Yeah, I know. When I heard you were an ER doc, it rang a bell, and I looked up your case."

As always when I'm reminded of that, shame fills me, and my cheeks heat in embarrassment. "Not my finest moment."

"You're human, Kinsey. Don't think I've never been tempted."

"Thank you."

"But am I right that you haven't dated anyone since you're out?"

"To be honest, I wouldn't even know where to start."

He studies me as he takes another sip of his coffee. "I think you'd start with Ben. God knows the sparks between you basically set the room on fire."

And my cheeks heat right back up again. Frank chuckles. "That blush is delightful," he teases.

I groan. "It's embarrassing as hell. A grown-ass man who still blushes, what kind of message does that send? I might as well tattoo *virgin* on my forehead."

Oh god, did I just say that? But Frank laughs. "I wouldn't

do that if I were you, since it won't stay true for long. It's charming, is what it is. Don't change."

"It is?" Or is he just saying that to make me feel better?

"I bet Ben would love to make you blush for him."

I shift in my seat, avoiding his gaze. "The thing with him is...complicated."

"The best things always are."

"He's one of my son's best friends."

Frank whistles between his teeth. "Oy. Yeah, I can see how that would make your relationship difficult."

"It seems I tend to make things difficult for myself." Since he's been so understanding so far, I might as well come clean about everything. "I've also discovered I'm submissive."

"That doesn't surprise me, but can you tell me in what sense? Are you drawn to BDSM?"

Again, I don't detect any judgment. "Not in the broad sense, but maybe domestic discipline?"

Frank smiles. "Which our Ben has experience in if I'm not mistaken. God, what I wouldn't give to discipline that boy. Mmm, he's mighty fine."

"Leif? You know him?"

"Through his OnlyFans. Well worth the money."

Ah, right. I'm not used to being so open about watching porn, but I guess that, too, is normal among gay men. The things I'm learning. "I haven't watched any of it, but I met him in person the other day, and he's super sweet."

Frank laughs. "You're an absolute delight, Kinsey. I can tell we're going to be good friends."

Warmth spreads through my chest. "Yeah?"

"Looks like you could use a friend."

I take a deep breath. "I could. But I don't want it to be

one-sided, okay? I want to be there for you as well. This can't be just about me."

"No worries. But let's get back to Ben. What's keeping you from taking him up on his not-so-subtle signals?

"My son. He didn't even want to talk to me for nine months, and he and I only recently saw each other again for the first time. Tomorrow will be the second time. If he finds out about Benoni and me, I'd lose him for good, I fear. Him and his sister. I haven't been a good father to them, and I want to grab every opportunity to set that right. A relationship with Benoni would jeopardize all that, as would me expressing my submissive side."

Frank is quiet for a long time. "It's hard as a nonparent to grasp that kind of love and devotion, but I understand what you're saying. However..." He searches for words. "It seems to me as if you're running ahead of yourself. How do you know if what you and Ben share now will last? Maybe he's not your forever guy but your right-now man, the kind you can experiment with safely and explore your newfound sexuality. If that's the case, would your kids even need to know? Aren't you entitled to some privacy?"

What he describes is so foreign to me. It's never even occurred to me that anything between Benoni and me would not be serious, that it could be temporary. I guess deep down I'm still conservative and old fashioned in that sense. But Frank is right. I don't know, and given Benoni's history, he probably doesn't want something serious anyway. "That's a new way of looking at it, one I hadn't considered."

"The same holds true for experimenting with your submissive side. That's not something they'd ever need to know in the first place, since it would be mostly in sexual activities anyway, I assume."

"Right." He makes it sound so logical, so easy. Have I been seeing problems where there were none?

"It's not my goal to convince you of anything. I hope you know that. But one thing friends are good for is offering alternative viewpoints that help you see things in a different light."

"True, and thank you. You've given me food for thought."

"Glad to hear it. One more thing and then I'll shut up, and we can talk about how hot the barista is, as two gay men our age should."

I chuckle. He's funny, and I'm so grateful I agreed to have coffee with him. All joking aside, this could be the beginning of a wonderful friendship.

"Kinsey, I want you to think hard about what sacrifices you're willing to make for your children or other family members. I know you love them and want a relationship with them, and I understand, but ask yourself at what cost. You've been hiding who you were your whole life. How much more pretending will you have to do to keep them in your life? Pretending to be single? To not be submissive? What other things will you have to suppress or not act on just to appease them, and will it be worth it? If they can't accept the true you, you have to ask yourself if that's a price you're willing to pay."

His words hit home, each one like a dagger that stabs my heart. I'm so tired of pretending and hiding. There's nothing I wish more than to be myself, to not be afraid of how people will react, but I'm so scared of losing Jonathan and Judith forever. Of abandoning what last hope I still harbor for reconciling with my parents, feeble as it may be. And perhaps even of my relationship with Caroline. Despite everything, I'm still clinging to the hope that she'll forgive me and that we at least can be on friendly terms.

But Frank is right. What price am I willing to pay for this? Will I be comfortable with still having to hide parts of me just to be accepted by them? In a sense, I'd be exchanging being a good Christian for being a good gay. The conservative kind, one that will still be palatable to them and won't offend them too much. I've spent my entire life being what others wanted me to be just so they'd love and accept me. And it never worked.

Who's to say it will this time? I could sacrifice it all, a possible relationship with Benoni, exploring all facets of my new identity, living a full life as a gay man...and still end up never gaining their approval. The thought sits bitter on my tongue, but I can't deny the truth of it, the penetrating honesty of Frank's words. "You're right," I say hoarsely. "It hurts to admit it, but you're right. I'm that idiot who lives to please others, and it's brought nothing but heartbreak."

"I'm sorry." Now it's Frank who takes my hand, and it's a comforting gesture. At least I'm no longer alone in my journey.

"Don't be. I needed to hear this. I don't have the answers, but I'll have to think about it. Thank you for saying this."

"My pleasure." A last squeeze and Frank lets go of my hand. "Now, tell me, on a scale of one to ten, how would you rate our barista's ass?"

31

BENONI

It's been two weeks since our almost kiss, and neither Kinsey nor I have brought it up. Oh, the attraction between us hasn't gone anywhere. I still catch him watching me from across the room when he's on the treadmill or the bike and I'm assisting another client. And I do the same to him, studying him when he's not paying attention.

When I touch him, which I still do when I help him stretch and his muscles cramp, he always reacts. He's become careful about making sounds, but he brings a towel, which he covers himself with when needed. But he's getting less anxious about it, and I take that as a win. Two days ago, he even made a self-deprecating joke about it. This progress is amazing. I want nothing more than to see him freed from that sense of guilt and sin and be able to experience all this without shame.

It shouldn't be so hot that a man his age gets so turned on by a simple touch, but it is. I daydream and fantasize about how he'll react when I get to touch him for real, when I explore every inch of his body. He'll be so responsive, so wonderfully needy, and every time I think about it, I get hard and have to jerk off. My right hand has had a lot of action, let me put it that way.

But I've been patient, and I intend to keep that up. As much as I want to press Kinsey for an answer, for the next step, I resist. I can't endanger our relationship, this beautiful friendship we have, by putting pressure on him. And the last thing I want is to run even the slightest risk of bringing his recovery process in peril. That has to be his priority, and I will respect that.

Doesn't mean I'm not curious about where he stands. I know his objections, and they're valid. How can I tell him they're not when his son is one of my best friends? I know Jonathan, and while his recent statements at Dash's party were encouraging, the peace between him and Kinsey is fragile. They're hanging out right now, and I'm hoping Kinsey will call me again afterward, like he did last time. We've been texting daily as well, short exchanges about what we're doing and pictures of whatever interesting caught our eye.

Kinsey likes me, that much I know, and it will have to be enough for now. Luckily, I've always been a patient man.

"What's going on between you and McDreamy?" Leif asks. He must be a mind reader.

Leif and I are lounging on the couch after our episode of The Great British Bake Off has finished. He's addicted to that show, and since he's been really good the last two weeks, I decided to reward him by watching it with him.

"I don't know, and that's the honest truth. In fact, I was just ruminating about that myself."

"Yeah, I figured. You get this dreamy look on your face when you think about him that I recognize by now. You like him."

"I do, and it's only getting stronger."

Leif frowns as he pulls up his legs and drapes a fleece blanket over himself. I prefer the AC set to sixty-nine, since I run hot, whereas he'd dial it up to seventy-five if he could. "He doesn't want you back?"

"It's complicated."

"The age difference?"

Leif may look like a total airhead, but he's not. "Among other things, but also..." I hesitate. "I need to know you won't talk about this with anyone. Anyone, Bun."

"I promise. You know I've never broken a promise like that."

No, he hasn't. "He's new to all this, only recently out and just divorced. I have to let him set the pace."

"Oh, he's a baby gay?"

"Yes, and he comes from a conservative Christian background, so he's been sheltered and not exposed to gay culture at all, other than what he's seen at work or through the media."

"Wow. That'll be quite the adjustment. I can't even imagine having to learn to navigate all that at his age."

Like me, Leif grew up with a single mom as a parent, and like mine, his mom was supportive. She comes over for dinner regularly, and it always warms my heart to see her obvious love for her son. The first time I met her, back when Leif and I were roommates at college, she told me she's known he was gay since he was two years old, and I can totally see that. She said it gave her plenty of time to educate and prepare herself, so when he came out at age eleven, she was ready for him. His current job is a point of contention for her, which I can understand, but she's accepted Leif is an adult who makes his own choices.

"Same. We've been lucky, Bun. I wish everyone had a mom like ours."

Leif bobs his head. "I agree."

He was close with my mom as well, and he was devastated when she died. Usually, Leif leans on me, but at her funeral, he was right there next to me, a literal shoulder for me to cry on, just like Dash, Bricks, and Jonathan. Friendship isn't about showing up in the good times. It's about being there in the bad ones, and I chose my friends well.

"I bet him being in recovery makes it more complicated as well," Leif says.

The one time Kinsey had dinner with us, Kinsey told Leif he was a recovering addict. I later asked him if he hadn't felt uncomfortable sharing that, but he said he'd rather be open about it with the people around him so they'd know. I liked the idea of him telling Leif because he'd be seeing him more as a consequence of hanging out with me.

"It does. I've read a few books about it, and it's unbelievably tough to kick an opioid addiction. I don't want to do anything to endanger his sobriety."

"Tougher than with other drugs?"

"At the same level of heroin, from what I understand. People think it's no biggie because they're prescription drugs, but they work in such a way on your brain that you can become addicted in mere weeks, and you need more and more to get the same effect. That's why people escalate to higher doses, stronger opioids, and often end up switching to heroin."

Leif taps his chin with his index finger. "Are we talking about a physical or a psychological addiction?"

It always amuses me how good Leif is at playing the sexy twink, as if he has two brain cells, when in reality, he's smart.

The guy speaks three languages and reads a lot and not the fluffy kind of books either.

"Mostly physical. I read this memoir of a father who lost his son to it, and he described the withdrawal symptoms as insanely tough. Pain, nausea, the shakes... And I'm not entirely sure how it works because that's advanced neurobiology, but long-time use alters your brain. Your dopamine levels go up and up, and you need more each time to feel that same high. So when you detox and even months later, you can struggle with depression because of low dopamine levels."

"That sounds distinctly unpleasant. Kudos to Kinsey for managing to get sober. That can't have been easy."

"We haven't talked about any of it. I don't want to ask because I don't want him to be triggered or bring back bad memories. I'll wait until he's ready. Anyway, that's why things have been moving slow between us. I'm letting him set the pace."

"Mmm, I get it. Do you know if he's into being spanked and shit?"

I can't betray Kinsey like that, not without his permission, not even to Leif. But before I can say anything, he holds up his hands. "Forget I asked. I know you can't tell me."

"It wouldn't be fair to him."

"I understand. I didn't mean for you to go behind his back or anything, but I was curious because it seems like domestic discipline has become as important to you as it is to me. And I know it turns you on."

Did I mention Leif has no filter? He says whatever pops into his head, and it's refreshing and frustrating at the same time. "It does, both emotionally and physically. I usually have to jerk off after spanking you."

Leif bats his baby blues. "You know I'd be more than happy to take care of that for you."

I snort. "Sure, because right after you've bawled your eyes out, your ass is hurting like a mother, and you being all tear-stained and snotty is when you're in the perfect mood for a blow job."

"Good point," he concedes.

"Besides, you know we're much better as friends, Bun."

He sighs. "But shouldn't I do something in return for everything you do for me?"

"You cook and clean. That's worth a lot to me, considering I work full time."

"True, but I know you haven't had sex in ages. Seems to me you could use some."

I frown. Has it been that long since I hooked up? I did one at least once a week, but it has been a while. I count in my head. Have I even had one since Kinsey became my client? No, I haven't. My last hookup was the weekend before he walked into Fit & Fun, which is...three and a half months ago. I haven't had sex in fifteen weeks. Jesus, how did I never realize this?

Kinsey. He's the answer to that question. It never even registered with me how long I've been dry because all I can think about is him. I wasn't lying when I told Frank I might be ready to settle down, though I wasn't even aware until now how serious I was. From the moment he walked into my gym, Kinsey is all I've been thinking about. He's become the sun to my solar system, the center of my universe, and if that all sounds cheesy and tacky, so be it. It's the truth. He's the reason I have zero interest in anyone else. I want him, and I'm willing to wait as long as I have to.

"Oh," Leif says softly, jerking me out of my thoughts.

"What?"

"You *really* like him."

"I do." Denying it is useless. Leif knows me too well, and he's seen it on my face. "That's why I'm willing to wait for him."

"But what about Jonathan? What if he finds out you're dating his dad? He'll blow a gasket."

I rub my temples. "Yeah, I haven't figured that one out yet. All I can hope is that it won't ever come to making a choice between them."

"You'd choose Kinsey."

Leif's certainty makes me smile. He has indeed understood the depth of my feelings for Kinsey. "I would." Then I sober. "But I'm not sure who Kinsey would choose if he had to make the same choice. Between me and his son? I never want to put him in that position."

"You won't," Leif assures me. "Your heart is way too big for that."

He comes over to my end of the couch, wraps the blanket around us both, and snuggles up to my side. "It'll be okay," he whispers, and how badly I want to believe him.

32

1994: KINSEY

I'm not an idiot. I know I'm running out of time. Caroline and I have been dating for well over three years now, and it's time for the next step. We're both twenty-one, and with me accepted into med school and her halfway through her teaching degree—I applied to the University of North Carolina so I could be close to her—we're in the right place to make things official. She didn't want to leave the state so she could help her father take care of her siblings, so when I got accepted into med school there, we both saw it as an answer to our prayers.

My parents already offered to pay for the wedding, since we all know her father won't be able to contribute much. She has three younger sisters he needs to provide for, so her father can't spare the money for a wedding.

There's one problem, though. I haven't asked her yet. I know I should have by now. Getting married at our age is pretty common in our church, especially for people who have been dating as long as we have. We're expected to start a family soon as well, and though that prospect is frightening, it's exhilarating to imagine myself with a son or a daughter. Maybe once I'm a father, I can finally put all these...urges to rest and make my parents and grandparents proud.

But to do that, I'll have to man up and ask her. Every time I want to pop the question, my stomach clenches, panic clawing at me. Caroline and I have talked about pretty much everything you can think of. She knows more about me than anyone else, but I haven't been able to confess the one thing that weighs so heavily on me. I've kept it hidden from everyone else, but I can't ask her to marry me without her knowing the whole truth. But how do I tell her this, knowing it could break her heart?

After months of going back and forth, even praying about it, I know I have no choice but to be honest with her first. I don't intend to ever mention Daniel, but she deserves the truth. Oh, I debated not saying a word. She'd never know, now would she? But I would, and I don't want that on my conscience. It's no way to start a marriage. No, even though I'm confident that once we're married, God will take these sinful thoughts away, I want to be honest with her. I don't ever want her to be able to accuse me of keeping this hidden from her. Our marriage is until death do us part or Jesus Christ returns, and she needs to enter it with open eyes.

Tonight is the night. It's our three-year dating anniversary, and I promised to take her to our favorite Italian restaurant. I can't tell her this in a restaurant, though. If she reacts badly, everyone will see. No, I'll need to do it before, so I park in the parking lot, switch off the engine, and I shift toward her.

"Sweetheart, there's something I need to tell you."

She stiffens, then turns toward me. "What is it, Kinsey? You know you can tell me anything."

I take a deep breath. *Please, God, let her understand. If you want me to resist this temptation, make her understand. I can't do this without her.* "You know how much I love you. You've been the sunshine in my life from the moment we met, and I can't wait to spend the rest of my life with you."

Her smile is careful. "I love you too, Kinsey. I'm excited about our future."

"I want to take the next step, but before I can do that, I need to tell you something. Something I'm deeply ashamed about, but you deserve to know the truth."

Her smile fades, and her body grows rigid. "What is it?"

Another fortifying inhale. "You know how the Bible says we all have our temptations, right? Well, God is allowing the devil to tempt me with...with thinking about other men...in a sexual way."

Her eyes grow big. "L-like, homosexual thoughts?"

I nod quickly. "I don't want these urges, Caroline. You have to believe me. I resist them, and I'll keep fighting them until God answers my prayers to take them away. I want to be with you more than anything. I love you, and I want to be with you and raise a family together."

A heavy silence fills the car, my whole happiness in her hands now.

"You're praying?" she finally asks in a small voice.

"Every single day. You're the best thing that ever happened to me, sweetheart, and I have faith that with you, I can beat this temptation. I can do this, in God's strength and with your help."

She sucks in a noisy breath. "Thank you for being honest with me. You haven't sinned, Kinsey. You're aware the devil is tempting you, and you're resisting. I know we can pray this away. God will be faithful if we are obedient."

The wave of relief that barrels into me takes my breath

away, and tears fill my eyes. "Caroline Marianne Walker, will you marry me?" I blurt out.

Her face breaks open in a smile so big all my fears disappear. "Yes. Yes, I'll be your wife and stand by your side. I love you so much, Kinsey."

I kiss her with a mix of desperation and gratitude. Once again, she's saved me. Or maybe God has saved me through her, I don't know. But I'm good. We're good. We're getting married, and I can leave all those sinful thoughts behind me.

33

KINSEY

"I want you to kiss me."

I blurt it out as soon as Benoni opens the door. He blinks. Then a slow smile spreads across his face. "I'm sorry, what was that?"

My cheeks heat, but I'm determined to push through it. "I want you to kiss me."

He leans against the doorframe, arms crossed over his chest. "Do you now?"

"If you still want to, that is. And maybe not outside?" Come to think of it, I shouldn't have opened with it. It's a bit forward, isn't it? "Or maybe talk first?"

God, how stupid can I be? But Benoni chuckles.

"I think it's customary to start with a greeting. Something along the lines of 'Hello, Benoni. Can I come in?' Then I would let you in, maybe give you something to drink, and we'd chat and catch up. And then would be a good time to casually drop this line."

He's teasing me. The little shit is teasing me. Again. He keeps doing that, and it's time I paid him back. "Or I could just conclude you don't want to kiss me after all and walk away."

I take a step back, but before I can make another move, Benoni has my wrist in an iron grip. "Stop! I didn't mean it!" Only then does he realize I wasn't serious. "Oh my god, you were messing with me."

I quirk an eyebrow. "I wonder where I got that from."

He grins sheepishly. "I know. You're so fun to tease, though, especially when you blush so prettily."

Hmm, maybe Frank was onto something with his comments about me blushing. "Now can I come in?"

He steps back and opens the door wide. "Yes, please."

When he closes the door behind me and we're standing in the hallway, my nerves return in full force, and I can't look at him. What if he changed his mind? What if I and my baggage are too much for him after all?

"Hey," Benoni says in that low tone I can't resist. "Look at me, Kinsey."

I lift my eyes to meet his. He cups my cheek. "That took courage. I'm proud of you."

His approval and pride bloom inside me. Is it strange or maybe even a little sad that I need it so much? Maybe, but I don't care. It feels wonderful. "Thank you."

As always, I lean into his touch, and he brushes my lips with his thumb. "What brought this on? Not that I'm complaining, but it's been two weeks since we talked about this, and since you never brought it up, I figured you'd decided you didn't want it."

"You didn't talk about it either."

"I didn't want to put pressure on you. All this is new to you, and I wanted to give you space to process it and make up your mind."

The man is a freaking saint. "I'm a relic, I know."

His hand travels from my cheek to my neck, where it curls around me tenderly. Delightful tingles skitter over my skin. "Not a relic. Special."

"Difficult and complicated," I counter.

"Unique." His voice drops lower, and I can't help but surrender.

"Okay."

"Hmm, good. Now tell me what brought your change of heart."

We're still in the small and impersonal hallway, not the best place for a discussion of this magnitude. "Can we maybe sit down?"

"Oh, *now* you want to take all the steps?" But he laughs as he lets go of my neck, only to grab my hand and pull me into the living room. "We have to be quiet because Leif is in a session."

"A session?" Moans come from his bedroom, and the red light above the door is on. Session. Right. He's having sex right now, filming it. Such a foreign concept. "Got it."

Benoni grabs me a water, and we sit down on the couch, our knees touching as he turns toward me. "Talk to me, Kinsey. Help me understand."

"Remember I told you I went for coffee with Frank two days ago?"

"You said you guys had a good talk."

"We did. He held up a mirror and dropped some hard-hitting truth bombs that got me thinking. He was asking me if I would forever sacrifice what I wanted and needed to appease others."

"Wow. That's... How did that make you feel?"

"Conflicted." I let out a sigh. "You know how much my kids mean to me. I'd do almost anything to reconnect with them, but Frank made me realize I have to draw the line somewhere. If I came out only to still have to hide parts of who I am, what's the point? I feel like that Meatloaf song. I would do anything for love, but I won't do that."

Benoni grins. "Meatloaf never specified what he wouldn't do."

"No, he didn't, but I do. I can't hide again, Benoni. I can't. It would slowly kill me. I've chosen to come out, and I want to live my life as a gay man. That includes"—I have to swallow, my throat dry—"having a relationship and having sex. And maybe being submissive?"

If Benoni smiled any wider, his face would crack. "I can't tell you how proud I am of you for realizing that. That's powerful stuff."

His words wrap around me like a hug, his acceptance seeping through my last defenses. "It hits me so hard when you say things like that," I whisper.

"I know. I can see it on your face, in the way you react. You've missed out on a lot of affirmation and approval, Kinsey. Let me give you that, please. It means a lot to me that I get to be the one to do that."

He inches closer to me, and my heart skips a beat. He cups both my cheeks and looks me straight into my eyes. "And I'm even happier I get to be the first man to kiss you."

He's waiting, a silent question in his gaze if I'm still okay with it, and sweet relief washes over me. No matter what happens, I'm safe with him. And so I nod...and close my eyes.

His breath drifts over my skin. His lips press against my forehead, the tip of my nose, my cheek...and then they meet my mouth in a featherlight touch, a soft brush, a ghost of a kiss. Still, my heart is racing. He's kissing me. Benoni Healey is *kissing* me.

He presses a little harder, and the tip of his tongue traces the seam of my lips. Oh, how can something so simple feel this good? Heat bubbles in my belly, and I'm already hard from that slight contact. I open up for him with a little gasp, and he slips his tongue into my mouth, where it encounters mine.

He gently pushes against my shoulders, and I let him, falling backward onto the couch. Benoni crawls on top of me, and the sensation of having a man this close is almost too much to take. The subtle smell of his cologne surrounds me, even as the coffee he must've had earlier hits my tongue, which swirls around mine. His weight presses me down, his arousal undeniable as it nudges mine. I'm too overwhelmed to do anything but lie there and take it all in.

His lips are soft and warm as they cover mine, effortlessly moving along with his tongue, which is doing wicked things. Roaming my mouth, exploring every corner, dancing with my tongue until I'm dizzy and panting. I've never been kissed like this, not with this erotic seductive undertone, this unashamed expression of desire and lust. Benoni's not holding back. With every touch, he tells me how much he wants me, and it's electrifying. The voice in my head that always reminds me of my sin is drowned out by the cascade of emotions until it's quiet for the first time in my life.

I stop thinking and let it all wash over me, sinking into the kiss, clinging to Benoni as he takes me apart with his lips and his tongue. My skin feels too tight for my body, like it's about to burst, and so does my cock, which is throbbing. He's making me fall apart with just a kiss.

"How are you doing?" he whispers against my throbbing lips as he breaks away.

I blink, coming back to reality from a sort of dream state. His pupils are dilated, his cheeks flushed, and his sexy smile makes my belly flutter as our chests rise and fall in the same rhythm. Panting. Out of breath. Kissed within an inch of my life. "I'm... Good, I think? That was...amazing."

"Yeah?"

"I never knew kissing could be like that."

A flash of sadness clouds his eyes. "I'm sorry you missed out on so much. It would be my honor and my pleasure to show you how amazing and wonderful sex can be in every form, even something as simple as kissing."

"The way you kiss isn't simple."

His smile returns. "I love kissing."

"I never did, but now I'm a fan."

He brushes my lips with his thumb. "Anytime you want to explore your newfound hobby, let me know. I'll gladly volunteer."

He rolls off me, and an involuntary sound of protest, akin to a little mewl, escapes me. Benoni chuckles. "I'm not going anywhere, McDreamy."

He turns onto his side, and I do the same. Thank god his couch is extra wide, so we fit on it together, facing each other. "McDreamy?"

"The hot doc from Grey's Anatomy? Patrick Dempsey?"

Oh, right. That rings a bell. "Is that what you're gonna call me now?"

I won't admit it, but I do like the idea of him having a pet name for me, just like he calls Leif *Bun*. It's cute and sweet and strangely intimate, and I want one too.

"I could call you McSteamy, who was the other hot doc. Or Clooney, from ER."

I roll my eyes. "You'd better not start calling me Mark Greene. He wasn't hot."

"Nah. He died. Way too sad. That said, so did McSteamy and McDreamy, so let's find someone else. How about Carter?"

"Carter? He was an intern!"

"He was cute, though."

"I'm not cute. I'm sexy, handsome, a silver fox. Not cute like a puppy or a kitten." I pout, and Benoni laughs.

"McDreamy is definitely a silver fox now, though so are McSteamy and Clooney," he argues.

"Yeah, so?"

He sighs dramatically. "Okay, okay, I'll call you something else. How about *honey*? Can I call you that?"

I nod, ridiculously happy he wants to pick a name for me.

"Honey it is."

I never realized you can tell if someone has been making out, but now I do. Benoni looks rumpled and flushed. It only makes him sexier and more attractive.

He leans in for another kiss, and I eagerly respond, kissing him back. His lips travel from my mouth to my cheek, then down my neck, my throat. He kisses and licks, then sucks on a tendon in my neck in a way that makes my cock ache. He groans and returns to my mouth, slipping his tongue back in and sucking on mine until I'm squirming.

His hand slips around my waist, finding my skin under my T-shirt. Everywhere he touches me, it tingles as if his fingertips transmit tiny electrical charges. He curls his other hand around my neck in a firm grip, holding me in place, and the strength and possessiveness of that gesture send shivers down my spine.

Oh, maybe I should touch him too? I put my hand on his back, where it encounters smooth, warm skin. But the sensation of his tongue against mine is too intense, too distracting, to focus on anything else, and I let my hand just rest there as Benoni kisses me senseless. He nibbles on my bottom lip, licks into my mouth, then does this swirl with his tongue in a gesture I copy, resulting in a delicious low moan from him.

"Mmm, you're a quick student," he rumbles. "Do that again."

Not obeying isn't even a choice, and I repeat the movement. This time, he meets my tongue and twirls it around mine, kissing me as if he wants to devour me. I know the feeling. I could kiss him for hours and not grow tired of it, though I have to admit that my shorts have never been this tight. Probably because I've never been this hard for so long.

He slides his leg between mine, pulling it up, and his thigh is now pressed against my dick. It's as if he knows I need the pressure, and instinctively, I move against him, rubbing myself against his leg. It's uncoordinated, and somewhere in the back of my mind concern gnaws that it's not dignified or sexy, but I ignore it. I need it. I need him.

"You're so hard..." Benoni's voice is low and sexy, settling deep inside my balls. "Are you getting close, honey?"

Hearing that pet name fall off his lips sends a jolt through my system. I want to be his honey. I want to be his everything. But right now, more than anything, I want to come. And so I press myself against him harder, burying my face in the crook of his neck as I chase my release. He pushes his leg up farther, and I moan. It's dirty and perfect, and I shamelessly rut against him, panting now.

His hand travels lower, cupping my ass through my shorts, and that simple touch is enough. My body convulses, and white bright light flashes before my eyes as I come in my pants, groaning as spurt after spurt releases from my cock until I'm left trembling.

"Holy shit, that was the single hottest thing I've ever seen," Benoni whispers.

My instinct is to avoid his eyes. What will he think of

me, coming like that? It's so...amateurish, for lack of a better word. So revealing of my complete lack of experience. But then his words register. Benoni doesn't lie, so if he says it was hot, he's telling the truth.

I raise my eyes to meet his, and he's staring at me with the sweetest look. "Ah, there you are," he says softly. "I'm proud of you for facing me."

He knows me so well by now. "It's not easy. The impulse to be ashamed is deep."

"You have nothing to be ashamed about. That was beautiful and erotic."

I swallow. "You didn't come."

"No, but this wasn't for me. This was about you."

I lean my forehead against his. "Thank you."

Then the enormity of it all sinks in. We kissed. We made out. Benoni made me come. We're...together? I think?

Oh god, what have I done?

~

To be continued in *New Daddy at Forty-Seven*. Turn the page for a sneak peek!

SNEAK PEEK OF NEW DADDY AT FORTY-SEVEN
JANUARY 2020 - KINSEY

It's been an insane day in the ER, and I'm happy to finally take a quick lunch break shortly after two. We had two big MVCs coming in, plus a couple of construction workers who got injured when their scaffolding half collapsed. I like it busy, since that's why I chose to be an ER doc, but this level of crazy is a little too much.

I've grabbed lunch from the cafeteria—pasta Alfredo, which is pretty edible—as well as a fresh cup of coffee from the doctor's lounge, and I'm on my way back to the ER. Usually, I try to eat in the cafeteria, but with today being so hectic and several patients of mine still waiting for results from scans and bloodwork, I figured I'd better wolf down my food in the nurse's break room.

"Incoming trauma," Sheila, our ER coordinator, shouts at me as I walk through the doors. Shit. There goes my lunch break. I'll have to put it in the nurse's lounge and heat it up afterward.

"What is it?"

"GSW with a single victim, shot multiple times in the

chest and abdomen. He coded in the ambulance, so they're coming in hot. ETA two minutes."

"Okay. Let me put this in the fridge."

"Watch out for the—"

My foot slips in something wet, and instinctively, I try to prevent myself from dropping my tray. My feet scramble for purchase, but it's useless, and my right leg shoots sideways in a way that no knee should ever go. The pain is instant, white hot and blinding, and I scream out.

"Oh, fuck," Sheila says, and after that, it's all a blur as I fight against the nausea and the urge to pass out.

They lift me onto a stretcher and wheel me into exam room 4, where Victoria, my intern, cuts off my scrubs and examines me. She's gentle, thank fuck, but even the lightest touch makes me sick to my stomach. I've never felt pain like this, so all-consuming.

"How did you fall?"

"I slipped sideways, landed on my thigh," I say between clenched teeth.

"Did you hit your head?"

"No."

"Does it hurt anywhere else but your knee?"

She's examining me as she asks questions, checking my lungs while Mark, the nurse, takes my BP and pulse. It's all as expected for someone who's in a hell of a lot of pain. "My thigh feels bruised, but nothing serious. It's my knee."

"What's your pain level?" she asks me, and despite everything, I'm proud of her for keeping her cool and following protocols.

"Nine out of ten."

"Okay."

"What do you see?" I grunt. I might as well make my misfortune into a teaching moment.

"Tenderness, even without touch, no obvious deformities, and it's beginning to swell."

"Differential diagnosis?"

"Bone fractures seem unlikely, considering the direction of the fall, so I'm most concerned about a torn ACL."

"Ding, ding, you win a gold medal."

"I need an attending," Victoria says to Mark. "I can't order tests."

"No attending available right now. It's all hands on deck with that GSW coming in and Dr. Lindstrom here incapacitated," Marks says with an apologetic look at me.

"Page Ortho." I have to force the words out, the pain coming in waves that seem to get higher and higher. "And in the meantime, order an MRI."

Mark nods. "On it. I'll make sure to mention it's you so they won't take forever like usual."

"Do you want pain meds?" Victoria asks me, a question she'll hopefully phrase quite like that to other patients.

"Just a gram of acetaminophen IV. Ortho needs to assess me first before I can take anything else. I may need surgery."

Ortho puts a rush on, thank God, and only minutes later, Mariah, the orthopedic surgeon, rushes in. "Kinsey, what the hell happened?"

"Ask my intern to present."

I don't have the energy anymore, and besides, she needs to learn.

"Kinsey Lindstrom, 46, presenting with a knee injury after a fall where his leg slipped sideways. No obvious deformities or other injuries. The patient didn't hit his head. The knee is swollen and extremely painful to the touch. Patient rates the pain nine out of ten. BP 140 over 95, pulse 86. Patient has been alert and responsive the whole time."

Mariah tips her head at her. "Excellent job. What's your diagnosis?"

"Torn ACL?"

Mariah clicks her tongue, then turns toward me. "It certainly looks that way. Can I?" She gestures at my knee, and I give her a terse nod.

She probes with gentle hands, but the pain still rolls over me, making me sweat from nausea. "Did you order tests?"

"Dr. Lindstrom ordered an MRI for himself, since no other attending was available. Mark already put it in."

"Good. We'll wait for the results, but I'm confident we're looking at an ACL injury. Page me when the results are in."

She puts a hand on my shoulder. "I'm sorry, Kinsey. This is a nasty one."

"Yeah, I was afraid that was the case."

"I'm gonna hold off on pain meds in case you need immediate surgery, but we should start icing."

"I'll do it," Victoria says, even though that's technically not her job. "And I'll page you when the MRI is done, Dr. Scholes."

"Perfect."

I try to relax as we wait for the MRI to become available, and when it does, I zone out, letting it all happen. It costs too much to be involved and present.

Mariah responds quickly to Victoria's page, and by the look on her face, I know. "Bad news, Kinsey. It's indeed your ACL. You tore it completely."

I groan. "Shit. What do you recommend? Can I get this fixed without surgery?"

She shakes her head. "I doubt it. Not with how much you are on your feet all day. No, I'd recommend physical therapy for several weeks to see how you do with that, but I suspect we'll end up operating. If we go in now, you'll risk complications, what with how swollen it is. I don't want you to end up with arthrofibrosis."

I close my eyes. Several weeks of therapy, then a surgery with the recovery period afterward. "I'm looking at, what, three months at the minimum?"

"At least, but probably longer, depending on how quickly you recover."

"Shit," I say again, unable to come up with something more original. "This is going to be utter hell."

I open my eyes again and find her looking at me with compassion. "Yes, and the pain is no joke either. You're gonna have to take the good stuff for the physical therapy, Kinsey, or you'll never be able to push through the pain and do the exercises. And trust me, you want them after the surgery as well."

I hesitate. I've seen the effects of opioid addiction too many times to take this decision lightly. "Can I do it with a mix of acetaminophen and naproxen?"

"You could, but I don't recommend it. Patients who don't take opioids need a longer period of physical therapy before surgery, and their recovery after surgery is longer as well. Do you have a history of sensitivity to opioids?"

"No, not at all. In fact, I've never even taken them. Never needed to, thankfully."

"Then I wouldn't worry about it. You're a doctor. You know all too well what these things can do, so I doubt you'll grow too used to them."

She's got a point. I'm overreacting. This is a serious injury, and my doctor is recommending I take them. Why would I argue with that and pretend to know better? I'm no orthopedic surgeon.

"All right, hit me with the good stuff. What's the drug of choice in this case, Percocet?"

"Yeah. We'll start with 2.5 milligrams, but I expect we'll need to increase to 5, one tablet every six hours. You know the drill."

"I do, thanks."

"Do you have a physical therapist who has experience with pre-surgery ACL protocol, or do you want me to recommend some?"

"I'll take some recommendations."

An hour later, I'm home, courtesy of Victoria and Mark, who volunteered to drive me home. I'm propped up on the couch with a filled prescription and my physical therapy appointment set up for tomorrow. Caroline is fussing over me, and even though I know she means well, all I want right now is to be left alone. It fucking hurts, and I'm not in the mood to play the role of the doting husband. That already drains me on a good day.

Then the first dose of Percocet hits me, and all is good with the world. For the first time in twenty-five years, I can look at Caroline and not feel a damn thing. No frustration that no matter how wonderful she is, I can't make myself love her. No anger for her being beautiful and the kind of wife every heterosexual man would kill for, but being unable to ever be the man she needs me to be, the husband she deserves. No sadness over the fact that I'll be forever stuck in this marriage with no way out. And no guilt over the hours of gay porn I've watched without Caroline ever suspecting a thing.

This stuff is amazing. No wonder people get addicted to it.

SIGNED PAPERBACKS AND SWAG

Did you know I have a web store where you can order signed paperbacks of all my books, as well as swag? Head on over to www.noraphoenix.com and check it out!

BOOKS BY NORA PHOENIX

If you loved this book, I have great news for you because I have a LOT of books for you to discover! Most of my books are also available in audio. You can find them all on my website at www.noraphoenix.com/my-books.

Forestville Silver Foxes Series

A brand-new contemporary MM romance series set in the small town of Forestville, Washington, featuring characters in their late forties. These silver foxes think they missed their chance at happiness...until they meet the love of their life, right there in Forestville. A feel good small-town romance series!

The Foster Brothers Series

Growing up in foster care, four boys made a choice to become brothers. Now adults, nothing can come between them...not even when they find love. The Foster Brothers is a contemporary MM romance series with found family, sweet romance, high heat, and a dash of kink.

Irresistible Dragons Series

A spin off series from the Irresistible Omegas that can be read on its own. With dragons, mpreg, stubborn alphas, and a whole new suspense plot, this is one series you don't want to miss.

Forty-Seven Duology

An emotional daddy kink duology with a younger Daddy and an older boy. Also includes first time gay, loads of hurt/comfort, and best friend's father. The third book is a bonus novella featuring secondary characters from the duology.

White House Men Series

An exciting romantic suspense series set in the White House. The perfect combination of sweet and sexy romance, a dash of kink, and a suspense plot that will have you on the edge of your seat. Make sure to read in order.

No Regrets Series

Sexy, kinky, emotional, with a touch of suspense, the No Regrets series is a spin off from the No Shame series that can be read on its own.

Perfect Hands Series

Raw, emotional, both sweet and sexy, with a solid dash of kink, that's the Perfect Hands series. All books can be read as stand-alones.

No Shame Series

If you love steamy MM romance with a little twist, you'll love the No Shame series. Sexy, emotional, with a bit of suspense and all the feels. Make sure to read in order, as this is a series with a continuing storyline.

Irresistible Omegas Series

An mpreg series with all the heat, epic world building, poly romances (the first two books are MMMM and the rest of the series is MMM), a bit of suspense, and characters that will stay with you for a long time. This is a continuing series, so read in order.

Ignite Series

An epic dystopian sci-fi trilogy where three men have to not only escape a government that wants to jail them for being gay but aliens as well. Slow burn MMM romance.

Stand-Alone Novels

I also have a few stand-alone novels. Some feature kink (like My Professor Daddy or Coming Out on Top), but others are non-kink contemporary romances (like Captain Silver Fox). You'll find something that appeals to you for sure!

Ballsy Boys Series: *Cowritten with K.M. Neuhold*

Sexy porn stars looking for real love! Expect plenty of steam, but all the feels as well. They can be read as stand-alones, but are more fun when read in order.

Kinky Boys Series: *Cowritten with K.M. Neuhold*

More sexy porn stars! This is a spin off series from the Ballsy Boys, set in Las Vegas...and with some kink!

MORE ABOUT NORA PHOENIX

Would you like the long or the short version of my bio?

The short? You got it.

I write steamy gay romance books and I love it. I also love reading books. Books are everything.

How was that?

A little more detail? Gotcha.

I started writing my first stories when I was a teen...on a freaking typewriter. I still have these, and they're adorably romantic. And bad, haha. Fear of failing kept me from following my dream to become a romance author, so you can imagine how proud and ecstatic I am that I finally overcame my fears and self doubt and did it. I adore my genre because I love writing and reading about flawed, strong men who are just a tad broken..but find their happy ever after anyway.

My favorite books to read are pretty much all MM/gay romances as long as it has a happy end. Kink is a plus... Aside from that, I also read a lot of nonfiction and not just books on writing. Popular psychology is a favorite topic of mine and so are self help and sociology.

Hobbies? Ain't nobody got time for that. Just kidding. I love traveling, spending time near the ocean, and hiking. But I love books more.

Come hang out with me in my Facebook Group Nora's Nook where I share previews, sneak peeks, freebies, fun stuff, and much more: https://www.facebook.com/groups/norasnook/

My weekly newsletter gives you updates, exclusive content, and all the inside news on what I'm working on. Sign up here: www.noraphoenix.com/newsletter/

You can also stalk me on
Twitter:
twitter.com/NoraPhoenixMM
Instagram:
www.instagram.com/nora.phoenix/
BookBub:
www.bookbub.com/profile/nora-phoenix

Made in the USA
Monee, IL
05 February 2024